DEMON
CREED

A DEMON OUTLAWS NOVEL

DEMON CREED

A DEMON OUTLAWS NOVEL

PAULA ALTENBURG

Entangled Publishing, LLC
2614 South Timberline Road
Suite 109
Fort Collins, CO 80525
Visit our website at www.entangledpublishing.com.

Entangled Edge is an imprint of Entangled Publishing, LLC.

Edited by Kerri-Leigh Grady and Marie Loggia-Kee
Cover design by Kim Killion

ISBN 978-1502872449

Manufactured in the United States of America

First Edition June 2014

For Annie Fox, Katie Armstrong, and Patricia McKinstry.
Loved and missed.

Chapter One

Three against one were not good odds for the thin young
boy with the dark hair and angry eyes.

At first glance, however, it seemed like any other
adolescent dispute, with at least one bloody nose or black
eye inevitable, so Creed paid it no mind and moved on.

He had not come to the very edge of what was once
demon territory to intervene in children's squabbles.
Rumors of their quiet disappearance from several villages
in and around the Godseeker Mountains were what had led
him here, to a town called Desert's End, when duty called
him elsewhere.

He was supposed to be hunting a demon spawn named
Willow on behalf of the Godseekers. While the rest of the
mortal world rejoiced over the banishment of demons after
more than three hundred years of occupation, Willow had
somehow raised one and used it to slay an entire village of
innocents. Creed intended to see her brought to justice. Not

only was it his duty as a Godseeker assassin—trained to enforce the goddesses' will by use of any means necessary—but Willow's actions had nearly killed his half-sister, Raven.

Demons hated spawn. The thought of them working together was troubling, and a possibility that Creed dared not ignore. He'd been informed that Willow was fleeing Godseeker territory and appeared to be headed for the Borderlands, where the world ended. Creed couldn't risk losing her trail. If his curiosity about the missing children wasn't satisfied soon, he would have to move on.

Children, however, deserved justice too. Facing it, as well as receiving it. If they were being abandoned rather than sold, as the stories intimated, then a man had to wonder if there was something unusual about them.

Frightening, perhaps.

He was pushing his way through the throng of people swarming the boardwalk, seeking the local jail and its sheriff, when it struck him that the altercation in the alley he had just witnessed was not all it seemed. He had passed over it too quickly, as if his attention had been turned from it.

Which meant at least one of the boys had the ability to sway people's actions and thoughts—a talent for demon compulsion that was almost as great as Creed's own.

He retraced his steps.

A narrow dirt alley separated the stable from the postal station and hotel next door. Inside that alley, out of the sun and away from prying adult eyes, two boys, approximately fourteen years of age, lay gasping for breath on the ground. One held his stomach. The other, his ribs. Neither appeared inclined, or able, to move.

A third boy, heavier set and taller than his companions,

possibly a year older, dabbed at the blood trickling from his nose with the blunt of his wrist. He faced the smallest and youngest boy—the one with the angry eyes Creed had first noticed.

So far the combatants had not noted his presence, and Creed pressed himself against a wall to watch and listen. He saw nothing wrong with a boy defending himself against bullies. It was how he chose to do so that could lead to problems.

"I warned you. I can take care of myself," the skinny boy said. He might have been thirteen, at the most. He doubled his hands into fists and held them clenched at his sides, ready to use.

The cruelty in the older boy's expression indicated to Creed that he was unlikely to concede defeat to what he perceived to be a punier victim. "And I told you that you aren't wanted here, you little freak."

One of the younger boy's fists lashed out in response to the insult.

The bully's head rocked backward. The flesh over one cheekbone splotched a deepening red that would purple by morning. Instead of backing off, he dropped his chin and charged at the younger boy like an incensed bull kyson. As the younger boy skipped to one side to avoid him, the subtle yet familiar tug of demon compulsion touched the edge of Creed's thoughts.

The older boy did not veer from his original course but plowed on, ramming headfirst into the side of the hotel. He staggered a few steps, reeling, before his eyes rolled back to expose the whites. With a soft, almost surprised-sounding sigh hissing from his throat, his knees buckled, and he dropped to the ground, unconscious.

The other two boys, seeing their friend fall, rediscovered their mobility. They scurried, scorpion-like, from the alley on their hands and knees, ignorant of Creed's presence even as they brushed past him. Out on the street, they got to their feet and ran as if the Demon Lord himself were chasing them.

In the alley, the dark-haired, angry-eyed boy kicked the one he had felled, now semi-conscious and drooling in the dirt. The blow was halfhearted and had no real malice behind it.

"Stupid," the boy muttered, his voice low, as if speaking to himself.

"Him or you?"

The boy looked up at Creed, his expressive eyes widening with caution at the discovery he was not alone. He glanced behind him. The alley ended in a huge manure pile at the back of the stable. It would be too soft from the rain and the heat for anyone to safely climb, and there were few worse deaths imaginable than suffocating in dung.

The boy bolted for the street.

Creed peeled himself away from the wall of the hotel. He easily caught the collar of the boy's homespun shirt, swinging him off his feet and holding him up so that their noses were inches apart.

"What's the matter, boy?" he asked, keeping his tone conversational, testing him to see how he'd react to discovery. "You think you're the only one in the world who can make others see and do what you want? Or that you're the strongest and fastest spawn who ever lived?"

The boy didn't deny the accusation, but instead struggled

in earnest. He kicked a boot at Creed's knee, but Creed, now that he knew for certain what he was dealing with, was prepared for a fight and easily evaded it. He could have compelled the boy into submission, but that was not how he wanted to deal with this situation.

He continued to dangle the boy at eye level. "What were you thinking, using your talents like that?" he asked. "No one will believe you bested three boys in a fight — and all of them bigger than you. Questions will be asked."

The boy's face turned sullen, rebellion displacing the anger in his gray eyes. "I don't care what anyone believes or what they ask. I don't have to hide what I am from mortals anymore. I don't answer to them."

Creed was not unsympathetic. The problem, however, was far greater than this boy and his talent for compulsion. The world had once believed that any offspring produced through demon matings with mortal women were male, and born in monster form. These monsters, whenever discovered, had been killed at birth.

Although still less than a year since demons had been banished from the earth, in that brief time it had become increasingly apparent to the Godseekers Creed served that the number of half demons left behind had been underestimated. They were not all male, and not all born in monster form. Many had managed to hide what they were, either out of a natural instinct for self-preservation, or because of mothers who protected them despite knowing what they were.

Even more troubling, any powers inherited by demon offspring seemed to be strengthening and developing.

The mortal world was ill prepared to deal with such spawn. Hatred for them ran deep and was almost universal.

Already, mortals were taking steps to eradicate them, and the boy would be foolish not to understand the danger he faced. No demon talents he had inherited would save him in the end.

Creed set the boy on his feet but kept a grip on his arm. "Even so," he said, "the memory of demon rule remains too fresh. There's widespread fear that they might someday return. If you can avoid such confrontations with mortals, why not do so? What if your actions today draw the attention of someone who's more dangerous to you than those three bullies could ever be?"

The boy's lip curled. "I'm not afraid of anyone."

His arrogance did not surprise Creed, who possessed a fair amount of his own. Half demons, like their full demon fathers, did not experience fear in the same way mortals did. They instinctively suppressed and controlled it, and used it to their advantage. Sometimes that confidence made them stupid and overbold, as this boy's actions proved today.

But half demons were not always evil and dangerous. Creed and his sister were proof enough of that. Or he liked to believe so.

He wavered, torn between doing his duty and what he believed to be right. He was not without sympathy for a child who would have experienced a lifetime of injustices, and he sensed there was little harm in this one—at least not yet. The lessons he'd learn over the next few years would prove crucial in shaping the type of man he became. The boy needed guidance, not persecution.

It made this decision a difficult one.

"You don't need to be afraid," Creed said. "You should, however, exercise more common sense. Do you know who

I am?"

"Why should I care?"

His belligerence was a strike against him.

"Because I'm a Godseeker assassin, tasked to hunt spawn and bring them to justice. Dead or alive," Creed added, after a significant pause. "What if I were to turn you in?"

The boy flipped a hank of dark hair from his eyes with a toss of his head. "I know what else you are, Assassin. I would turn you in, too."

The threat amused Creed. "Of the two of us, who do you think people would believe is a spawn? A skinny child who somehow bested three larger and older boys in a mismatched fight, or a trained assassin who serves the Godseekers?"

The boy scraped a toe in the dirt. "I can make anyone believe what I want."

"And you want me to believe you did your best to walk away from that fight," Creed said. "But I don't. So now what?"

Guilt flared in the boy's eyes. "They started it."

"I have no doubt. But you could have convinced them to leave you alone instead, if you'd wanted."

A hross kicked a heavy hoof against the wall of the stable next door to the alley. Out on the street, traffic rumbled past.

Again, Creed hesitated. While it was his duty to ensure that any spawn he discovered were brought before the Godseekers for judgment, he did not want to condemn a child. Not without first determining if there might be enough support in his life to bring out the potential Creed sensed in him. Spawn had only demon instincts. They lacked morality. Half demons, on the other hand, tended to be far more complex. More mortal.

At least they could choose to be.

"Where is your mother?" Creed asked. The boy said nothing, his lips pressed in a thin line of rebellion, and Creed lost patience. "I can return you to her, or I can give you to the sheriff to be passed on to the Godseekers, who will then determine your fate. Which is your preference?"

"She's selling corn cakes at a stall near the goddess temple." The words dragged unwillingly from the boy's mouth.

Creed tightened his grip. The mother's reaction to having her son presented to her by a Godseeker assassin would decide the matter for him. "Come on."

Larger than any other structure in Desert's End, built on higher ground and constructed entirely of colorful stones, the temple was simple enough for Creed to locate. It was not meant to be inconspicuous.

He drew his young prisoner through the crowds.

The land around the town was a farming region, and the noisy market square stank of old kyson droppings and sodden scafhoof wool. While recent spring rains had not done the streets any favors with regard to their stench, the wooden buildings surrounding the square had been cleansed and left gleaming in the noonday sun as if freshly painted.

The town had other features to redeem it in Creed's eyes, as well. Sinkholes were rare so close to the mountains, and Desert's End had been built with confidence on the eviscerated ruins of an Old World city. Ancient and hardy gardens remained determined to flourish despite the various indignities the years had wrought. Rose bushes, from a time before demons had razed the earth with fire, bloomed pink and red in unexpected places—to either side of a creosote-blackened boardwalk and from beneath one cornerstone of the town hall.

In front of the temple, a number of tarpaulin-capped wooden stalls had been erected with a variety of goods displayed on long counters.

An older woman with delicate features, golden brown hair and vivid green eyes, and wearing an expression of trepidation mixed with concern, watched their progress toward her, her attention divided between them and a customer.

Creed stopped beside her stall, keeping a solid hand on the boy's shoulder, and waited for her to finish with the transaction.

As he did, he quietly observed her. Soft-spoken and displaying a gentle weariness, she reminded him more than a little of his half-sister's mother.

Raven had always considered her mortal mother to be weak, but Creed, several years older than Raven and more aware of the harshness of the world, had adored Columbine. She'd always been kind to him, even though he was not her child.

Columbine was long dead now. He'd not been able to save her from an abusive husband. Raven, however, was safe in the mountains with her lover Blade, a former assassin who did not need or want Creed's help in protecting her.

That left him without any responsibilities other than to the leaders of the Temple of Immortal Right—and therefore, to the Godseekers. Their mandate in this post-demon world was to establish a universal law across the entire land.

Blade had not shared the Godseekers' faith in the simplicity of their mandate, or their law. He'd quietly suggested to Creed that if it became necessary to go as far as the Borderlands because of spawn, then Creed should seek out the Demon Slayer and give him Blade's regards. He'd said the Slayer would understand what that meant.

Creed hoped it would not come to that because he understood too. The Demon Slayer and his wife, the half demon known as Airie, were reputed to be responsible for the banishment of demons from the world. To call the Slayer back meant the Godseekers were far out of their depth.

An overladen cart filled with sacks of grain cut through the market, its contents spilling over its sides, the wooden wheels sprawling wide. An enormous black work hross, head bent and back swayed with age, strained at its traces. Feathered fetlocks were caked in a fine red dust that puffed in small, dirty clouds with each step the animal took. The cart's load brushed against several stalls, threatening to knock them over, and the vendors shouted their displeasure at the fat driver.

As Creed continued to wait to speak with the boy's mother, he noted there were no signs of a husband or master about. He wondered why not. Women were not free, and despite her obvious maturity, she retained far too much of the physical perfection that had once captured the interest of a full-blooded demon for her to go unnoticed in a market such as this. Her young son could not possibly provide sufficient protection for her here.

Unless, of course, the boy had a demon gift for compulsion, and directed attention away from her.

The woman finished with the customer and turned to her son, as if by ignoring Creed's presence she would somehow avert an unpleasant confrontation. While she pretended not to notice him, Creed was well aware of her sidelong scrutiny.

And what she saw.

He was not unprepossessing. Most women found the vibrant contrast between his golden skin and unusual, crystalline blue eyes attractive. In the past he had shaved his head because his black hair, which had a tendency to curl, had made his physical resemblance to Raven too obvious, and he had not wanted others to suspect they shared a father. If they had, they might also have begun to wonder who—or what—that father had been.

After the departure of the demons, however, Creed's scalp had gone naturally smooth. The flaming tattoo that now covered his back and shoulders had also emerged, although he had no idea what its purpose was or if it held any demonic significance. He had no one to ask.

The woman ran a palm down the front of the tidy apron that covered her simple dress, smoothing imaginary wrinkles from the heavy fabric, an action that betrayed her nervousness at his presence. Women usually loved Creed, and while under other circumstances he was not above using that attraction to his advantage, normally he would not be passing judgment on one of their children. Most mothers placed their child's welfare above everything else.

But not all of them did so. His own had not. And this mother's child, too, was half demon.

"Where have you been?" she asked the boy. "I expected you here to help me an hour ago." Her tone held reproof and anxiety, as well as an undercurrent of unmistakable affection. Soft green eyes darted from the masculine hand on her son's shoulder to Creed's face. "He's a better salesman than me," she added, with pleading in those eyes as if she already knew without being told what was at stake. "I need him."

A gift for compulsion would indeed benefit her sales and keep them both from starvation. Creed's gut tightened. There was no husband or master. Not that he could discern. Without the boy, this woman's fate would be uncertain and undoubtedly hopeless. Condemning one would mean a death sentence for them both.

Since Creed sensed nothing but truth in either of them, he saw no pressing reason to remove the boy from his mother. The only fear in her was for her son, and of Creed.

He released his prisoner. "I don't doubt your son is good at sales," he said. "He seems less inclined to use his skills of persuasion to avoid trouble. You might want to impress upon him the advantages of walking away from a fight rather than diving in without careful consideration for the consequences. No one willingly draws the attention of Godseekers."

"Thank you," the woman whispered, her green eyes filling with tears of gratitude and relief.

Creed walked away without further comment, confident the implicit warning he had delivered was enough. He threaded his way through a crowd that paid him little attention even though he dwarfed most other men. One of an assassin's greatest attributes was an ability to move about unnoticed, and Creed, thanks to his demon father, was better at it than most.

He finally located the jail on a narrow street backing the temple. It was flanked by green-fingered desert palms and a faded mercantile. He climbed three stone steps and entered the low building. Inside, the high, narrow windows positioned beneath the ceiling beams offered interior lighting while protecting the room from the worst of the dry desert heat.

A tall man, seated in a straight-backed chair, bent forward over a heavy oak desk. He coughed into a crumpled handkerchief, his bony shoulders shaking. His face was as gray as the walls. The rattling cough, combined with the unhealthy pallor to his flesh, suggested the odds were good that he was also dying.

Creed waited in silence until the coughing fit subsided.

"I'm looking for the sheriff," he said.

The man mopped at his mouth with the handkerchief. Although reflecting ill health, his gaze was intelligent and thoughtful, as if he had not yet given up on living. He tapped the badge on his chest, then extended a hand. "You found him. The name's Fledge."

Creed took the offered hand, shaking it as he introduced himself. "I represent the Temple of Immortal Right and the Godseekers. I was told you might have information regarding several children who have gone missing in recent months."

Sheriff Fledge tipped back in his chair. "Why would an assassin be interested in a few missing children?"

"It's not the children who interest me as much as the circumstances in which they're rumored to have disappeared."

Fledge hooked a chair near the desk with the toe of his boot and flipped it around, then gestured for Creed to take a seat. Creed dragged the chair to the far corner of the desk so that his back faced a wall, not the door. A slight grin crossed the sheriff's thin face as he noted the action.

"I don't have much hard information," Fledge said. "Besides, there are all kinds of rumors flying these days."

"Such as?"

The good-natured smile faded. "The kind that says those children are spawn. That there's a whore hiding in the Godseeker Mountains who's one of them, too. That maybe the Demon Slayer is to blame for them by taking up with a demon when he should have been protecting people from her kind instead. He's abandoned us, leaving his work half done."

The sheriff had strong opinions.

Creed could ignore his use of the term *whore*. It was not meant with any disrespect, only as a distinction. Women, owned by men and used as they pleased, were one of three things—wives, daughters, or whores.

But Creed disliked the term *spawn* when used by a mortal. It was a slur against all half demons—and an intentional one.

He especially did not like hearing it associated with Raven, who was the "whore" on the mountain Fledge mentioned. She and Blade had begun a new settlement in one of the many abandoned mining towns, where they welcomed any half demons who wished to live in peace.

Once he stripped off the prejudice, he sifted through everything Fledge had said for what was important. The sheriff had heard rumors that those missing children were spawn. The last time Creed had seen Willow, she'd had a misshapen and feral demon child in her company. The memory of that pitiful creature, and how she had used it, haunted him.

Perhaps Raven was not the whore Fledge referred to after all. Creed had assumed that feral child was Willow's. It was possible he'd been mistaken about that. The thought of her raising children made his blood run cold.

"So you've heard of a woman hiding in the mountains who might be spawn, and blame the Demon Slayer, who's reported to be in the Borderlands, for her existence," Creed said. "It doesn't sound to me as if either of them could be held responsible for children who've gone missing in the area around Desert's End."

The sheriff's gray face reflected his agreement before another coughing spasm overtook him. By the time he recovered, his whole body was trembling.

"If you're wanting someone to hold responsible for their disappearance, maybe you should disregard the rumors and consider slave traders instead. The man to discuss that with lives about three miles out of town on a kyson ranch." The sheriff paused again to catch his breath. The rattling sound in his chest filled the silence of the empty jail. "He sold his whore's son to them about a year ago, and he would have driven a hard bargain. Maybe this season the slavers decided to bypass him and save money."

That was a reasonable assumption, and one worth checking. Creed got directions to the ranch.

As he rose to go, the sheriff stopped him.

"If it turns out slavers aren't responsible, have you asked yourself what else might have happened to them?" The sheriff leaned forward, steadying himself against his desk. "What if they were abandoned, and for good reason?"

So the sheriff, too, thought the children were spawn.

Creed understood people's fear. But half demons were not entirely to blame for the changes taking place. No longer under the rule of the immortals—goddess or demon— the world had no true law anymore. As far as Creed was concerned, people could choose to make a better place of it or a worse one. What was guaranteed was that it would not be the same. And if mortals were to coexist with half demons, a new path needed to be blazed.

Creed believed he had an obligation to help make that happen. He had a sworn duty to the Godseekers, but an inherent responsibility to others like himself. No matter what the world wished to think, he and his kind were mortals too.

"Whether it was slavers who took them or they were abandoned," Creed said, "what I do know is that those missing children deserve justice, the same as anybody else."

• • •

Nieve pressed both palms to her tired back as she stretched out the cramps she'd acquired from bending over all day, planting seeds in the kitchen's vegetable garden. Every bone in her body called her by name.

The ranch had been her home for the past four years. It stretched for miles beneath a seamless roof of royal-blue sky. An impressive herd of long-haired, mammoth beef kyson roamed wild in the blowing grasses and scrub brush littering these farthest edges of the demon desert, where the animals would forage and fatten until roundup in the fall.

The unpredictability of the kyson made it unsafe for Nieve to wander too far from the protective fencing of the compound surrounding the house. The beasts were as ill-tempered as their owner, Bear, and she feared them both equally.

Wolven, another threat, had been heard howling the past three nights. A cross between an old world mountain lion and a wolf, they were the result of an unsuccessful attempt by mortals long ago to protect the desert region against the invasion of demons. Instead, wolven became the scourge of farmers and travelers. And slaves.

Bear had ridden out early that morning to check on his herd. While adult kyson had little to fear from them, calves and yearlings were a different matter. The horns and thick frontal skull bones that kyson used for defense did not fully develop until their second season, leaving their young vulnerable to wolven fangs and claws.

Despite a dull ache of loneliness she could never quite escape, Nieve preferred these hours of solitude. In another lifetime, before her world had been turned to blackened ruins by a demon who had professed to love her, her days had been filled with light and laughter.

Demons might be gone from the world now, but it would be a long time—if ever –before she lost her fear of them. And while she had given up on hating Bear a long time ago, she would never lose her fear of him.

She stared across the desert foothills to the jagged mountains with emptiness gnawing at the raw edges of her heart. She could not shake the belief that she had lost something of inexplicable and infinite value. Yet no matter how hard she tried, she could not recall what it was. At night she dreamed of it, but in the morning the dreams were gone, leaving seeds of discontent and sorrow sown in their wake.

Nieve shook herself. The sun was beginning to set and Bear would return soon. When he did he would want his dinner on the table, and the bruises from the last beating she'd received were not yet faded.

She turned to the low, sprawling log house and saw a stranger, larger even than Bear, striding toward her. Alarm rippled up her sore spine. At first, with the last of the day's light at his back, she could not see much about him other than his outline, but it was the stealth of his approach that truly frightened her.

It made her think of demons.

He stopped a discreet and reassuring distance away. She had a better view of him now, and the small trowel poking from the hand-harrowed dirt at her feet seemed an inadequate weapon when she compared her slight size to his.

With wide shoulders and long, lean legs, he wore typical desert clothing—a homespun cotton shirt and neckerchief, thick denim trousers tucked into knee-high leather boots, and an oiled canvas duster. He wore no hat, and his shaved head was as bronzed as his face. The golden hue of his skin made the mesmerizing blue of his eyes even more vibrant and compelling. Kindness and good humor radiated from him. She could not look away.

She blinked several times to dispel the unexpected, hypnotic appeal. The harmlessness he transmitted no doubt served as a lure to calm most people's fears, but served to increase her suspicions. Nieve was not an innocent and impressionable child. She knew danger when she saw it. She tore her eyes from his to fix her attention on his hands and any threatening movements he might make toward her.

"I'm sorry," the giant said, the gentleness in his voice matching the kindness of his eyes, at odds with the rest of him. Those strong, agile-looking hands remained motionless, however, and he maintained a discreet distance. "I didn't mean to startle you."

A pulse thrummed in Nieve's throat, and she fought an

urge to run. If she'd thought it would do her any good, she would have.

"No?" she asked, her unsteady voice betraying her nervousness. "Then why approach me on foot? Where is your hross?"

Those beautiful blue eyes beamed benign innocence at her from his too-handsome face. "Beside the stable."

He'd been spying on both her and the ranch and had seen she was alone. That made her even more afraid.

He realized it too, and his expression changed again, this time to sympathetic understanding. "I swear I'm no threat to you."

That might well be true enough. But since Nieve could not recall the last time anyone had been deliberately kind to her, suspicion ran deep. She'd taken great pains to ensure she did not attract undue notice from men. The few she came in contact with on the ranch rarely spared her a single glance, let alone two. She sensed that this one, however, saw past her dowdy, shapeless dress and the faded black neckerchief covering her white-blond hair.

"I'm looking for a man named Bear," the stranger continued. "I was told he might have some information I need." He considered the purple-streaked horizon. "If possible, I'd like a place to stay for the night, too. I saw wolven tracks on my way out here, and my hross is nervous."

Nieve inched toward the house, ready to bolt if her knees would allow it. "My master will be back at any minute," she said. "You can wait in the yard by the stable if you wish to speak with him."

The stranger did not make any move to follow her. He simply watched with observant eyes, very quietly. When she was close enough to the kitchen door to make a run for it, she turned and dashed inside. She slammed the door shut behind her, then dropped the wooden bar that locked it into its brackets. Her heart hammered beneath her ribs the entire time.

Coward.

She pressed her back against the solid door, and closing her eyes, tried to steady her uneven breathing. Her trembling knees gave out, and she slid the door's length to the floor.

Whoever the unsettling stranger was, he was Bear's problem now.

Chapter Two

Creed did not so much as twitch a facial muscle as he watched the woman vanish inside the sprawling log house.

The fear in her eyes had astonished him. It left him feeling dirty, as if she had somehow read his carefully guarded thoughts regarding her. Underneath the plain clothing, and despite her thinness of frame, she was startlingly and undeniably beautiful. Brilliant green eyes alone, enormous in a waifish face, were enough to mark her appearance as extraordinary and render him nearly speechless. That white-blond hair was another. Creed had been forced to work hard to keep from staring at her.

He frowned at the closed door. Perhaps he had not worked hard enough. Or it was possible the woman had been so beaten down by the life she led here that she was incapable of trust.

If the latter was the cause of her fear, there no hope for her. A woman needed to be strong-willed in order to survive a harsh world. He could not make this one his problem. She was another man's property. He would get the information on the missing children he came for and get out. He could not right all of the wrongs in this world single-handed.

Creed went to wait in the yard in front of the stable with his hross, as he had been instructed.

It was not long before a man on a sand swift—a large, ugly, lizard-like beast—rode at a lazy pace toward the ranch. Distance out here could prove deceptive, and it was almost an hour before the man entered through the ranch's gates. By then the sun had already set.

The old man proved to be as large and ugly as his mount, and equally irritable. Shaggy gray hair touched mammoth, stooped shoulders. Much of his muscle had gone to fat with age, but Creed suspected what was left remained formidable enough. Black brows met over a hawk nose, and equally black eyes scowled as he brought the sand swift to a halt too close to Creed's already agitated hross. The hross shied away from the long, razor-sharp tongue that lashed at it, and only Creed's firm hand on its reins kept it from bolting.

If this was Bear, then he had been aptly named.

"The sun has gone down," the man said to him. "Whoever you are, you should have been on your way hours ago if you expected to avoid wolven. The sons of whores have killed and eaten six of my best calves."

That explained some of the ill temper.

The dead calves could only be partly to blame for this man's demeanor. Anyone who could sell his own child into slavery would have little or no natural softness to him. Creed suppressed a flicker of pity for the tiny woman who had locked herself in the house. She stood no chance of survival against this rough-worn man. She would be dead in a few years, either by his hand or her own.

Since there would be no offer of hospitality for the night Creed would ask his questions and be gone. Wolven did not frighten him, and he would rather not involve himself in private matters that did not concern the Godseekers.

The sand swift's body color remained constant. That meant it was not alarmed or threatened by Creed's presence as it snuffled its broad, ugly snout back and forth along the ground.

With an unpleasant jolt, Creed realized that it was trailing his footprints in the dirt. He stroked his hross's neck, soothing the nervous animal.

"It's a pity about your calves," he said. "My name is Creed. I serve the Godseekers and I'm looking for a man named Bear. The sheriff in Desert's End said he might have some information I need."

The old man did not dismount. Craftiness entered his ferret-black, unblinking eyes. "You were told wrong. I don't know much about anything except ranching."

"Then you know nothing of slave traders who bought a young child from you last year?"

His weasel eyes tracked to the house, then back to Creed. "I know very little of them."

Creed read truth in his words. Yet also, a lie. This man might not know much about them, but what he did was most likely significant—if not to Creed, then to someone else. His thoughts went to the woman he had surprised. The sheriff had spoken of a slave whore. Since Creed had yet to see signs of another woman, or anyone else here, it stood to reason that she was it. If it was her son the old man had sold, she'd have paid attention. Most mothers would.

Unless it was a child she had not wanted either.

"What of the woman in the house?" Creed asked. "Would she know more than you?"

The old man spat a wad of chewing tobacco on the ground. It glistened, brown and wet, near the toe of Creed's boot, although not so close as to seem deliberately offensive.

"Why are the Godseekers interested enough in slave traders to send one of you to investigate them?"

Creed did not miss the slight emphasis on the word *you*. Bear knew he was an assassin, and it was not likely to make him more forthcoming. He did not wish to cooperate with the Godseekers. It was doubtful he ever willingly cooperated with anyone.

Creed recognized him as someone who enjoyed the suffering of others in an attempt to ease his own. His sister's stepfather had been a bully such as this. Still, Creed had to try.

He studied the sand swift, wondering what it would do if he chose a different method of getting what he needed from its master. Adult sand swifts tended to be loyal and aggressively protective, and quick to sense any threat to their masters no matter how subtle. The only creatures more dangerous were the juveniles.

He concentrated, sending out calming thoughts as he spoke, not wanting to alert either Bear or the sand swift as to what he was doing.

"Since the end of winter, several children have been reported missing in the area," Creed said.

"Children are a dime a dozen," Bear replied. "If they

can't earn their keep, farmers sell them to be rid of them. Or they leave them for the wolven to have."

Certain slave traders made their profit selling children to brothels. Some might argue that it was kinder of parents, or owners such as Bear, to leave them for wolven if they could not feed them. Such an action would be politely ignored by neighbors who well understood the problem. It would not be remarked upon. Word would not spread.

And yet both things had happened.

Creed was unconvinced that slave traders were responsible for these latest disappearances. The sense he got from Bear was that he did not believe they were either. Therefore, if the disappearances were being remarked upon, it was because there was something unusual about the children. The sheriff was most likely correct, and they were half demon.

Frustration filled him. Regardless of who had fathered them, they were innocents.

The sand swift had not raised an alarm at the slight amount of compulsion Creed unleashed, so he released a little more, although even more carefully. He wanted that invitation to spend the night and Bear was not the sort of man to be magnanimous. If pushed too far, he would question why he did something so out of character and against his instincts.

But Creed did not intend to leave here without more complete answers to his questions. He could not ignore instincts telling him that the spawn woman he hunted, and the children he'd heard whisperings of, including this one of Bear's, were somehow connected.

• • •

Slave traders had bought a young child from Bear.

Nieve, eavesdropping at the open window beside the front door, let the plain lace curtain drop from her numb fingers. She braced herself against the wall as the blood rushed to her head and her vision grayed.

He had sold her son. That was what she'd sensed missing from her life. What had caused this raw, gaping hole in her heart.

Once the dizziness passed she pressed a shaking palm to her stomach, afraid she might be sick. She could not decide what was worse—the fact that Bear had done such a thing, or the discovery that she had forgotten. She prayed it was because her son had not wanted her to remember him. He'd always been protective of her, even as a baby—an old soul in a child's body.

But even so, what sort of mother could allow herself to forget her own child?

A part of her wished she had not eavesdropped on this conversation, because she was not strong enough to deal with it. She had no idea what had inspired her to do so. Perhaps it was a compelling and insatiable interest in the stranger with the beautiful eyes and this one last opportunity for her to gaze at him.

No matter the reason, she could not undo the damage now done. The floodgates opened and memories washed through her, as did the knowledge that an entire year of her son's life had been wasted. Somewhere in a harsh and unforgiving world, Asher waited for her to come for him.

Pain sliced her heart, so unbearable that she had to pant her way through it. Ash would be almost four years old now, and she knew what could happen to children too young or unable to do physical labor. Most ended up in brothels, where they were used and then discarded.

But Ash was not like other children, and had a knack for deflecting unwanted attention. He'd been slow to speak, preferring to sit and listen to what went on around him. He'd always known when Bear was in a foul mood, and to hide from him.

Was he still alive? If he was, did he think of her?

She had thought all her old hatred for Bear long dulled and expended, but it resurged now along with her grief. Tears streamed down her face.

She brushed at them with the back of her wrist. She did not want Bear to discover her like this. She did not want him to get any joy from it, so she buried her emotions as deep as she could and focused on actions.

For a moment she gave serious consideration to killing her master. Believing her broken, he would not expect it. But she discarded the thought. If she did it, she would never find out where Ash had been taken. For her son's sake, she had to be strong. Somehow, she had to get the information she needed from Bear.

Then she would kill him.

By the time Bear entered the house Nieve was back in the kitchen and at the wood stove, removing an orange custard pie from the hot oven. She placed it on the counter.

Squeezing his large frame into his usual chair, he settled at the head of the long, bristlewood table.

She dared not look at him as she dished up his steaming

dinner from a pot on the stove before setting it in front of him. The glow from the oil lantern sitting in the center of the table reflected off the black windows.

"Fill another plate," he said. "And take it out to the stable."

At first, Nieve could not think why he would give her such a task. Her thoughts had been so wrapped around Ash that it was a second before she remembered the stranger.

"That man you spoke with is spending the night?" she asked, unable to hide her surprise. Bear never gave anyone permission to stay for longer than it took them to conduct business.

His harsh black eyes lingered on her, thick, wiry brows casting them into shadow. "What difference does it make to you?"

He was not happy about the stranger's presence. She tried to gauge the depth of his displeasure, wondering how best to answer him, although it was possible she was too numb to feel it if he struck her anyway.

"I need to make sure I have enough food prepared for an extra person," she said.

Bear dipped his spoon in his stew, indifferent. "You're skinny already. If you have to, missing a meal won't make much difference to you."

He stopped, the dripping, overfull spoon partway to his mouth, as if arrested by a sudden and important thought. He dropped the spoon back in his bowl and lifted his head.

She did not like the unexpected scrutiny, or the speculation in his eyes either, because she realized it was not indifference she read in him, but preoccupation.

The stranger's presence troubled him. Premonition and long experience suggested it was about to trouble her too. His eyes swept her from head to toe and made her feel naked.

"If you changed your clothes and did something with your hair, you'd be a decent-looking woman," Bear said. "Go clean yourself up. There's information I want you to get from him for me. If you were once good enough for a demon, you're likely still good enough for a Godseeker assassin. As long as he doesn't find out about the demon you slept with," he added. "It's possible he'd kill you for it. Something I should have done."

She inhaled a sharp breath. It had been four years since this was last mentioned, at least to her face, and the past slapped her. This, she would gladly forget. Bear had agreed to marry her when her father first approached him, thinking the baby she carried was mortal, but then Bear had heard the rumors. He had not wanted to so much as buy her after that, let alone marry her. Instead, her father, who she had foolishly believed loved her enough that she could tell him the truth about her baby, had paid Bear to take her.

Bear, however, maintained he would have no demon's leavings. Other than to beat her, he'd never touched her. She cooked and cleaned for him, and in the yard surrounding the house, did the work of a grown man.

But then last year, with no warning, Bear had sold her son into slavery. And now he wanted her to whore for him.

Hatred bubbled inside Nieve, so thick and hot she could barely breathe. She had endured this life for four long years. The need to do something—anything—to find her son compelled her. Sleeping with a Godseeker assassin, if that's who this stranger was, would not be the worst thing she had done at another's command.

She would not, however, do it for nothing. While Bear might own her, she also wanted information.

"I'll whore for you if you tell me what you did with my son," she said.

Bear was out of his chair so fast she had no time to do more than take a few steps back, toward the stove, and cover her head. He grasped her shoulder with one hand, then slammed a fist into her stomach. When he let her go, all she had strength to do was fall to the floor and curl in a ball.

Pain and nausea washed through her. She was not as numb as she had thought.

He loomed over her with fingers clenched. "You'll do as I say."

If she had no one to worry over but herself, Nieve would simply acquiesce, even though the thought of being possessed by the intimidating stranger terrified her, because she had relinquished her pride long ago. But knowing Ash was all alone, with no one to love and care for him, was far worse than any beating or indignity she might suffer.

Desperation motivated her. Now that she had remembered him, her wrenching heartache was as fresh and raw as if it had happened seconds ago. She might not get another opportunity to find out anything about his whereabouts, and she dared not back down now. Bear could not beat her into submission, then expect her to be able to entice a man. She would do what she had to in order to get her son back, or at least to discover what his fate had been.

She curled in a tight ball. "You'll only get what information I manage to extract from him. How hard do you think I'll try if you deny me this?"

Bear glowered down at her. "What difference can

knowing who bought the spawn make to you after all these months? He's probably dead."

He was not used to opposition from her and sounded truly perplexed. Nieve could hardly blame him. In the past year she had asked no questions about Asher—but only because she had not remembered him. She could not imagine how she had ever forgotten something so important and she swore she would not forget again.

Something else said by the men when they were outside in the yard niggled at her. The assassin claimed children were missing and the trail he followed had led him to Bear. Hope flared like a torch. There had to be a connection. She could ask the assassin a few questions of her own. If whoring got her that opportunity, then she would do it.

But Bear would only get what he wanted if he told her what he had done with Ash.

She got to her knees in the over-warm kitchen, one hand pressed to her sore stomach, the other ready to protect her head from any more blows. "I want to know what you did with him," she said. "I'll do anything you want if you tell me where he went."

"You'll do it regardless." Bear stared at her, his anger with her changing to ugly frustration. Rather than striking her again, he lowered the fist he had raised. "There's something not right about that assassin. I can't quite place it. I don't want him coming back here, or spreading stories. If you find out anything I can use against him, something that will discredit him with the Godseekers, then not only will I tell you who I sold the spawn to, I'll set you free to go find him."

Nieve's heart expanded in her chest, squeezing her

lungs. Under any other circumstances being set free was not something to anticipate, but to fear. A woman alone would have protection from nothing and no one. Wolven, while fearsome enough, were far from the worst predators she might face. But Nieve had grown up in the desert's foothills.

"I'll do my best."

He brought the back of his hand hard across her cheek, a blow she was not expecting, and her head snapped to the side, wrenching her neck.

"That's not enough to earn your freedom." Bear went back to the table and his meal. His chair legs scraped along the floor as he sat.

Nieve groped for the counter and drew herself to her feet. Even though her cheek throbbed and her stomach ached, nothing seemed ruptured or broken.

He swung his head around to glare at her as he swallowed a mouthful of the thick, hot stew. "I want to know what led a Godseeker assassin to me. I want him to stop asking questions. And I don't want him ever coming back here again. Even an assassin has a weakness."

He glanced at her bruised face as if well satisfied with what he saw.

"And I think his might just be the weak."

• • •

The small jailhouse in the tiny mining shantytown was not as secure as Willow had feared it might be.

Little more than a hastily erected shack, it had not been intended to hold anyone for more than a day at most. It had never been meant to contain a half demon. From her position in the shadows behind an abandoned shed, she waited for an opportunity to approach it without being seen.

The smells of human waste and the rotting, discarded remnants of meals filtered past the fresher tang of the surrounding mountain pine, and had her pressing a hand to her face. Willow's disgust for the mortals who lived here, and in this manner, could not be suppressed. She had grown up in slavery. Never again would she—or any other half demon if she could help it—serve crude, filthy men such as these.

Her demon father had once ruled this world. He was dead now, killed by the Demon Slayer after another of his daughters betrayed him. That daughter had then joined with the Demon Slayer against her own kind.

Willow planned to avenge her father's death. Then, she intended to rule the world in his stead. Godseekers would not be allowed to determine the futures of half demons. And no true daughter of the Demon Lord would be allowed to consort with the Slayer.

All was silent in the neighboring shanties, and had been for quite some time as the moon shifted position above her. Willow moved with swift, cautious steps toward the sagging door of the jail. She inched it open a crack, peering inside.

The lone man on guard duty sprawled in a crudely crafted chair, a stoppered flask clutched in his hand. Soft snores drifted from beneath the hat tipped to cover his face. His chest rose and fell in a deep, even rhythm. Other than that, he showed few signs of life. She wrinkled her nose. The stale smell suggested he was drunk.

So much the better.

She slipped inside and eased the door shut behind her. It closed with a faint snick and she leaned against it, listening for any unexpected movements. The sleeping man stirred, shifting in his creaky chair, but did not awaken.

A lantern hung from a hook on the wall. Its frail streams of yellow light saved her from having to expend valuable energy by summoning demon fire. Willow snapped her fingers shut over her outstretched palm and lowered her hand as she examined the prisoner she had come to rescue.

A sullen boy lounged on the dirty cot in the single jail cell. He had a knee pulled up to his chest, one foot on the tattered gray wool blanket and the other firmly on the floor. His back rested against the wall. Unwashed brown hair, with a fine curl to its tips, touched the collar of an ill-fitting, thick plaid coat. A small hole, edged by a large, suspicious stain, plus an enticing coppery smell that made Willow breathe a little deeper, suggested that the coat's previous owner had fallen victim to a gunshot wound.

"What are they holding you for?" Willow asked the boy.

He stared at her long and hard before answering. Then, "Claim jumping," he replied with a shrug, as if speaking of an inconvenience and not a charge that was about to get him hanged.

"Is that how you got your coat?"

"So what if it is?" His eyes, filled with insolence, came back to her face and ran over her in a way that made her itch to slap him. She had killed the last man to look at her that way, but this was a boy—and if he wished to be a part of her growing family, he would learn some respect. Half demons would not turn on each other the way mortals did, and females would not be the servants of males.

"Do they know you're a half demon?"

"What makes you think that I am?"

She did not think it. She knew. One of the children she had adopted in the past few months sensed others of their kind. Willow stayed clear of the ones living deep in the Godseeker Mountains. The mortal Blade, and his half demon whore Raven, had formed an alliance with the Godseekers and were too strong for her to confront on her own. She was not yet ready to raise another demon against them. Her ability to control the last one had proven too precarious.

Soon, though, when her children were grown and had learned to use their talents to defend each other, the Godseekers would die. Raven could either join her own kind or die with them. That choice was hers.

Willow gripped the bars of the cell, bringing her face between her clenched knuckles. The guard in the chair behind her remained asleep, but she had no idea for how much longer, and she was not taking unnecessary risks for someone who did not deserve it. The boy's demon talents did not appear to be so great that she would endanger herself to have them, and the children she had already rescued became unruly if left unsupervised for too long.

"You can wait here for Godseekers to judge you, and possibly discover what you are, or you can come with me," she said. "I won't make this offer again."

"I'm here for the three meals a day they bring me." He shrugged. "When the time comes, I can save myself."

Either he was lying, or he was not ready to reveal himself to mortals. Many of their kind, having suffered years of persecution at the hands of mortals, weren't able to trust enough in their newfound talents to expose them. Willow wondered which it might be, and if this boy was already too old for her to have any positive influence on him.

Or perhaps he really did want those three meals a day. He was very thin.

She started to turn away. "Then by all means, do so."

The boy rose from the cot and walked to stand in front of her. She'd been told he could shift to a partial demon form that gave him the outward appearance of one, with some added physical strength, but little else. She'd hoped his talent had grown over the past months, but it appeared that was not the case.

He blinked several times. His face broadened, flattening, and his shoulders hunched forward. Two tiny curved horns split through the skin above his temples. From the neck and cuffs of his coat, hard, red flesh encased in bone plating emerged.

She had seen real demons before. Had bound one of them to her with demon fire. So far, this child's talent did not impress or alarm her.

"What is your name?" she asked him.

"Stone." The word rumbled from his throat like gravel grinding sand. He thrust his shoulder at the cool black iron bars. They creaked, and a trickle of plaster sifted from the ceiling, but they did not bend.

"Fool!" Willow snapped, whirling, but there was nothing she could do to prevent what happened next.

The guard was no longer asleep. His flask clattered to the floor. The sharp smell of whiskey splintered the air, along with a few blistering words. Bleary eyes captured her, registered her presence, and shifted to Stone. Willow saw the guard's confusion, then the dawning fear at what appeared to be a demon standing inside the cell. His chair tipped over in his scramble to get to the door.

Willow had to act quickly. She withdrew a long knife from the sheath hidden in the folds of her skirt at her hip, and ran to intercept him. She caught him by the arm, intending to drag him back, but he was larger than she was and fear gave him added strength. He swung his head out of reach when she tried to catch him by the throat, and thrust one elbow into her chest as he shook off her hand. His fingers grazed the door handle.

Willow could not allow him to escape and alert anyone else to what he had seen. She drove her knife into the soft flesh at the base of his skull. The man was too tall for the blow to do what she intended. He clawed at the knife's handle protruding from the nape of his neck, and screamed— horrible, mewling sounds, like those of a rabbit trapped in a snare. He went to his knees. Blood bubbled from the wound. The heady smell of it made Willow shiver.

But, while she could resist it, it sent Stone into a full, blood-lusted frenzy. He threw himself against the bars, again and again, despite her sharp commands for him to calm himself.

She snatched a handful of the greasy hair of the man she had stabbed, drew back his head so that it rested against her hip, and slashed his throat from ear to ear. The screaming ended abruptly. Hot blood spurted over her wrist and gushed onto the door and wall. She brought her wrist to her lips, tasting the blood with a flick of her tongue, then dragged the wet blade of the knife across the dead man's shirt to wipe it as clean as possible before slipping it back in its sheath.

Already, shouts echoed outside as the miners in the dozen or so surrounding shanties called out to each other, demanding for someone to check on the jail. She had only a few minutes until they became even more curious about the sudden silence.

"Shift back to your mortal form," she commanded. "I don't want anyone else to see you like this. If they do, I'll leave you here for the Godseekers to deal with. Do you understand me?"

Stone gave a single, jerking nod of his head. The red bone shell he wore melted back into his body, leaving flesh in its place.

Willow reached between the bars and grabbed him by the front of his coat to shake him. He might be half demon, but he was also very stupid. She was not certain any longer that she wanted or needed him. Or even if she could manage him.

She most certainly did not need this aggravation. Outside, in the path that served as a street, the sound of men's voices was coming closer.

If Stone could not keep up with her, she would abandon him.

She released his coat, then forced fire through her palms and into the metal lock of the cell door. The metal smoldered and smoked before turning a bright, cherry red. When it was hot and melting, she pried the lock off.

It fell to the wooden floor. The planks turned black as they charred, then smoked, and finally, dry as tinder, caught fire. The hate darkening Stone's expression turned to grudging respect as he swung the door open and stepped from the cell.

The fire on the floor was spreading fast. Willow ran through her options in her head. Her use of demon talent, even though slight, drained her physical strength. Her real abilities lay in her instincts.

They could not go out the front door. There were too many people blocking the way. That meant they had to make a back exit for themselves.

She grabbed the lamp from the hook and smashed it against the wall. The splattered oil ignited. That would slow anyone down if they tried to enter from the front. A window at the back, low to the ground and too small for Stone to climb through, was now their only means of escape.

"Give me your coat. I'm going to break out the glass," she said.

She wrapped the coat around her fist, and drove her hand through the glass. It shattered into glittering splinters. She tossed the coat back to him and examined the opening. She would have to make it bigger somehow.

"Let me."

Stone took a few steps back, then, as his foot began to enlarge and his leg to lengthen, he rammed it against the wooden frame and widened the hole. Without stopping to see if she was behind him, he went over the broken ledge and vanished into the night.

Flames licked at her heels as Willow climbed from the burning jail to freedom. She followed Stone's trail through the pines.

He could shift individual body parts. That could prove a useful talent to her, after all.

Chapter Three

The stable smelled of warm hross, and grain mixed with molasses.

It was not long past the end of winter and the few bales of dusty hay that remained in the loft were no longer fit for consumption, so Creed cut the twine on one bale and threw it down for bedding. He then fed his hross a liberal amount of feed from the well-stocked bin. Bear might not offer much by way of hospitality to people, but signs indicated he was good to his animals. The other hross in the stable appeared well tended.

Bear's sand swift, thankfully, did not share a roof with the other animals, but had been turned loose to fend for itself. Creed assumed the creature did not wander far from the ranch, and suspected the reason Bear released it was because it served as an excellent watchdog. That made Creed doubly glad he had gotten an invitation to stay. The thought of a hungry sand swift following his scent in the night held little appeal.

It also meant he was effectively trapped inside the stable until daylight. He hoped to have better luck using compulsion on Bear in the morning. Without the sand swift around, he would not hesitate to use his talents to get the information he required so he could then be on his way. This place disturbed him, leaving him restless.

He was not used to the sensation.

He spread his blankets in an empty stall and dug out some hardtack from one of his packs. It was fully dark outside now. The moon had not yet risen, and the faint light from the tiny windows beneath the rafters of one long wall was inadequate. Even so, he chose not to employ his kerosene lantern. Stable fires were too common. He planned to spend his time sleeping.

His thoughts returned to the pretty, timid young woman and the possible reasons why she had been eavesdropping on his conversation with Bear, and could only reach one conclusion. The child had to be hers. That was all he could think of that would make her so bold, because in every other respect, she gave off an air of the utterly defeated.

Raven would despise a woman like that.

Creed did not often think of his sister these days. Leaving her had been the hardest thing he'd ever done, but the moment he'd met Blade, he had known that disengaging himself from her life was the right thing to do. The former assassin might have his hands full with her, but he would protect her in a way Creed could no longer do. She'd needed more. And Raven, for her part, would tear the soul from anyone who tried to harm Blade.

The two women could not be more unlike, and yet in

their own way, each was equally vulnerable.

He wondered why Bear would sell off his son when it was obvious not only could he afford to keep him, but someday soon would have need of the cheap labor he would have provided.

A faint scraping noise at the front of the stable had Creed sitting upright, instantly alert. The door inched slowly back, and a thin stream of pale yellow light crept inside.

When he saw who it was, Creed could not have been more surprised. She had made it clear he frightened her to the point of incapacity.

She juggled a lantern and a large basket as she wrestled with the door. Creed took swift advantage of her distraction, and was out of the stall and across the stable in an instant to help her. He took the basket from her hand and manipulated the door, pushing it wider on its runners to let her inside before drawing it shut again behind her.

She turned her face toward the closed-off escape route, and Creed saw that he frightened her still. He put as much reassurance as he could into his manner.

"There's a sand swift roaming free," he said. "I'd prefer it to stay out there."

She made an excellent attempt to return his smile. "It's been trained to leave me alone, but I still run when I see it coming if Bear's not around."

Creed doubted if running would save her. Sand swifts were faster than they looked, especially when hunting, but at least she did not simply stand and do nothing to try and save herself.

"Grab a rock or whatever is handy and hit it on the snout," he advised her. "But avoid its tongue if you can."

A sand swift's tongue, meant to capture prey, was covered in coarse buds that could tear a woman's delicate flesh to shreds with one flick. He looked at the basket. An enticing aroma of cooked kyson meat and vegetables wafted from it, and the hardtack he'd been planning to eat no longer held much appeal. He hefted the basket. "Is this for me?"

"Bear told me to bring you some dinner. It's stew," she added.

She exuded waves of discomfort at being alone with him. She shifted her eyes to the closed door, and Creed wondered why she did not leave now that the meal had been delivered.

He wondered, too, why Bear had really sent her. He was not the type of man to be concerned over the welfare of an unwelcome guest. The odds were good that she had been sent to question Creed, and there could be only one way he thought she could get information from him. Although whoring women to guests was a common enough practice, Creed's distaste for Bear increased. A man should protect a woman under his roof, not place her in a position such as this.

Since she seemed in no hurry to leave, and he thought it likely she might have answers to some of his own questions, he tried to make himself appear as non-threatening to her as possible.

Normally that was not difficult for him to do. This woman, however, seemed immune to him. He found that both intriguing and a challenge. If most women loved him, and his intentions toward this one were harmless, why did she continue to shy away from him?

This one's life was difficult enough without him adding to that. While he would like to question her about her son, he wanted to win her confidence more.

"Thank you," he said. "Since you know my name, do you mind if I ask for yours?" He sent out a tiny bit of compulsion with the question, although not enough to do more than give her a choice as to her response. She could answer him or not, whichever she preferred.

She bit her lip. "Nieve."

The name meant *innocent*. He could not imagine a more appropriate one. Except, perhaps, for *Mouse*.

"Well, Nieve. Would you like to sit with me while I eat, so you can take the basket back to the kitchen with you?"

She nodded, her relief at being handed a reasonable excuse to stay palpable, but she had so many other emotions swirling in her that he found them difficult to sift through. Fear was most prevalent. Almost equal was determination.

He dragged two new bales of hay from the loft above for them to sit on, and positioned them so that he faced her. Nieve said nothing as he proceeded to eat the contents of the basket.

He chewed slowly, watching her without appearing to do so. In the light from her lamp, which he'd hung from a hook on a gray-cobwebbed, dusty beam, he saw a darkening bruise spreading, finger-like, across her face. The bruise had not been there earlier.

His grip on the fork he held tightened, and he forced himself to remember that she belonged to another man. He had a duty to uphold the laws of the land, and right now, like it or not, the laws did not favor her. It was incomprehensible to him, though, how Bear could treat a sand swift with more patience and kindness than a fragile, beautiful woman such as this.

"Is it true that the Godseekers are hunting down spawn and putting them to death?" she blurted out, breaking the silence.

Creed, his mouth full of food, took his time to think about that before answering. "Yes and no. It has to be proven they're half demon, and dangerous," he replied. "All I'm tasked with is bringing them to justice."

Nieve looked at her fingers, which she had twisted together in her lap, as she asked her next question. "If you're seeking spawn, then why are a few missing children of such interest to the Godseekers?"

"It's a matter of who they belong to that makes them of interest." And they were not of interest to the Godseekers. Only to Creed.

"Do you believe there's a connection between spawn and these missing children?"

The deeper Creed investigated the matter, the more certain of that he became, and while he suspected the answer, he could not yet say for sure. What he did know was that the questions Nieve asked were of far more importance to her than to Bear. He might have wondered if she had demon in her own background if she were not so meek. He wiped his mouth with a cloth napkin she had provided him, then packed his empty plate and his fork into the basket and closed it.

"I'm sorry," he said quietly, "but I know nothing of your son or what might have happened to him. Bear readily admits to selling him, so he doesn't fit the same pattern as the others who've disappeared. Tell me what Bear sent you to find out from me so I can help you provide him with satisfactory answers."

Her face crumpled. Enormous tears, captured by the lamplight, tracked like melting diamonds down both of her cheeks.

Creed rubbed the back of his neck, torn between an instinct to offer comfort and use of common sense. With a faint, muttered oath, he crossed the short distance between them to sit at her side. She did not stiffen or pull away, as he'd half-expected and hoped, but lost in some private world of her own, seemed not to notice his presence at all.

She doubled over with her arms clutched tight around her waist and sucked in loud, agonized breaths that shook her slight shoulders. Hair the color of cream spilled from her bent head and over her arm to hide her face from him. Her grief, so enormous and fresh that it hurt him to be this close to her, swept over and around him.

He was at a loss for an explanation for her behavior. Something was not right. Her son had been taken from her a year ago, yet she reacted as if it had happened much more recently than that.

Again, he ran his hand along the back of his neck, and up the smooth lines of the tattoo winding from the nape of his neck to his crown. He was reacting to her as if he had never been this close to a woman before. He tried to imagine her as his sister, and how he would deal with her in this situation, but could not. Raven was fire and passion. She would be plotting a murder, not sobbing as if she had lost all reason to live.

Nieve seemed a broken woman.

Another man's property or not, Creed could not walk away from this and ignore it. He draped an arm around her and drew her to him so that her cheek rested against his thigh. His other hand stroked the top of her head, his fingers tangling through her soft hair. He was large in comparison to her, and he did not wish for her to be frightened by him again, so he sent a faint tendril of compulsion to belay her fear while he whispered a few nonsensical words of comfort.

It was a long time before her shaking stopped and the sobs died away to become muffled sniffles and sighs. He reached for the basket, on the floor not far from their feet, and pulled it closer. From inside, he retrieved the cloth napkin and used the clean side of it to wipe her face as if she were a child.

Up close in the pale lantern light, even with her bruised face splotched from crying and her eyes red, it was plain she was even lovelier than his first impression of her had intimated. What was equally obvious was that she had no wish to bring any attention to it.

She did not object to him holding her, however, so he did not release her. She shifted her head so her cheek pressed against the front of his shirt. He rested his chin on her crown but otherwise allowed her the freedom to withdraw from his touch whenever she chose. There was very little he could do for her except treat her with kindness, something he was certain she rarely received.

"You have yet to ask me Bear's questions," he said to her.

When she answered, she sounded tired. Defeated. "I have nothing more to ask, other than that we sit here like this for a few minutes. That's all."

The raw emotions that had bombarded him dissipated, as if she had drawn them back into herself and somehow buried them. In their place ran a thin thread of psychological steel, bent but not yet broken. Perhaps she was not as defeated as he'd thought.

He eased them apart, worried that she would soon grow aware of the awkwardness of their too-familiar position, but she slid her arms around his waist. Instantly, desire for her shot from his groin to his chest. Her action, and his response to it, startled him in equal measure. He blamed it on the compulsion he had extended to her, and worried that this might not be the best time for him to withdraw it. But she could not continue to fear him while he held her, at her own request, when so far he had posed no threat.

She rolled deeper into his arms before lifting her face. Their eyes connected. It seemed he was not the only one equipped with emitting compulsion. He dipped his mouth to hers. She tasted sweet and warm, and made him forget his resolve not to frighten her further. It was as if a switch had gone off in his brain, telling him that she was his and he had to have her.

His mouth moved from hers to the soft curve of her neck. He slid his fingers into the collar of her dress, plucking at the buttons, easing them undone until her breast filled one palm. She let out soft cries of pleasure, her fingers clutching at his arms, her green eyes closed and her head thrown back. Creed carried her from the bale of hay to the stall where he'd spread his blankets. She shivered in his arms, as if suddenly uncertain, and he again sent out a waft of compulsion—not enough to sway her against her wishes, but enough to overcome any fears she might yet entertain. He wanted her, but of her own will, not his.

Certainly not Bear's.

The thought of the other man made Creed too reckless. The compulsion he discharged became more intense than he'd planned. Nieve's eyes widened, her small hands tightening on his biceps as he settled her on the blankets beneath him.

It was darker here, and he could not read her expression, but the sudden stiffening in her body, and the heightened caution in her mood, were unmistakable.

She pushed against his chest with both tiny hands, surprisingly strong for such a small woman, and he rolled away, not resisting.

She sat up, drawing the front of her dress together as she scrambled to her feet, then stumbling as the blankets tangled around her. He reached out to steady her, fingers brushing the length of her skirt, but she swept it out of his reach.

"You're a *demon*," she spat at him.

She backed way, and he called out a warning for her to mind the lantern hanging behind her, but she either did not hear him or was too panicked to understand his words. Her head brushed the base of the lantern, rocking it on its hook. The light spun crazily around the stable, bouncing off the walls, before the lantern crashed to the dirt floor. Kerosene licked along the ground, followed in seconds by flame.

Nieve bolted for the door.

Creed grabbed up one of his blankets and the bucket of water he had set aside for the animals. Within a few moments he had extinguished the fire, and the stable was once again plunged into darkness. By now the moon was up, and the windows offered enough light for him to find his way to the stalls. It took him longer than he liked to calm down the animals, even though he sent out soothing compulsion as he checked on each one.

Nieve was gone long enough to raise an alarm with

Bear, but so far, the old man had not stirred from the house. Creed would have known, although he could not believe how stupid he was for misreading her.

He did not blame her for this. He had pushed her too hard, and tried to sway her emotions too abruptly, with all the finesse of a teenage boy. He should never have tried to compel her in the first place, and could not explain to himself why he had, other than he had wanted her.

He wanted her still. It made no sense to him. Nieve was fragile, and while not completely broken she was badly damaged, and would prove too much of a burden for any man. Particularly one in his position.

Creed, however, could not disengage his thoughts from her. To complicate matters his demon, on edge from the moment he'd met her, refused to settle.

Frustration coiled through his belly. He had always been a fool for women in distress. He had adored Raven's mother, partly because she had been willing to love him as if he were her own son, but mostly because she had needed his love in return. Her mortal husband had not been kind, and Raven, half demon and bold, had not understood her timidity.

One more thing about this evening troubled him immensely. Other than Raven's mother, who had loved his father, no one had ever recognized Creed as being half demon before.

Yet quiet, innocent, mouse-like Nieve had managed to do so.

· · ·

Nieve closed the door as quietly as possible behind her

despite the unrelenting terror that clawed at her throat. The house was still, and she thanked the goddesses for that. She did not want to attract Bear's attention. He had expected her to be gone for the entire night and would not be pleased to see her back so soon. Despite the early hour, he must be asleep already. He was no longer a young man and would be tired from riding on the back of a sand swift all day.

With a bit of luck she would not have to answer his questions until morning. At least she had found something he could use against the assassin.

Creed.

The name had to be someone's idea of a joke. Demons did not live by creeds. They killed men and used women, luring them against their will even while inside their heads they were screaming.

Leaning against the wall for support, she bent at the waist and tried not to be sick to her stomach. Memories, unwanted, washed into her thoughts, images she had tried to suppress for too long. She loved her son more than her own life. She wanted him back. He was hers, and had nothing to do with his demon father.

But her fear of Asher's father could not be restrained, and as the flood gates opened, her whole body shuddered at her recollection of every intimate detail of his touch on her flesh. She had never wanted him. She had known the things he did to her were wrong, and had not wanted to receive pleasure from them, but had been helpless against his allure. No matter how hard she had tried, Ash's demon father had been impossible for her to resist. Not until she became pregnant.

Tonight, she had let another demon touch her. Had in

fact welcomed it. And she loathed herself for that.

She despised Creed for it as well. His methods might have been different, but the result, very nearly the same. He had feigned gentleness and kindness at first, and then he had tried to lure her. But she was older now, and wiser. Possibly less attractive to a demon, too—because she had been able to resist Creed, which made her suspect he had not tried as hard as he might have if truly interested.

She thanked the goddesses for that as well.

She scrubbed the heel of a trembling hand across her mouth where his lips had been on hers, but the lingering warmth of him, and the spellbinding taste, would not be erased.

The front of her dress remained undone. She fumbled with the buttons, the tips of her fingers numb and next to useless. In spite of everything, she could not forget his considerate words to her, and the offer of help. *Tell me what Bear sent you to find out from me so I can help you provide him with satisfactory answers.*

How pitiful she was that she could be swayed from her purpose, even for a moment, by such a small gesture that was undoubtedly empty.

She crept through the great room and into the hall leading to the bedrooms, making her way by memory and the moonlight dappling the floors. She stepped around the loose board in front of Bear's door that had a tendency to creak. The long, low, familiar rumble of his snores followed by the heaving of bedsprings told her he slept soundly.

She reached her own door and slipped inside.

The room was plain, with its chipped furnishings that had seen better days, but clean and private. Next to the tall window a low commode held a neat runner, a wash basin and pitcher, a warped mirror, and her hairbrush. Along the back ran a rack for her drying cloth. Inside the commode's cupboard was a chamber pot. Three drawers housed her intimates—undergarments, clean washcloths, and other personal items. A wardrobe held three dresses, a plain, raw-cotton blouse, and a pair of trousers. On a stand beside her narrow bed was a stub of a candle. Her night gown hung over the back of a hand-strung chair.

All traces of Ash had been removed, and she could not say when or how.

She curled her feet under her skirt as she sat on the floor beneath her window, her arms on the ledge, her chin on her arms, and stared at the stable. She had to be stronger than this. She had no tears left in her anyway.

As her terror and self-loathing eased, she pulled her thoughts into order. The demon posing as a Godseeker assassin had said something else that was of importance to her. *I know nothing of your son or what may have happened to him.*

If he was to be believed, that meant she had no one to turn to but Bear. She stared pensively into the night. Whether or not she believed him, she would not get any answers from him. Demons took. They did not give.

She wanted her son back. But how was she to tell Bear what she had discovered and be certain he would fulfill his promise to her? Would he tell her the truth about Ash if she gave him the information about Creed that he wanted?

Would he really let her go so she could find her son?

She went to bed, although she did not sleep well.

• • •

The next morning brought her no closer to answers. Dawn stole over the mountains to settle in the foothills and around the ranch.

She lifted her head from her pillow, blinking awake with eyes scratchy from poor sleep and spent tears. She swung her feet to the floor and gripped the edge of her bed. She had not taken the time to undress, which was just as well. Bear would be up early and expecting his breakfast on the table.

No allowances would be made for the whoring he had also expected of her.

She smoothed her clothing as best she could. She had no urge to face Creed again. If she was lucky, he would be long gone. She could then tell Bear that yes, she had discovered something about the assassin he could use, and force him to tell her about Ash before revealing anything to him. Let him try to beat it from her again. He had not succeeded in doing so last night.

Bracing herself, she reached for the door. She had also resisted the lure of a demon, and should take pride in that, too. She was not as weak as she had thought.

Bear was seated at the table when she entered the kitchen.

Instinctive, ingrained fear leaped in her chest despite her determination to contain it, leaving her dizzy, but then she saw he did not seem bothered by her late appearance. She moved to the stove.

"I'll have your breakfast ready in a few moments," she said.

"Leave it." He splayed a giant, work-worn palm on the table. As his fingers flexed a splash of sunlight caught the fine, graying hairs on his knuckles, transfixing her attention so that she could not seem to look away. "What did you learn?"

Now that the moment of her rebellion had arrived, Nieve

discovered she was not as brave as she'd thought. Then Ash's small face flashed into her thoughts and strengthened her courage.

She forced herself to lift her eyes to Bear's.

"First, where is my son?" The tremble in her voice felt very faint to her, hopefully leaving it undetectable to him.

The fingers on the table curled. "Don't play games with me."

She was too terrified for games. "You made me a promise."

Thick gray brows formed a single, ominous line above the bridge of his nose. His expression turned ugly. He hooked an elbow over the back of his chair and stared at her with cold eyes, and she tried not to shudder.

"I don't have to make promises to you, or to keep them," he said. "I could kill you and no one would care. You have no one but me to look after you, and if I don't want to keep you here any longer, what do you suppose will happen to you then?"

A sick sense of dread edged out her fear. Bear did not like to be opposed and he'd had all night to think about how best to deal with it.

She had lost everything. He had no intention of telling her where her son was. Once she told him what she had learned about Creed, he planned to kill her. No one would care if he did. It would matter to no one.

Except to Ash.

She had one card left she could play.

"What do you suppose a demon might do to the mortal man who harms a woman it's claimed?" she asked.

He laughed, ugly and mean. "Demons are gone."

"No," she said. "They're not."

Chapter Four

Creed awoke to a feeling of pressure crushing his chest that caused him difficulty in drawing breath. A sense of impending disaster had him on his feet in an instant, his gun in his hand.

His demon, normally so easily contained, had come unleashed while he slept. That could only mean trouble.

As he cast a glance around the stable's gloomy interior, struggling to inhale, all appeared to be in order. He peered between the wide doors into the yard outside, and listened for long moments, but saw and heard nothing.

And yet he knew there was trouble close by. His demon refused to be calmed. He slid the pistol into the waistband of his trousers at the small of his back so that it was within easy reach but left his hands unencumbered. The threat of doom had not faded although he could breathe again. Someone's life was in danger, and if not his, then whose?

Nieve.

He had been dreaming of her, and her name came to him with such certainty that he could not ignore it. If he did not act now, she would be dead.

He squeezed through the stable doors, not wanting to open them enough to allow the sand swift access to the restless hross inside, then loped across the yard and around the ranch house to the kitchen.

The door, when he tried it, was locked.

Through the long, narrow side window, he saw Bear. The man's back was to him. Facing Bear was Nieve. Creed tasted her terror, burning like acid on the back of his tongue.

There were other emotions bleeding from her, but as Bear drew back a fist, Creed did not take the time to identify them. This was why he had awoken, unable to breathe. The demon inside him was struggling for freedom in response to her distress.

Always, in the past, Creed had been able to restrain it without effort. Now, the flesh across his shoulders crackled and split, and strained against the seams of his clothing before he managed to subdue it. He capitalized on the physical strength it unleashed in him to smash through the kitchen door with his shoulder, blasting it back on its hinges. It struck the interior wall with a solid crash.

Bear half-spun to face him, fist still cocked. "*This* is your demon?" he demanded of Nieve. "A Godseeker assassin? Are you certain of it?"

Nieve nodded, even as she took a step behind him so that he formed a barrier between her and Creed.

A shard of incredulous outrage slid into Creed's thoughts, still partially possessed by his demon, that she had turned to a man who beat her and intended to kill her for protection from him.

He set aside a stinging sense of betrayal. It hardly mattered that in her fear, she had revealed a secret about him to an enemy. What did matter was that she had nothing to fear from him—even if she did not yet understand that.

Creed said nothing as he waited to see what either one would do next. He had already decided he could not leave Nieve here with this man.

But Creed was the one in the wrong in this particular situation. No laws protected Nieve. The old man owned her and could do with her as he pleased. If Creed tried to take Nieve away, Bear had every right to appeal to the Godseekers for restitution.

To protect her, Creed had no choice but to kill him. That was the one action an assassin would have no need to explain.

His demon rumbled agreement.

An unpleasant smile curled Bear's thick, sun-cracked lips. "No. Not a full-blooded demon," he said, staring hard at Creed's face. "But no doubt a demon's spawn. Do the Godseekers know what you are, Assassin?"

They both knew they did not. Godseekers had spent countless years as faithful servants to the goddesses. They had little love for half demons. They would never trust one in a position such as Creed's.

With a speed born of long hours of training, Creed reached for his pistol, then shot the man twice in the chest, careful with his aim so that Nieve, behind Bear, would not be hit.

Both bullets passed through Bear's body. One struck the cast iron stove and ricocheted into the wall. The other buried itself in the frame of the door leading to the rest of the house.

Shock edged out the old man's self-satisfied expression. His hands clutched at his chest. Blood seeped past his fingers to spread across the front of his thick plaid work shirt. It dripped from beneath his palms. He folded at the knees, then crumpled forward and was still.

Creed set the pistol on top of the table, the barrel too hot to holster in his waistband, but he did not want her to feel threatened by him.

Nieve backed away. Her heel caught the potbellied stove's cast iron poker, knocking it over with a clatter. It scraped against the blistered linoleum flooring to catch on one leg of the stove.

"I'm not going to hurt you," Creed said.

Hate, as well as fear, flowed from her now. "You've ruined everything."

Creed strained to hear her soft-spoken words and struggled to understand them. At first, they were incomprehensible. He had saved her.

But when he examined the situation from her perspective, he thought perhaps she was right. He'd had no right to interfere. Perhaps she preferred death. Many women did, and she was far from the strongest one he'd ever met. What future could she possibly have now?

He had ruined things for himself as well, or at least created a serious setback. Bear could no longer give him the information he wanted regarding the missing children.

They remained his priority. The world was changing with the immortals gone, and Creed hoped it would one day become a better place for it. That meant he had to do his own part to help in its transformation. Children, mortal and half demon alike, were the key.

Now that the danger to Nieve had passed, his demon had settled. He could tuck away these complex and baffling feelings he harbored for her. She hated him and feared him, but he could not walk away and abandon her to an uncertain fate. Anything could happen out here, in such isolation, to a woman alone. He would take her to safety, then move on with his journey.

The house was silent except for the harsh breaths Nieve drew in. She brushed back a length of pale hair from her cheek with an unsteady hand. Fat teardrops clung to her long lashes, making her eyes sparkle like green pools of light.

A significant change had manifested in her. Gone was the despair from last night. She had made some sort of decision, and whatever it was, he was wary of it.

"Do you have somewhere to go? Somewhere I can take you?" Creed asked. "Any family?"

"I'm not going anywhere with you." She spat the words at him.

The tattoo between his shoulders itched. Again, he experienced an inexplicable, stinging sense of betrayal but shrugged it off. He understood self-preservation and the things it made a person do. She did not owe him loyalty or gratitude for helping her, especially when she did not seem to want it, but right now, she needed to hear truth. This was not a woman used to, or capable of, taking care of herself.

"You'd rather stay here with a dead body?"

Those too-large green eyes widened as at least part of the reality of her situation slowly settled in. "I can bury him."

It would take her days to dig a hole in the baked earth

that would be deep enough.

"Let's say you do. After that, how will you explain his disappearance?"

"I'll tell the sheriff what happened."

"Fledge won't believe that a Godseeker assassin left a witness behind." Creed punched holes in her logic in an attempt to make her see the entire picture and the hopelessness of her situation. "No one will believe any man left a woman—especially one as pretty as you—behind, either. Besides," he added, "Bear claimed there are wolven hunting in the area, killing his calves. Don't forget about the sand swift roaming free in the yard, or that it's going to grow hungry soon."

Men also traveled the area with as much frequency as wolven or sand swifts and were more dangerous to women than any of the desert's many natural predators.

He went in for the kill. "You have a ranch that will be left without an income, or at least any avenue for a woman to claim it. What do you think will happen to all of Bear's possessions when it becomes obvious to the locals that he's gone and is not coming back?"

She seized on that final point. "It will be a long time before anyone notices he's missing."

"Not long enough. And if it takes them too long, you'll die of starvation. Or worse. Right now I'm your only hope."

A hint of steel touched her eyes. "You don't know what I hope for."

Creed was at a loss. As much as he'd like to, or his demon would like for him to, he could not take her with him. Not hunting spawn. Especially not one such as Willow.

He could leave her with the sheriff in Desert's End, who

seemed to have some honor to him, but that was no real solution. The sheriff was dying, and it would not be long before Nieve was back in this same situation, with no one to look out for her.

He did not have time to find somewhere else for her to go. If she had been the least bit like Raven he might consider taking her with him, but the best thing for him to do would be to leave her here, for now, and hope for the best. She was too timid and delicate for the hardships imposed by his line of work. He lived out of his saddlebags.

He would come back for her after he tracked down Willow. Nieve should be fine for a few months, at least if she were adequately armed, although he did not hold much faith in her ability to defend herself if she were threatened.

His demon stirred in protest at the thought of walking away from her. Creed suppressed it, although with greater difficulty than usual.

A puff of dust kicked up at the stoop of the broken door that swayed on its one remaining hinge. He made one last effort to make her see reason, and to find a better solution that might appease his protesting demon.

"What about your family?" he asked again. "Is there no one you can return to?"

"My family is gone."

She said it with such finality that he believed her. She had no one.

While he did not like it, nor did his demon, he would repair the door for her and bury the old man's remains. He would leave behind what he could spare of the weapons he carried, and check to see what others Bear kept in storage, and ensure she knew how to use them. Then, he would have to leave her here.

At least until he could return for her.

• • •

The coppery scent of Bear's blood made Nieve nauseous, although there was not as much of it as she might have expected. It seemed the demon assassin knew his trade well.

While she could hardly mourn for a man who beat her, and in the end intended to kill her, she had never seen someone murdered before. Or in such a cold, dispassionate manner.

Inside, she shuddered. The compulsion he had weaved last night might have cloaked Creed's violent nature from her for a short time, but she would not fall victim to it again. She would never be able to trust a man like this, even had he not been a full-blooded demon. Bear might have taken him for spawn. She did not. She knew the difference.

And now that she knew of Ash's existence, she could not give up on finding him. Bear had been her best hope for information, but she refused to accept that he'd been her only one. If she did, she'd go mad.

She would rifle through his possessions for any possible clues as to Ash's whereabouts. If she found nothing, she would head into Desert's End and ask questions there. Somewhere, someone knew at least something of what had happened to her son.

But first, before she could do anything, she needed to be rid of the demon assassin.

The kitchen resounded with silence as he continued to ponder her, an expression of doubt on his face. "I know you believe you have no reason to trust me," he said, "but I've given you no reason not to, either. If I'd wanted to harm you I would have done so before now."

The sympathetic kindness spilling from those warm, deep blue eyes captivated her, making her want to believe him, but she didn't dare. She did not trust that his idea of harm and hers were precisely the same. Memories from the previous night, and a more distant past, assaulted her.

He had no reason to care about her safety.

She had nothing with which to protect herself. She glanced at his gun on the table behind him, then as quickly, away. She could never reach it fast enough and they both knew it. Not with Bear's body sprawled between them.

The morning sun shining through the broken doorway created a halo effect of red and golden light around Creed as he retrieved his weapon, tucking it into the waistband of his trousers at the small of his back. A flaming tattoo winged upward from beneath the loose collar of his shirt to wrap around the nape of his neck and the back of his smooth-shaven, perfectly shaped head.

Even without the use of compulsion he would be a captivatingly beautiful man, but it was another, and indefinable, air surrounding him that convinced her he could be nothing less than a full-blooded demon. It could almost, but not quite, make her forget this terrible, soul-crushing and urgent need to find Ash.

It terrified her that she might forget her son again. She could not hide that fear.

"Then please, leave me alone," she said. "Go away."

Stubbornness crept past the warmth of the assassin's eyes.

"I'll bury the old man and fix your door before I leave."

Nieve pressed a hand to her stomach and turned away as he grabbed Bear's legs at the ankles and hauled him across the blood-slickened floor. She left the kitchen without another word.

Bear kept his papers and records in an office off the front parlor. That was where she went now, to search through his effects.

As she pushed the door open, she held her breath. It was foolish of her to feel such nervousness. Bear was dead and could not harm her anymore, so it no longer mattered that she was not supposed to enter this room.

It was stuffy and dirty, but more in a neglected way than a truly untidy one, although the floor was piled high with well-thumbed books. The room had no shelves on which to store them.

She'd had no idea that Bear enjoyed reading.

A wide, overstuffed chair with curved, threadbare arms sat near the window. Its fabric might once have been white. Now, it was gray and somewhat yellowed. A solid, ornately carved desk flanked the other side of the window, although it was obvious that Bear never sat there. It had been shoved against the wall so that the matching chair was pinned behind it. A pen and ledger lay on the outer edge of the desktop, not the inside.

Three filing cabinets overflowed with papers crammed so tight inside the drawers that they could no longer fully close.

She surveyed the room with growing dismay. It was clear that she had considerable work ahead of her, when a foolish part of her had expected to ride out this same day, on the assassin's heels.

• • •

Hours later, with the angle of the sun shining through the window indicating it was at least midday, she heard steps outside the closed door, then a soft knock and her name.

"Nieve?"

She sat on the round, braided rug in the middle of the floor, suddenly conscious of the frenetic chaos she had created, and the papers strewn haphazardly in every direction around her. She went very still, praying that if she did not answer, he might go away.

Instead, the door inched open. He peered around it, first at her, then at the mass of papers she could not hope to hide, before pushing it farther. The bottom of the door caught on some of the sheaves, dragging them across the rug and crumpling their edges, and she stifled a sharp cry of dismay because she'd not yet had a chance to examine them.

He stooped and gathered them, smoothing them against his muscular thigh with the palm of one hand while he continued to regard her with a thoughtful frown.

"I found a few weapons and some ammunition in Bear's storage room that you should find easy enough to use," he said. "I've also got a small handgun that I thought I might leave behind. Do you know how to use a gun?"

She'd never had any reason to learn. It was not something she'd had to know growing up, and certainly not anything Bear would want to teach her. Bullets were expensive and difficult to obtain. He would not have wasted them.

"Of course," she lied. "Most women do."

"No," he said. "Most women do not." His mouth twitched into a faint almost-smile. The creases it created at the corners of his lips surprised her because they suggested he smiled often, or at least he had at one time. He held out the papers and she took them, adding them to the unread pile on the floor beside her. "Why don't you come with me for a few moments and I'll give you a quick lesson in the yard? Just to ease my conscience about leaving you here alone?" he added, before she could object. He looked at the papers. A dark eyebrow lifted. "Unless you'd like me to help you find whatever it is you're looking for in here?"

She could think of nothing she wanted less. "You don't need to worry about me. I'll be fine."

"But I will worry. You can either convince me you know how to fire a gun, or you can let me give you a quick lesson. I'm not leaving until I've seen evidence that you can protect yourself."

She did not want his concern. Neither did she care to be in the close proximity to him that such a lesson would require. She did not trust him, or the troubled warmth in his eyes no doubt meant to lull her into a false sense of security, because inside, and from past experience, she knew she should be screaming.

Yet she did not dare let him see how afraid of him she was. Demons fed on fear. Standing strong against him was her best defense. She would show him that she could, indeed, protect herself.

For Ash, she would do what she had to.

"Very well." As she stood she kept her head down, pretending not to see the hand he extended to help her. She would not let him touch her again.

His hand dropped to his side. He stepped out of the doorway, giving her plenty of room to walk past him.

• • •

Creed did not care to contemplate her aversion for him. He did not want to know anything about her anymore, other than that she would be safe.

Because what he did know was that his demon half was far too attracted to her, making it difficult for him to control, and that was not good.

Not for anyone.

He followed her past the parlor and out the front door, into the yard, where he had set up a few targets for her to practice on. A row of tin cans crested the top of a rough wooden sawhorse he'd found in an outbuilding. She would need to be able to use Bear's rifle from a reasonable pace in case wolven came prowling around. She would not want to let them get too close. His handgun, conversely, would be more useful to her at a closer range, because she could not shoot a man from any great distance and call it self-defense. It was a small, single-shot pistol with a pearl grip, and she could hide it in her skirt.

First, he taught her how to load each weapon. Then he showed her how to hold the rifle.

"Not into your shoulder," he said. "The kickback's too much for a woman your size. Prop it on top. Like this."

The crown of her head skimmed the underside of his chin as he shifted the butt of the rifle into a better position for her. His nearness made her nervous. He sensed it in the same way he smelled the soap she used and felt the hot sun on his skin. His demon rampaged inside him, tortured to have her so close and yet be forced to maintain a distance.

She lifted those wide green eyes, casting him a look of anxious suspicion as if she sensed the internal battle he fought. He forced his attention away from her and onto the target.

She crooked a stray length of white-blond hair behind her ear with a slender finger, bit her lip in concentration, took aim, and fired the rifle. The barrel shot skyward on the recoil, and he grabbed for the butt to keep it from sliding backward off her shoulder. The bullet missed the target entirely.

It was not long before she had better control of the weapon, and he decided she could manage to practice with it on her own.

He picked up the small gun. It looked like a toy in his hand.

"All you really need to know with this weapon is how to pull the trigger," he said. "Always keep it well hidden, because it's something you don't want your opponent to see. The aim is poor and it's unlikely to kill a man from any real distance. Even up close, it will probably do nothing more than wound him."

With his mind more focused on the demonstration now, he took her hand in his and placed the gun in her palm. He pressed her fingers around the grip. Then, as the sun beat with relentless heat against the back of his neck, his gaze brushed against hers.

She froze, her wariness of him unwavering, but beneath it there existed a thin layer of curiosity. The attraction between them might be unwanted by her, but it was not unnoticed. He could not seem to read her true wishes. They were jumbled and complex, and he would have to untangle them in a more traditional way. He lowered his head, giving her plenty of warning so that she could avoid him if she wished, and while she did not make any move to encourage him, neither did she pull away.

After another second's hesitation, he covered her mouth with his.

The barrage of sensations left him weak at the knees. She tasted delicate and soft, and the feminine scent of her warm skin bombarded his thoughts so that nothing mattered to him but this splintering effect she had on his senses. That switch clicked again in his head, releasing a truth he had not been more fully aware of last night because the timing had not been right.

He belonged with this woman. He was hers.

He slid his free hand to the small of her back and drew her against him, deepening the kiss. His demon growled with satisfaction, possession, and a rising, impatient desire.

Creed must have responded in kind, because with a gasp, she broke off the kiss. Time crawled to a standstill, then shifted to a sprint. Nieve shoved the gun lodged between them into his ribs. His hand still covered hers, and with the well-trained instincts of an assassin, he jerked the gun to the side so that the bullet she fired embedded into the ground, kicking up dirt, and not in his heart.

Shock roared in his ears.

"I'm sorry," she gasped.

For what, he could only imagine. For trying to kill him? Or for allowing him to kiss her?

His face felt wooden. Immobile. Time slowed again as

he stared into those beautiful, terror-filled eyes. Her fear washed over him.

All at once, the very sight of her infuriated and frustrated him. He had not compelled her, or threatened her in any way. He'd been nothing but kind. He had not earned her fear of him, but instead, kept his demon well in command.

At least now he knew she could shoot a man if she wanted. It made it far easier for him to leave. A stupid part of him had begun to worry that he might end up neglecting his duty in favor of her well-being. Sooner or later he would have resented that, and then her, regardless of what his demon wanted.

"I'm sorry, too," he said, and went off to the stable to gather his belongings.

A short while later he rode from the yard. As he passed through the gates, he did not look back.

• • •

Some distance away, in the Borderlands at the far edge of the desert, a blond-headed child sat on the top rail of a wooden corral where his friend Hunter was training an unbroken hross.

He swung his legs, kicking his heels against the next railing down. Hunter and Airie called him Scratch, but that wasn't his name. His real name was Asher—Ash, for short—but he kept that to himself. His mother was coming for him, and until she did, he had to be careful. Names had power, and he didn't want the mean woman, the one who could summon demons from the demon boundary, to know his. If she had it she might try to summon him, too, when he traveled the boundary.

But the big man—the one who was different, like Ash and Airie—had gone to the ranch where Ash used to live, and now his mother remembered him again, and she was going to come for him. The big man would help her. Ash had protected his mother for as long as he could, and kept her hidden from demons, but now the mean woman was following her. She'd be coming here, too.

And she didn't like Airie.

Hunter's wide-brimmed hat had fallen in the dirt. Now, sun-bleached hair hung in his eyes and he flipped it back with an absent toss of his head, his attention on the young hross on the end of the long lunge line. The nervous animal reared onto its hind legs, giant hooves pawing at the air inches from Hunter's face, but he did not seem concerned, so Ash wasn't either.

Airie, however, was another matter. As if sensing danger to him, she came out of the log house across the yard and carefully descended the wide plank steps. She always moved more slowly these days. The heavy weight of the baby she carried in her stomach disrupted her balance.

Airie was tall and very pretty, and Ash would not mind having her for his mother if he didn't already have one he loved. He loved Airie, too, but his mother needed him whereas Airie did not. Not in the same way.

She came to stand beside Ash as he sat on the fence. She slipped an arm around him and gave him a hug, although her eyes were on Hunter, but she knew better than to distract him when he was working.

When Hunter was finished he released the hross from the lunge line, picked up his hat, and came over.

"It's lunchtime," Airie said. She said nothing to him about being worried. Hunter always knew without being told.

He climbed over the fence, lifted Ash from the top railing to the ground, then turned to give Airie a kiss. Ash placed a hand on her stomach and the baby inside rolled over in her sleep. Airie said the baby would be born in a few months, but Ash knew she was going to be several weeks longer than that. Hunter was worried the baby might be a monster, and that she would be born in a demon form that might hurt Airie, but Ash also knew he was worrying for nothing.

Ash knew lots of things that he kept to himself. As he followed Airie and Hunter into the house, he glanced over his shoulder at the road winding back to the desert. Right now, he knew that his mother was coming.

But so was trouble.

Chapter Five

Willow waited in a rocky cleft at the base of a broad mesa for the wagon train of slavers Imp had assured her was coming.

The little girl had a talent for travel over vast distances, and could cover many miles by flitting in and out of the boundary between this world and the one where demons existed. She said that time had less meaning there.

But Imp did not like to travel the boundary now that demons had returned to it. She told Willow that if she hesitated too long within it they searched for her, and if they should ever manage to find her, she could not protect herself from them.

Of course Imp could not. She was only a child, barely eight years of age. Even Willow used caution when she reached into that boundary to summon her fire.

But no matter how hard Willow tried, she could not physically cross into the demon boundary as the little girl did. Imp would have to continue to travel and simply be as cautious about it as possible.

You are half demon, Willow had reminded her. *You do not show fear. They smell it on you. That's how they find you.*

A cloud of dust and a shimmering wave of heat, low in the sky beneath the ragged edge of the horizon, warned Willow of the approaching wagon train. Satisfaction filled her. It was as Imp had predicted.

She stifled her thoughts. Her talent for demon fire had grown to breathtaking proportions after the Demon Lord's murder. She had used it against the last slavers to own her, buying her freedom, but it required complete concentration. While burning, it was nearly limitless. Afterward, it took her several days to recover. During that period she was almost completely defenseless. She sometimes wondered how great her talent for demon fire might have been if she did not have to share it with the Demon Lord's other daughter, the traitorous one who lived in the Borderlands.

There was one additional risk. Her increasing talent for fire had come with an extra component. When she reached into the demon boundary for fire, she could also summon demons. The last one she'd brought to the mortal world had escaped her, and she was warier now. Demons disliked the feel of the sun on their flesh. Bringing one forward while it was still daylight, when the demon was not at full strength, would be safest.

All around her the desert held a collective breath, as if in wary anticipation of what was coming. A kettle of vultures circled high in the blue sky, then settled like sentinels on the lip of the mesa. Fire tingled at the tips of her fingers while she waited.

The wagons rumbled into view, their spoked wheels

jouncing over the rough trail. Willow remembered all too well how it felt to rattle around inside one of them until her entire body was bruised and aching.

Willow hated slavers.

She counted only five wagons in the train. She stepped into the trail to halt the first of them, forcing the teamster to rein his hross in as he yanked on the brake lever by his knee. She saw the speculation in his eyes as they settled on her after he'd looked around and decided she must be alone.

She did not wait to see what he planned to do about it. She did not want him to approach her, which would place him outside the ring of fire she was about to release.

Willow stretched her thoughts into the demon boundary, calling for fire. She captured it as the slaver leaped from the footrest to the ground. It danced from her fingertips to her palms, where it grew into great balls of red and gold flame. She juggled them briefly before tossing them to the ground. They dashed down either side of the approaching train, left and right, to connect in a complete circle behind the last wagon.

Then, with her thoughts, she retraced the fire's path into the boundary in search of a demon.

It emerged within the circle of fire, three times the size of any ordinary man. Horns curled from its ugly head. Rather than flesh, thick red bone plating protected its body. Two humps formed on its back over the shoulder blades that contained its set of furled wings. Massive thighs bore its weight as it paced inside the circle. The flames would contain it, too, but would not harm it. While the fire burned, the demon would play with the mortals trapped with it.

And demons despised mortal men.

Pandemonium broke out. Rearing hross snapped their harnesses, flipping the wagons and dashing them to pieces. Women's screams mingled with the shouts of the men. Willow had no pity for the slaves within. If they were half demon, they could reveal themselves and she would save them. If not, they would die. Mortal lives had no value to her.

Maintaining the wall of fire was not the most difficult part of this endeavor for her. A slender young man darted from one of the wagons and ran at the flaming barricade, trying to break through, and within seconds was completely engulfed. High-pitched shrieks of terror and pain threatened to distract Willow. She loved this part. But even the slightest shift of her attention could free the demon, so she closed her eyes and ears, and her thoughts, to the carnage.

The sun had significantly lowered by the time the fire burned itself low, leaving only the demon behind for her to contend with. Willow was exhausted inside, yet knew better than to reveal any weakness. She held the last of the fire in its circle. As long as the flames remained, so did her strength.

Chest heaving, the demon watched her with hungry, feral eyes.

Elation overrode her own fatigue. She'd trapped it, leaving it subject to the same limitations of this mortal world as she was. It had no more strength than she did. When the fire died away, fading back to the demon boundary, the demon would be dragged with it.

But nighttime was coming. The demon's strength would increase.

It shifted to man form, one easier for it to maintain beneath the glare of the mortal world's sun.

She sucked in a breath at his beauty. He was tall, broad-shouldered, and narrow-hipped. Long brown hair, tied in a braid as thick as her wrist, hung down his back to his buttocks. He was naked, and from all she could see, perfectly formed.

Magnificent blue eyes caught hers and held them. The smoldering look he cast over her burned as hot as any demon fire.

She could not look away.

"Tell me. What is your name, pretty lady?" he asked. His voice was like music. It lulled her, dulling her thoughts.

"Willow."

"Well. I've done what you wished for, Willow," he said to her. He extended a hand. Long, elegant fingers beckoned for her to come closer. "Now. A favor for a favor. I have something I'd like from you in return."

Willow had not freed herself from slavery to mortal men to become one to a demon. She deserved better.

But she had made a mistake with this one just now, and she was uncertain as to what she'd done wrong. She moved closer, but stopped well away from the flames. He might be beautiful, but his were the eyes of a reptile. Dark. Soulless.

Willow was fascinated by him in spite of the danger. Or perhaps because of it.

"It depends on the favor."

He chuckled softly. "I want you to find someone for me."

Her brows lifted. Demons hated mortal men, yet she sensed no hostility in the request. "A woman, then."

She saw by the faint tightening of displeasure around his lips that she was correct. There was only one woman a demon would seek. She'd be someone he'd claimed—who he believed was his reason for existence—and therefore, of infinite value to him.

Willow pushed aside a niggling worm of concern that she'd made some mistake. Delight filled her instead. This wasn't a small favor he asked. It would leave him indebted to her.

"I think we need to talk more about what I want," Willow said.

He shifted his weight, folding his arms and cocking his head to the side as he studied her. The tip of the thick braid of hair swept, pendulum-like and hypnotic, along the curve of one naked hip.

"I know what you want. I can feel it, every time you draw demon fire from the boundary. You want to crush mortals. You want to claim their world as your own. You want demon power." He leaned forward, as if imparting a great secret. "I can give that to you."

He did not know everything. She wanted demon power, but specifically, she wanted that of her Demon Lord father. With it, the world would be hers.

As would the demons he'd once commanded.

"But can you give me the Demon Lord's daughter?" Willow asked. "Because I want the one they call Airie."

· · ·

Creed slouched in his saddle, deep in thought, ignorant of the passing miles.

He traveled at a steady but leisurely pace, skirting the edges of what had once been the beginnings of demon territory. This isolated route cut all the way to the Borderlands. It was a very old road, little used for the past three hundred years, but now that demons no longer patrolled it, it was safe enough for an assassin to travel. In some places broken bits of asphalt could still be found, thrust up through grass and dirt. In others, it peeked through desert sand in long stretches that came and went with the scattering effects of the winds. He expected to pick up Willow's trail in the sparse towns and villages along the way. She had to be hiding somewhere. And someone would have seen her. A woman traveling alone, or possibly accompanied by children—at least one of whom was misshapen and feral—would have been noted.

Creed had stopped in Desert's End the previous night to tell the sheriff about Bear. Fledge had seemed neither surprised nor concerned by the news.

"The old man was tough, but no match for an assassin. He rubbed any number of people the wrong way," was all he had said on the matter. "I may get around to writing a report on it." He coughed, then spit bloody phlegm into a can. He cast Creed a rueful smile. "Or I may not."

As for Nieve, the sheriff had been more troubled. "There's not much I can do about it except maybe drop a word to someone who might be willing to take her in." He correctly interpreted the doubt on Creed's face. "And who'd be kind to her," he added. "There are plenty of good men around here, Assassin. They aren't all like Bear. Most people aren't without sympathy for her circumstances."

Even so, Creed had not felt good about the sheriff's solution, or his part in it, when he'd left Desert's End the next morning, but he had already decided that he would not be returning for her. Despite his best efforts, he despaired of her ever learning to trust him. He certainly could never trust her again after she had tried to kill him.

Not even his demon could make him forgive her for that.

A half day's ride on the other side of Desert's End, and well away from Nieve and the ranch, Creed came across the burned remains of a small wagon train at the base of a tall, lopsided mesa.

The ashes were cold. He could not tell what kind of train it had been or the goods it had carried, if any. The devastation was that great. He did estimate that there had been five wagons in it. He dismounted, wrapping the reins around the horn of his hross's saddle, knowing the well-trained animal would remain steadfast despite its obvious nervousness.

Given the remote location, he could think of no adequate explanation for this attack. The fire had burned around the wagons in an enormous circle, then moved in to consume them in a controlled pattern, which suggested demon fire.

While Willow had this particular talent, that did not mean she was the only one. Creed rubbed the back of his neck. He wondered what trade goods the wagon train had been transporting, because what motive could there be to burn it out so completely other than to hide robbery?

Unless this was simply random destruction, and the train had been in the wrong place at the wrong time, which was a talent of Willow's as well.

That last thought was particularly disquieting. It spoke of an utter lack of conscience, as well as a high level of unpredictability. And danger.

Creed walked the length of the decimated train, examining the circle of scorched earth around it. Then he sifted through one of the piles of ash near the center of the fire. He found no traces of human remains. He moved to the next pile and found none there either. In the third, he uncovered what might have been the charred remains of a human thigh bone, the thickest in a man's body and most difficult to destroy.

He nudged it with the toe of his boot. Bodies, human or hross, did not burn easily or so completely. Not in a normal fire.

He had no idea if this was Willow's work. He widened his search, taking it outward now, but could find no tracks to tell him anything as to who was responsible, only that nothing had escaped.

The presence of spawn in the world could no longer be ignored or denied. He glanced at the sky, still clear and blue beyond the ragged bluff of the mesa above him. Although he should take this news to Desert's End, he did not wish to turn back. The temptation to return for Nieve was too great, and made his demon difficult to manage. But his conscience would not allow him to proceed on his journey without at least trying to warn the sheriff that what everyone feared, but no one wished to acknowledge, was upon them.

He would get in and out as quickly as possible.

His pace was not so leisurely this time. He arrived in Desert's End around suppertime and went straight to the jailhouse, but the door was locked and there was no sign of Fledge. A few questions confirmed that the man had passed away shortly after Creed left him. So far, there was no replacement.

Creed had ridden back for nothing. To tell anyone else of what he had found would be to induce panic.

He stood on the boardwalk, his enormous hross tied to the hitching post, and debated how long he dared linger in town. There was little point in riding back into the desert tonight.

Neither was he riding out to the ranch to see Nieve.

He stopped first at the stable to lodge his hross for the night. The animal took a half-hearted nip at one of the young stable hands with its long, yellow teeth before settling into a nosebag of feed.

Creed hefted his packs to his shoulders, crossed the alley where his young friend had fought the three bigger boys, and entered the hotel next door.

The hotel was a three-story building with a large dining area in the front and to the right of the vestibule. When Creed peered inside, he saw the room was half full. Straight ahead of the vestibule, in the main lobby, was the reception desk. Beyond it were wide swinging doors that led to a kitchen. Women's laughter could be heard over the clattering of dishes.

Creed walked up to the desk, dropped his dusty packs on the floor in front of it, and requested a room.

"What's on for dinner this evening?" he asked once he'd registered and been handed a key by the reedy young man who waited on him. Whatever it was, it smelled good.

"Chicken and biscuits."

He had been assigned a room on the third floor. Single men took the top rooms so that women traveling with men did not have to climb the extra flight of stairs. Women, single or otherwise, did not stay in hotels alone. Not if the hotel was respectable.

He had a quick wash in the men's bath house attached to the hotel, then went to the dining area to eat. He chose a linen-draped table near one of the windows that overlooked the main street and sat facing the door, making himself inconspicuous to the other diners in the room.

The flame of the candle on the table bounced off the dark glass of the window, but despite the settling night Creed had a clear view of the street outside. Warm light from the saloon across the way spilled onto the boardwalk. Even though he was not a drinker, he thought he might spend his evening in the saloon. Regardless of his profession, he liked people as a whole and enjoyed their companionship when he could get it.

He flirted with the pretty waitress when she came to take his order, making her smile. But his heart was not in it.

As much as he wanted to put the whole incident at the ranch behind him, he could not seem to contain these continued and unwanted thoughts about Nieve and her welfare. The people in that wagon train would have been better prepared to defend themselves than she, and they had not survived the disturbing attack. He had no idea where their attacker, or attackers, had been headed. He had not forgotten the ill-tempered sand swift roaming free around the ranch either. There had been no sign of it when he left.

Was she safe?

He was well into his serving of chicken and hot biscuits when a conversation at another table distracted him.

He guessed by the look of the table's two occupants that they were involved in the mining industry, possibly investors in the claim they were discussing, which would explain their presence in a place like Desert's End. They did not look like miners. Ranchers either. By its cut, their clothing was expensive and not locally made.

"The boy murdered a miner twice his size and got arrested for claim jumping. It took three men to bring him in. He cut the throat of his jailor before burning the jail down," a man said. "Then he vanished. It's fair to speculate that he's spawn."

There were a lot of mines in the mountains. Some were owned independently, some of them brought in investors, while others were run by the communities that had built up around them. No matter what, it was dangerous business and Godseekers served as the law.

Creed had already been handed his task and was stretching its boundaries to the limit. This one would have been given to somebody else to investigate. Nevertheless, if half demons were implicated, he was curious as to why. Especially after what he had seen with the wagon train that day, because this incident, too, had involved fire.

"It seems like every time something bad happens, the person's labeled spawn," the second man insisted. "Demons or not, if there were so many of them they would have revealed themselves long before this."

The first speaker made a sound of disgust. "Keep talking like that and people might start to wonder why you're defending the boy. You got something to hide, Treble?"

The man named Treble already had his dinner knife in one hand when Creed decided the rising hostility between them required his intervention. To suggest that someone was spawn was the worst insult imaginable. People had been murdered for far less.

He pushed back his chair and leaned the short distance between the two tables, ramping up his compulsion and sending out an air of good will.

Immediately, the hostility abated and both men relaxed.

"I couldn't help overhearing," Creed said. "I've been

away on other business. Something happened at a mine in the mountains?"

The men appeared startled to discover a Godseeker assassin sitting at the table next to them, but Creed made himself amiable enough that they were not alarmed by it.

The tale they told was a dark one. When they finished, Creed had to agree that the first man was no doubt correct. It sounded to him as if the boy accused of murder was spawn as well. The fire involved in his escape, however, appeared to have been ordinary, and caused by a lamp.

He returned to his meal, his thoughts even more troubled now, when an unusual movement across the shadowed street gave him pause. A slight, feminine figure mounted the steps to the saloon across the way, hesitated at the door, then with a stiffening of the shoulders, pushed inside.

His fork clattered to the plate. He would recognize her anywhere. And he could not quite believe that the timid creature he had met, one who did not seem to want to draw male attention, would ever enter a saloon unaccompanied.

Then he remembered that she had tried to kill him, and he had not expected that from her either.

He dropped a few coins on the table and abandoned the rest of his meal. A minute later, he was outside and striding across the street.

• • •

Hunter and Airie thought he was sleeping. Ash knew they would never be having this conversation otherwise.

Ash loved the house where he lived with Hunter and Airie. It was big, and old, and had lots of cupboards and corners in which he could hide. When Hunter had arrived home with a ready-made family, his parents had moved into a smaller house on the far side of the property and left the original farm house to their only son. They were nice to Ash. They were nice to Airie, too.

But not everyone else was. The town had gotten a lot bigger since Hunter had left it, and many people here were strangers to him. A lot of them weren't happy that the Demon Slayer had returned, and about whom he'd brought with him.

Yet Airie and Ash were only the beginning of who—what—was coming. They needed the big man to help them.

He lay on his stomach in the shadows at the head of the stairs, where their voices carried up to him from the warmth and bright light of the kitchen. Airie liked to putter around it in the evenings. Hunter said he helped her so that he could make sure she did not overexert herself, but Ash knew he simply enjoyed being with her because she was so pretty and happy.

She wasn't happy this evening. She sounded worried.

"They're rumors, Airie. Nothing more," Hunter was saying, but Ash knew he was worried too.

"It's the way people whisper," Airie said. A pot clattered. She was putting dishes away. "They don't know I can hear them talking. There has to be a bit of truth to what they're saying."

"Why now, all of a sudden, would there be spawn in the world?" There was a brief pause, then Hunter's voice, sounding chastened and grumpy, drifted upward again. "Sorry. *Half demons.*"

"That's the trouble," Airie replied. "They aren't all

half demons. Some are their grandchildren and great-grandchildren. We have no idea how many generations back they go. But they all have demon blood, and now that the demons are gone, they seem to have acquired at least part of their ancestors' traits. Or the traits they already had are gaining in strength, and less easy for them to hide." Another pot clanged as either Hunter or Airie put it into a cupboard. "My own talents are stronger than before."

"But you possess demons," Hunter said, "where before, you didn't. That might explain why you're stronger."

Ash knew that Airie wasn't like him. Not exactly. Her mother had been a goddess, which meant Airie could have been an immortal if she'd wanted. Airie, however, had chosen to remain with Hunter. But because she was born an immortal, she had to own the deaths of any of her kind that she caused—either directly or indirectly—and she owned at least five. Two of those were her parents. Her goddess mother and demon father did not struggle against her, but protected Airie's unborn baby from the other three. That was something Hunter did not understand and she didn't want him to know, because she believed he already worried about her pregnancy more than he should.

"That doesn't explain the rumors," Airie replied. "We know Scratch is at least part demon. There could be a lot more like him in the world."

"He doesn't seem any different now than he was when we found him." Hunter's voice came from the side of the kitchen nearest to Ash, where the table was.

"He's different," Airie said. She sounded quite definite, which surprised Ash. He thought he'd been careful, but then Airie was special. It was harder to hide things from her. "He's learning to control it better as he gets older. That's why you haven't noticed. But other people have, and they're talking. Add to it the stories about half demons coming out of the Godseeker Mountains, and sooner or later, there's going to be trouble. And they're going to say that we brought it here."

When Ash craned his neck, he could see Hunter and Airie were both at the table now. Airie was sitting on Hunter's lap, and he had his hands on her stomach so he could feel the baby if it moved.

"Let them say it. That won't make it true," Hunter said.

But it would be true, Ash knew, because his mother was coming for him. When she did, the mean woman wouldn't be too far behind.

Ash also knew what made people do the things they did, and he wasn't afraid of the mean woman. It was what she believed that was going to be the real problem for everyone. She thought life had cheated her. That it was unfair. She also thought half demons were better than mortals. She was teaching children who didn't know any better not to let life cheat them too, and that they should take what they wanted.

Ash knew it didn't matter if a person was mortal, immortal, or half demon. Life was about giving, not taking, or taking what one was given and making it better. That was what Hunter and Airie, and the big man with his mother, all believed.

But Airie was the only one who could convince the mean woman she had things all wrong, and Ash didn't think that would happen because the mean woman also believed Airie had betrayed her somehow. She planned to hurt Airie, and a lot of other people besides. In order to stop her, they needed the big man to help.

But getting the big man here meant having to put Ash's mother in danger, and make her remember things that were better for her to forget, and Ash didn't like that.

The floor was hard and he wiggled around on his belly to find a more comfortable position. He nestled his cheek against his folded arms. He loved his mother and he missed her, and he reminded himself he had no reason to worry.

The big man would protect her.

• • •

Heads turned, one by one, as Nieve came through the door. Within seconds, every eye in the room had fastened on her.

Under those unwelcoming, semi-incredulous stares, she almost lost her nerve. This was not a place intended for women unless they were working whores, and she had not yet reached that point in her life.

But she had finally made it through Bear's papers and there was nothing in them to indicate what had happened to Ash. Nieve had not been willing to wait another day for substantive information. She hoped the saloon's owner, who heard everything according to Bear, would know something about the traders who had bought her son.

All that had made the fruitless hours of searching bearable was the knowledge that the demon assassin would be long gone by the time she got to Desert's End, and she would never have to face him again.

She had not meant to pull the trigger. Fear had made her do so, but Nieve was honest with herself. She had been more afraid of what he made her feel, because until she found Ash, her emotions had to be set firmly aside or she would not be able to function. She was not strong enough to manage them.

The saloon was quite nice, and not at all what she had expected, undoubtedly due in part to the high quality of the hotel across from it. The floors were clean, and the patrons well dressed. Gas lighting spread deep into the corners.

Business resumed. Glasses clattered on brass trays carried by women wearing scandalous dresses, a song tinkled from the music machine at the back, and men, deep in private conversation, spoke to each other in hushed voices. Overall, it had the air of a private club. One in which Nieve was not a member, and in fact, an unwelcome interloper.

The owner, a stout, middle-aged man she knew only by sight, leaned with both hands on the polished mahogany bar at the far end of the low-ceilinged saloon. As she walked the entire length of the room to speak with him he eyed her with such disapproval that she wanted to run, but did not. The gun the demon assassin had given her caused a reassuring weight in one pocket of her full skirt. As instructed, she kept it well hidden.

"Bear knows better than this," the man said to her when she reached the bar. His thick, handlebar mustache quivered against his upper lip as he spoke. "If he wishes to speak with me, he's to come here himself."

With a start, Nieve realized that his disapproval was not aimed at her but at Bear. She could use this to her advantage. Her courage returned in a rush, along with giddy elation.

"Please, sir," she said, her voice soft and deferential, but also steady. She dropped her eyes and stared at his hands splayed against the polished wood of the counter. "He wants to know if there's been any word on the traders who came here last year, and when they're returning. He's been expecting them."

The man drummed his fingertips on the bar. He opened his mouth, then closed it, as if uncertain whether or not he should speak. Finally he said, "Any day now. They sent word a few weeks ago. They're late. If he wants to know anything more than that, he can ask me."

Their return had been a wild guess on her part, based on timing. She knew slavers regularly traveled into the mining regions, where women were in constant and high demand. Bear had intimated more than once that he would send her to one when she was of no more use to him. All she had to do now was be patient and await their arrival.

She risked asking one more question because she could not help but worry that she might somehow have missed them already, or they might have had a change of plans. "Where did they send the last message from?"

"Freetown." The owner leaned forward. His serious expression and darting eyes revealed impatience with her and a rising concern. "I understand that Bear isn't the easiest man to live with, and you're afraid to go back without the information he wants, but you need to get out of here. This is no place for a woman like you, and I don't want any trouble."

Nieve thanked him and turned away, already armed with more information than she had dared hope for. She did not look to the right or left, but kept her gaze fixed on the exit, so was surprised when a hand seized her arm.

Attached to the hand was a youngish man of about thirty years. He was not unattractive, or even unkempt, but there was a cruelty to his eyes that Nieve recognized all too well.

"If you're looking for light work, then I can keep you occupied for a few hours," he said.

She tried not to show it, but inside, she was shaking. "I work for Bear."

The man did not let go of her arm. "This Bear should be more careful with his valuables if he wishes to hang on to them. His loss is my gain. Not to worry. I'll be providing greater protection than this."

Desert's End was not a large town. Nieve had thought Bear's reputation alone would be enough to prevent such advances. She had not considered that there would be strangers in the saloon who did not know of him, or might not care if they did.

She faced a quandary. She did not wish to cause an even greater disturbance than she already had through her mere presence here, but did not know how to extricate herself. Even if she could reach the gun in her skirt, which she could not, she knew better than to shoot a man in a saloon.

Any further response on her part was not necessary, however. Another man, this time familiar, came out of nowhere. Preoccupied as she was with her problematic new benefactor, she had not seen Creed enter the saloon.

Her heart almost stopped at the sheer magnificence of him. Of his perfect-formed features and exquisite male beauty. He turned his head from side to side, scanning the room with eyes like shards of blue diamond. The tattoo running up the base of his skull, black against the gold-hued backdrop of his skin, undulated with each movement he made as if it had a life all its own.

Calmness assailed her with his appearance. He was using compulsion again, but what he exuded felt fractured to her this time, and erratic in its pulsing intensity, as if he had difficulty controlling it. It had a peaceful effect on the nearby tables because the men seated around them settled into their chairs and returned to their own business.

Yet, a bit farther away and closer to the door, people continued to stare.

Hostility crept beneath Creed's air of calm, and her assailant seemed to sense it. Nieve, standing between them and wishing to be far away from them both, watched the two men assess each other. Her heart slipped to her boots. Her assailant did not recognize Creed as either an assassin or a demon. There was about to be trouble, just as the owner had feared, and she was its cause.

"She has no need of additional protection," Creed said. He did not look at the hand on Nieve's arm, but watched the man's face. "But thank you for your concern."

Rather than release her, the man's fingers tightened to the point of pain. He twisted her arm, making her cry out.

Creed's compelling calmness vanished completely. One large fist flew past Nieve's cheek to land in the other man's face, emitting a wet, pulpy sound, and a drop of blood splashed on the floor at her feet. The blow knocked the stranger from his chair. He caught the edge of the table as he went down, toppling it onto its side.

The stranger bounced back to his feet. Anticipation brought a smile to his split and swelling lips. He dove at Creed, who shook off a well-aimed blow to one kidney as if he had not so much as noticed it.

The mood of the formerly genteel-seeming saloon degenerated to mayhem.

Nieve, now disregarded, seized her chance and darted

for the door, weaving between the emptied tables and around men more interested in watching the fight than in hindering her escape.

Outside, she ran across the street and scurried into the shadowed alley between the hotel and the stable. Breathing hard, her heart still pounding, she pressed her back to the hotel's plain exterior wall and listened to the chaos she had caused.

She closed her eyes. Creed was a demon as well as an assassin. He could take care of himself. She could not bring herself to worry for the safety of the cruel-eyed stranger. If given a choice between the two, she would throw in her lot with the demon.

A tear slid down her cheek, and she scrubbed it away with the heel of her hand. Waiting in town for the slavers to appear, especially after the events in the saloon, was now out of the question. If she stayed at the ranch she might miss them entirely.

One thing was certain—skulking in an alley off one of the busiest streets in town would not help her. She had to find a better place to hide.

As she pushed away from the wall, a large, shadowy figure blocked her path. Someone grabbed her, but before she could scream, a hand covered her mouth.

Chapter Six

Creed could not help but enjoy a good fight, and his opponent posed enough of a challenge to keep this one interesting. His demon needed an outlet for pent-up aggression as well.

Nieve had managed to escape the saloon unobserved, however, and as much as Creed wanted to stay until the end of this, he had no choice but to pursue her.

He divested his opponent's attention onto another man standing nearby. Then he walked out of the saloon as if he were an innocent spectator and not the instigator of the brawl.

While Creed was disappointed to abandon the fight so soon, it restored much of his natural good humor. It was also just as well that he decided to leave when he did. His demon had wanted to kill the man for touching Nieve and causing her physical pain, and it hadn't liked exhibiting restraint. Since Nieve should not have been in the saloon in the first place, by law Creed could not justify beating any man to death for accosting her.

The brawl in the saloon had not yet attracted outside attention. Soon people in the hotel, and attendants in the nearby stable, would catch wind of the ruckus, and come out to investigate. As long as Creed was with Nieve when they did, he could make her as inconspicuous as himself and no one would take any notice of her.

He looked up and down the dark, silent street, but saw no signs of her. He asked himself where he would go if he were a frightened woman needing to hide and gain breathing space to consider her next move.

Acting on a hunch, he loped across the street, skirting a pile of dried and crumbling hross droppings.

He found Nieve in the same alley where he had discovered the boys fighting a few days ago. She was leaning against the hotel's shingled exterior wall, likely unaware until after she'd entered that it held no rear pathway to escape. Because her eyes were closed, she did not see him.

Some of the resentment he carried for her sloughed away. While he was angry that she had tried to kill him, he found he was growing more sympathetic. He had stood not far from her at the bar, unnoticed by anyone while she asked the owner her questions.

Now that he understood she was searching for her son, Creed could only pity her. For her sake, he hoped the child was long dead. But he wondered why it had taken her a year to reach a point of such desperation.

Something about this situation was odd.

He watched her wipe a tear from her cheek, then from beside him, he saw the first of the onlookers dribbling from the hotel and onto the boardwalk.

It spurred him to react. As Nieve pushed away from the wall, he blocked her path and placed a hand over her mouth to stifle any screams.

She bit him. Hard.

He jerked his hand away in surprise, then fumbled to replace it, worried she would make noise and draw unwanted attention. He doubted if he could deflect the sight of a large man wrestling in the dirt with a small woman such as Nieve. He could only hide so much with his skills.

To her credit, she did not scream. Instead, she kicked at his legs and threw a punch at his face. The aggressiveness of her resistance startled him. Then he remembered the gun he had given her, and that she would not hesitate to use it on him, and grabbed for her wrists. He yanked them behind her back and jerked her toward him so that her chest was splayed against his upper abdomen.

"If I have to knock you unconscious to get you to safety, I'll do it," he said into her ear. Frustration made him sound harsh. He could not use compulsion to calm her because she did not respond well to it. "I'm trying to help you, but you aren't making it easy."

"Why would you want to help me?" she asked. Her head tipped back and her chin pressed into his chest, her voice a whisper that warmed the skin of his throat.

"I really don't know." He had no other answer for her.

It seemed to be enough. Either that or she realized the futility of fighting him. Her struggling ceased, but she remained wary and tense, as if poised for flight at the first opportunity.

He would not give her one.

The brawl in the saloon had finally spilled into the

street. The hotel's occupants milled about at the entrance to the alley, curious but as yet uninvolved. Past history warned Creed they would not remain so. The situation was a lit fuse on a full keg of dynamite. Most men, the same as demons, enjoyed fighting, and there was no longer a sheriff to stop them.

"Come with me," Creed said.

He draped an arm around Nieve's shoulders and guided her through the small throng of people. They entered the hotel foyer and climbed the stairs to the third floor without any opposition. Creed nodded to two men at the top of the stairs. They nodded back but paid no attention to Nieve.

He could not say the same for his demon. Its satisfaction at having her with him stalked hungrily at the back of his thoughts.

At the door to his hotel room, as he fumbled in his pocket for the key, Nieve finally balked.

"I don't want to be alone with you," she said, showing the first signs of panic.

His patience snapped at last. He fitted the key in the lock, turned the knob, and thrust her into the room ahead of him. He closed the door behind them and leaned against it, his arms folded across his chest.

The room was dark, but his night vision was exceptionally good. The thin moonlight streaking between the drawn curtains was more than enough for him to see her face clearly.

His jaw worked as he contained his temper. He did not unleash it often. When he did, it tended to be spectacular.

"You've lived with a man who abused you and was planning to kill you," he said. "You gave birth to his child.

You came to the stable the other night prepared to seduce me to get information. You walked alone into a saloon filled with men, most of whom would treat you with far less consideration and courtesy than I have shown so far. You tried to kill me. And still, I offer to help you. Tell me what I've done to make you so afraid of me when I would say I have more reason to fear you."

Muffled noise from the crowd in the street two levels below filtered between the floorboards and through the walls.

"You're a demon."

"I am not."

Nor was he. Demons did not belong to this world, and he did. He was as mortal as any other man alive, and he hated demons every bit as much as they did. He was not to blame for the other half of his nature. He kept it well under control. Besides, it had no wish to harm her.

Quite the opposite.

Her slight frame shook so that she had to reach for the footrest on the narrow bed to steady herself. "You use compulsion."

"Assassins learn how to manipulate others into doing what we want, or seeing what we want them to see," he said.

"Only a demon can force a woman to want him against her will."

He heard one thing. She wanted him.

His heart leaped, the anger in it slipping away entirely. She was right about compulsion, but also wrong. He had not used it in order to make her want him, only in an effort to gain her trust. If she did want him, it was because of her own natural desire—although there was another, far stronger, connection between them that she chose to fight.

A sense of impending disaster preceded his under-standing of the root cause of her fear. He should have known from their encounter in the stable that night at the ranch, and supposed on some level he had, but hadn't wanted to acknowledge it. Even now, possessiveness made the words painful to utter.

"You were once lured by a demon," he said.

She did not answer but dropped to the bed as if her legs could no longer support her weight, insignificant as it was. She then stared at her hands, which were clasped so tightly in her lap he could see the whiteness of the knuckles despite the darkness.

His throat went so dry that it hurt to swallow. With those disconcerting, deep green eyes underlined by thumbprint bruises of fatigue, and the halo of white-blond hair, she looked very beautiful to him, and yet also tragic and fragile. He longed to take her in his arms and protect her, but no one could shield her from her thoughts and memories.

He concentrated on the positive. The demon had let her live, so it had not been cruel or abusive. If it had sought nothing but pleasure it would have killed her as soon as it grew tired of her. If anything, Bear would have given her more cause for fear than the demon had.

Creed had given her no cause to fear him. He could not imagine harming any woman, let alone this one, who despite everything, he could not seem to walk away from. Since he had met her, it was as if the universe repeatedly led him back to her. He was tired of fighting it, and could not form any plan as to what he should do with her while in her presence.

His thoughts lay in shambles. He had missed something

important—another piece of information about her son that he should have seized on in all this. Yet try as he might he could not recollect what it was because one thought continued to edge out all others. Demons did not share, and his was no different in that regard. It had claimed her as his.

He wondered if the demon who had lured her had tried to do the same thing. If so, it was plain that Nieve wanted neither of them. And that was what mattered.

Silent and uncommunicative, she watched him from the edge of the bed. He had no idea what she was thinking. He did know that he could no longer leave her behind, alone and defenseless. The sheriff, his one hope for someone to help her, was dead.

He picked up one of the packs from the pile in a corner of the room. It contained weapons and a few personal items.

"I'll stay in the stable," he said, slinging the heavy pack over one shoulder. "Try to sleep for a few hours if you can, but it's best if we're gone from Desert's End before morning. I'll be back when things settle down outside. When they do, it'll be time to go."

He locked the door behind him, pocketed the key, and headed for the stairwell at the center of the long corridor. At least no one could get into the room to trouble her. And she could not get out.

His steps slowed as he reached the top of the stairs. He paused, wondering if he should be so certain. Then he returned to the door of his room and listened for a moment before setting his pack on the floor.

He sat down beside it, leaned his head against the wall, drew up his knees, and closed his eyes. His demon refused to settle.

It would be a very long few hours.

. . .

Nieve curled in a ball on the bed. He had locked the door behind him, and the coward in her was grateful for it. With no easy means of escape, she did not have to attempt one. That meant she might possibly be able to sleep, knowing there was nothing more she could do to find her son until morning.

She was well aware that she'd had a very narrow escape already that evening, and it was thanks only to Creed's intervention. He should no longer terrify her, but he did. Not in the same way as the man in the saloon. Creed was not cruel. Not to her. Even she could see that.

But he thought Ash was Bear's son. He had not yet figured out that Ash was half demon, although he would soon enough, and demons despised half demon offspring.

Despite his claims, Creed was more demon than not. She knew it because of the way he attracted her to him even when she fought to resist him.

She did not know if someone who hunted other spawn and turned them over to the Godseekers could ever have sympathy for a child such as Ash. In Creed's persistent refusal to admit what he himself was, would he dismiss Ash as having no worth?

She had no idea what Creed was planning to do with the missing children he sought—if or when he found them—if they should turn out to be like Asher.

Nieve's veins had turned into conduits of ice. She tugged the bed's top blanket over her in an attempt to grow warm.

She was so tired. She could not remember the last time she had truly slept.

Whenever she began to drift off, her dreams, interspersed with loud male voices from either the street below or a neighboring room, would begin, and then the pounding of her heart reawakened her.

When she finally did fall asleep, the dream that stayed with her was of Creed. The warmth of his smile drew her to him. He held out a hand, his fingers beckoning to her, and for the first time in years, she felt no fear at all.

She had forgotten what that was like, to be unafraid, and went to him willingly. He enfolded her in his arms and cradled her, whispering for her to trust him, and that he would help her find Asher.

Then she looked in his eyes, ready to do anything he asked of her, and saw they were not Creed's eyes at all.

They were the eyes of Asher's father, red and hot and filled with desire. In her sleep, Nieve shuddered from her head to her toes. She did not want to do the things with a demon that he compelled her to do, but she could no more deny him than she could refuse to draw breath. His hands on her flesh set her on fire. She wanted more, and yet it was not him that she wanted it from. Her father had called her a demon's whore, and he had been right. It was terrible, this mix of longing and self-loathing.

She flung out a hand to push the demon away, to prove that she could, and that her mind was her own.

Her palm struck solid warmth and she awoke with a gasp. A shadow loomed beside the bed. A hand touched her shoulder.

"Wake up." The voice sounded familiar, and soothing,

but she was too struck with terror to place its owner.

"I can't see," she choked out. Neither could she breathe. Her chest ached from ribs stretched to bursting as air flowed into her lungs but could not be expelled.

The curtains were thrust back to flood the small, serviceable hotel room with starlight. Strong hands lifted her to a sitting position and nudged her legs over the side of the bed.

Creed. Relief left her shaking.

Crouched in front of her, he took one of her hands in his while rubbing her back in circles between her shoulders with the heel of his other palm.

"Put your head between your knees," he said. "Try to breathe slowly."

Nieve groped at his shirtfront with her free hand to further steady herself. After several long, agonizing moments, her world ceased to spin. She lifted her head and blurted out the first nonsensical, stupid words that came to her. "I'm sorry I tried to shoot you."

She felt him smile. "You're hardly the first, although you did come closest to succeeding. You should take pride in it."

The knot in her chest began to unravel. He had not treated it so lightly at the time, but he appeared prepared to forgive. That gave her hope he might be willing to help find her son. She had nowhere else to turn.

Long seconds ticked by. Her breathing steadied.

"Why are you being so kind to me?" she asked.

He sat back on his heels and studied her face. "Why do you find it so difficult to accept?" he countered. "Never mind." He cut her off before she could reply. "I already know the answer to that." His fingers tightened on hers. "I swear to you, Nieve." His voice softened. "I won't hurt you. I won't compel you to do things you don't want to do. I'm not a demon."

He might not believe he was. But it was in him, just as she knew it was in Ash. But Ash was a good-natured, sweet, and loving child. Creed was a trained assassin.

Yet she wanted so much to trust someone. If she did not long for Creed in this manner—the way a woman desired a man—when she did not want to, then perhaps she could.

He seemed to understand what she was thinking, and where her greatest concerns regarding him lay. "Have you considered the possibility," he said, "that any attraction between us is natural, and not compulsion? I can state honestly that if I could somehow release me from you I would—but for my sake, not yours."

His face, such a short distance from hers, seemed so earnest in the star-dappled light. Despite his proximity, and with both her hands touching him, she felt none of the sway of compulsion.

Still, she hesitated. She could think of only one way to test his sincerity. Her fingers twisted in the fabric of his shirt. She shifted forward to the very edge of the sagging, creaky bed and pressed trembling lips to his.

Excitement, hot, sensual, and unlike anything she had anticipated, lanced from her breasts to her thighs.

He knew what she felt. A muscle jerked at the corner of his mouth, and he ran his thumb over the back of her hand, but other than that, he remained very still. Lightly, she ran her lips along the line of his jaw, then lower, to brush the length of his neck to his open collar. He swallowed, but still, he did not move. She pressed her cheek into the hollow at the base of his throat and closed her eyes as a deep sense of peace wound itself around her. Beyond a doubt, the attraction was there. It was two-sided, as he maintained. And he would not act on it. Not tonight.

She could not act on it, ever. He diverted her attention from finding her son, and she couldn't afford that. Not even for a single moment. The possibility she might forget him again terrified her more than any demon's allure.

From somewhere deep in the hotel, Nieve heard hushed voices and a stirring of activity. Although it was still night, it would not be long before the hotel's staff began to prepare for the coming day and the early departure of impatient travelers.

"We should be leaving," Creed finally said. His voice rumbled in his throat beneath her cheek.

"I can't leave Desert's End." She had to wait for the slavers to return.

Creed sighed. He extricated himself and pushed to his feet, looking down at her as she sat on the edge of the bed. His next words dropped like pebbles into unbroken water. "The slavers you're searching for aren't coming."

They had to come. They were the only known link she had to her son.

"I don't understand."

"I found the remains of a burned out wagon train a half day's ride from here."

She did not want to believe him. He had to be mistaken. Her stomach burned with anxiety now, not desire.

"You can't know it was them for certain."

He did not answer, but watched her with a kind of pity that convinced her more than any words could have done.

Yet she did not sink into the same despair she might have only a few short hours ago. A year had passed. Even if Creed had stumbled upon the slavers' remains, as he believed, Ash would not have been with them. Her baby was out there somewhere, waiting for her.

While she was willing to trust Creed with her own safety, she did not dare rely solely on anyone else to secure Ash's. She tried to think of what to do, or to say. Going back to the ranch would not help. Staying with Creed would at least give her a broader area in which to search, and protection while she did.

But if she stayed with him she would, in effect, belong to him. There would be expectations.

It did not matter. She would do anything to locate Asher.

"Will you help me find my son?"

She could not look away from his eyes but tried to read his thoughts through them.

He chose his words with particular care. "I'll help you look for him. But I need you to understand that I'm making no promises to you. My own work comes first. And we may never be able to find him."

She could ask for nothing more from him. She did not know what she would do if she never found Ash, only that it would not matter. Nothing would.

They left the hotel unnoticed. Nieve stood beside him as he claimed his hross from the stable. No one paid any attention to her when she was with him.

Out on the silent street, in the chill morning air, Creed lifted her into the saddle, then swung up in front of her. She rested her hands on his hips to steady herself. It had been a long time since she'd ridden a hross. It felt awkward, and yet familiar.

The sun was beginning to rise in the east as they rode out of Desert's End. Hope, once lost, again lightened her heart. For several miles she stared at what appeared to be the head of a phoenix covering the back of Creed's shaved skull. Otherwise, his skin was golden and perfect.

"Your tattoo is quite distinctive," she said. "Why is it I've never really noticed it before?"

She had seen it, of course, but paid no real attention to it. If asked to describe him, she doubted if she would have thought to include it. Now she could not seem to look away.

He glanced back over his shoulder at her. A smile filled his striking blue eyes. "It symbolizes rebirth. I received it when the demons were banished. To me it means that the world has been given a new start, and I have a duty to help it recover. I guess you weren't meant to see it until now."

His words, although uttered in jest, slapped her instead, reminding her again of what he was. The spell broke and she found herself frowning at the back of his coat. Creed could make people see what he wanted them to see. Whether he admitted to it or not, that was a demon trait.

Ash, too, had a talent for going unnoticed and deflecting unwanted attention, something she hoped had saved his life.

But would his talent also make Asher impossible for her to find?

* * *

Two days after the wagon train burned, shortly before midday in a darkening sky that threatened rain, Willow walked back into the small camp outside of Desert's End where her children awaited. Scruffy and dirty, and reeking of neglect, seven of them rushed to greet her. They ranged in age from six or seven years to twelve.

The enthusiasm of their greeting warmed her. Willow had wintered in a burned out village in the Godseeker Mountains with three of these children as her sole companions. All three were males, and quite feral. One of them, more mortal in appearance, was only now beginning to speak. The other two were physically deformed, retaining demon-like features that they could not shift. Willow guessed they all had either been abandoned by their families when it was obvious they were half demon, or that their mothers had not survived their births. Either way, the children had managed to forage for what they needed in order to survive on their own.

Now they were hers to love and protect.

Once spring had arrived, she'd moved them out of the mountains. Of the five additional children she had rescued along the way, swelling her family's numbers to nine, Stone was the oldest and most difficult to manage. He was also the one who needed her least, and yet she needed the most.

And he was nowhere to be seen.

Willow's lips thinned even as she hugged the smallest ones to her. Stone was a problem, and difficult to control, but his talent would no doubt prove useful to her in the Borderlands. She had to get past the Demon Slayer in order to get to Airie.

She also had to find the woman the demon sought. Willow had no intention of simply turning her over to it. As soon as she did that, it would forget its promises to her. Willow would have to get what she wanted from it first, and arrange some sort of trade, but she had to be careful.

She'd been given a name, a physical description, and a location in which to begin the search. She would send Imp into the boundary, where the girl could travel long distances in the shortest amounts of time, to search for the demon's woman. Once Imp found her, Willow could decide how best to proceed.

A pretty girl of twelve stood apart from the others. Her name was Thistle and she had golden brown, curly hair, and eyes that appeared purple depending on her mood and the lighting. With a smile that could soften the hardest of hearts she was easy to love, but not nearly as easy to trust. All three of her siblings had died of crib death as infants. Her stepfather had suspected that the crib deaths were not natural. Then Thistle had overheard him talking of selling her, and her mother had not tried to dissuade him. Thistle had run away from home when she sensed Willow's presence nearby, because that was one of Thistle's talents—an ability to sense others like her, and over significant distances.

Willow suspected the only reason Thistle had not yet harmed the younger children in their group was because they were so wild and skittish. It was difficult to get close to them, even when they were asleep.

"Where is Stone?" Willow asked her.

The girl shrugged. "Not far. He left the morning after you did. He said he'd be back before you."

Stone, as it turned out, was a compulsive thief. The greater the risk, the more he enjoyed it. He had gone off to steal, and undoubtedly from someone he should not.

Thistle tugged on her sleeve. Willow smiled at her, lifting her eyebrows in an unspoken question. The girl required a lot of devotion, and a great deal of patience, and Willow was willing to provide both since her mortal mother had failed her so miserably.

"There's a man coming," Thistle said. She raised one arm well above her head to indicate a great size. "He's big. His head is smooth-shaven. There's a tattoo of some kind of bird all over his back."

Willow's smile faded. For Thistle to know this, the man who approached had to be half demon. The description was vague, but also familiar. Willow struggled to place it, her instincts warning her that it was important. It took her a few moments, but when she did, it came as a shock.

There had been an assassin matching the man Thistle described in the mountains the night Willow had unleashed a demon on Raven, and he had not been on Willow's side. He had come to the defense of a Godseeker. But, if he was the man Thistle had sensed, then the assassin was more than he seemed.

While she had known the Godseekers would send an assassin after her, this would make him a bigger problem than she'd expected.

She needed to get the children away from the reach of the Godseekers, and this assassin in particular. She wasn't yet ready to fight — not him, and not the Demon Slayer — but it was a long road to the Borderlands. There would be time enough for her to prepare.

There would also be time to find the woman the demon wanted. Willow wanted to know where she was, but did not want to put her within the reach of the demon too soon.

She regarded eight-year-old Imp, who always managed to lose herself among the other children, with thoughtful eyes. Willow had a fondness for her. The girl was shy, but also sweet-natured and eager to please. At first glance she appeared plain, but it was an illusion the child had created. All half demons were beautiful, even the ones in their monster forms. It was a matter of recognizing that beauty.

Imp's talent for deflecting attention from herself protected her very well. More time in the demon boundary would do her no harm, and in fact, some good. The girl was too soft and gentle.

"I have a special task for you, darling," Willow said to her. "I want you to find someone for me."

"You mean through the demon boundary?" Imp asked. Uncertainty had her plucking at the skirt of a dress that no longer covered her knees.

Willow frowned. Imp had grown in the past month and needed new clothes, and Willow didn't like that she hadn't noticed it before now. She wondered if Imp had been deflecting her attention.

She also did not care for the child's obvious reluctance to follow instructions, and her tone hardened. "You are half demon, and you are strong. Nothing can touch you as long as you believe in your abilities. You can do this. Don't disappoint me."

Imp nodded. She listened carefully to Willow's instructions. Then, she disappeared.

A streak of lightning split the sky in half, followed almost at once by a deep rumble of thunder.

"Come along," Willow said to the other children. "A storm is coming. Once it passes we'll pack our belongings, and tomorrow, we'll be off on a new adventure."

Chapter Seven

Although Creed remained hyper aware of Nieve as she sat behind him on the massive hross, overall, she was not a difficult companion. If anything, as the morning wore on, he found her too quiet.

He had no way of knowing if she was comfortable, hungry, tired, or thirsty. She did not complain. Right now the inside of her thighs had to chafe where they rubbed against his denim-clad hips, which was awkward for both of them, and yet she said nothing. The skirt of her dress was not intended for riding astride, and hiked up to expose a great deal of bare skin to the heat and rays of the sun. Creed's solution was to drape a blanket over her legs to keep them from burning. He could do nothing about the distraction caused by her proximity, or the way it made his demon hum with a low buzz of pleasure. Not even ignore it, although he tried his best by thinking of other things.

He had finally pieced together what it was about her

story that he had been missing. She'd had a demon lover. Therefore the child Bear had sold was most likely not his but a demon's, and Creed did not believe their search would end well. Young children were peddled into brothels with a specific sort of clientele. Any child would be damaged — mentally, physically, or both — after a year in such slavery. If they did find her son, and he was in any way dangerous because of the damage done to him, Creed would have no choice but to hand him over to the Godseekers.

He had also seen what happened to mixed-blood children abandoned and left to die, but who possessed enough demon traits and skills to somehow fend for themselves. Cold and extreme heat did not affect them. They could survive on very little. He would never forget the horror he had witnessed in the Godseeker Mountains when a feral demon child, at the command of Willow, had slaughtered several men.

That child had been failed by everyone — mortal, immortal, and spawn alike. Creed hoped he never encountered such a sad situation again. He certainly had no wish for Nieve to see it.

He considered turning around and taking her to Raven and Blade for safekeeping but dismissed the idea almost at once. He did not want to be parted from her, or have her away from his protection, and his demon concurred. Raven would have little patience for her. He also suspected that Nieve would not stay behind. She might be a mouse, but she was a more determined one than he had foreseen and he worried this search for her son would get her killed. If he kept close watch on her, that, at least, might be prevented.

As well, Creed had wasted enough time on detours already. He was going to seek out the Demon Slayer, as

Blade had suggested, and pass on his message. Right now, that was more important even than hunting for spawn, because it was beginning to seem that it was a task too great for a single assassin.

The spring day was not unusually hot, but a swirling mass of gray that ate away at the horizon warned of an impending thunder and lightning storm. They passed beneath a sandstone bluff, following the same ancient and broken trail he had taken two days before. He planned to detour around the site of the burned out wagon train and move onto higher and safer ground. When this roadway was built hundreds of years ago, the lay of the land would have been different than it was now. Flash flooding could occur within minutes of a heavy rainfall, and he did not want them to be caught in this narrow depression of land that would act as a funnel. A nearby stand of green-leaved and healthy cottonwood trees confirmed his suspicions. They thrived in wet soil.

His tattoo itched between his shoulders, a sure signal of danger. He shifted his weight, his first thought for Nieve's safety, and heard the report of a rifle at the same time he felt the bullet whistle below his left ear and tear through the fabric of his coat.

He reacted the way he'd been trained to do. As he tumbled from the saddle, away from the shooter, he reached behind him to seize Nieve by the arm and drag her with him.

Creed was close to six and a half feet tall, yet when standing, the top of his head barely came to his mount's withers. That meant the drop from the back of the long-legged hross was a steep one. He did his best to protect Nieve from the worst of the fall, landing so that she was not underneath him, but he did not want her exposed to more gunfire either and tried to shield her with his body. He'd gotten his hand beneath the back of her head so it did not connect with the ground, but he could do nothing to save her shoulder and hip. A sharp inhalation and low, muffled groan were the only indicators that she'd hit the ground hard.

As the hross danced around in nervous anxiety, its heavy hooves presented another danger to them. A feathered fetlock stomped dangerously close to Creed's face and the top of Nieve's head. Then the hross galloped off, stirrups flailing.

Creed let it go. It was well-trained and would not go far once it got over its fright. Whoever had shot at them was a bigger problem. With the hross gone, they now had no cover at all.

Creed rolled to his feet, pulling Nieve up and in front of him so that his back was to the shooter. One of her feet got tangled in the blanket wrapped over her legs, and she stumbled. He scooped her up and, in a half-crouch, ran with her toward the safety of nearby rocks at the base of the bluff.

Another bullet chipped off a piece of the sandstone wall above their heads, showering fragments of dirt.

Nieve was shaking. His demon, already inflamed at the possibility she had been harmed, almost escaped Creed's restraints as it scented her fear. His skin stretched taut across expanding bone, and he breathed deeply, in and out, as he fought to contain it. If he'd had any cause to doubt the threat half demons posed to the mortal world, he need look no farther than himself. It had grown stronger over the past months, with an increase in physical power that showed no signs of abating. Nieve's presence, and the urge to defend her, amplified it yet again.

Several new shots rang out, kicking up more dirt and rock. From their trajectories, Creed thought there were three shooters. It was possible a fourth man had gone off to try and capture the runaway hross.

"Are you hurt?" he asked Nieve.

While her green eyes reflected alarm and her cheeks had gone pale, he saw she was not about to become hysterical or faint. Life with Bear had toughened her up that much, at least.

"No," she replied, her chest rising and falling. "Who are they?"

"Thieves."

Ammunition was expensive. Honest people would never waste it by firing on someone who posed no threat. Therefore, they were planning to rob him. He had two things of value with him that someone would want to shoot him for. His hross and Nieve.

Creed would also bet money that they were mortal thieves and not spawn. He understood how half demon thought processes worked. They preferred to use demon talents over mortal weapons. Under other circumstances, so would he.

But not with Nieve watching. Right now, he'd trade all of his demon strength for the rifle in the sheath strapped to the packs on his fleeing hross.

The space where they were trapped between the rocks and the bluff was low and cramped. Creed sat so that Nieve was pinned between his knees, protected from gunfire by rock on the front, and with his arms and legs around her so that he defended her back from potential ricochets.

Thunder cracked on the far side of the bluff, a loud bang

that made Nieve jump and the earth shake. The sky darkened as the black clouds of the approaching storm moved in. If it rained hard enough, they would be in far more serious trouble from flooding.

Their attackers would also be aware of that danger. Therefore, they would all have to act soon.

The shooting had already stopped. They would be moving in closer, attempting to trap them. Because Creed had not returned fire, they had to suspect he was unarmed. Which he was.

Nieve, however, was not.

"Do you still have that pistol I gave you?" he asked. He already hated the idea of leaving her here alone. He could not leave her defenseless, too.

She fumbled with the folds of her skirt, and he shifted a leg so that she could reach it. When she drew it out and pressed it into his waiting palm, he checked to see if it was loaded.

He passed it back to her, closing her fingers around its grip when she tried to protest. He would be taking a gamble that his ability to go unnoticed would work in this instance since they were already aware of his presence. The thieves thought they had him trapped, however, and he hoped they would not notice his movements.

But he was not gambling with Nieve's life. He was confident that she could use the pistol to defend herself.

He started to stand. She clutched at his arm. When he looked into her pale face, he read panic.

"What are you doing?" she asked.

He wished he dared use compulsion on her, to give her a sense of security, but it was too risky when she was already this agitated.

He touched her cheek with his fingertips. "Not abandoning you. And not committing suicide either, if that's what you think," he said. "I don't intend for either one of us to die. They won't be able to see me, just like no one could back at Desert's End. Not if I don't want them to. You have to trust me."

It was tempting to lean forward, kiss her upturned mouth, and tell her not to worry, but she wasn't really worried for him, only of what might happen if she were left on her own.

Still, even understanding that, it was difficult for him to know she was afraid and unable to control it. He naturally suppressed his fear. That was part of his demon heritage. But Nieve's filled him almost to the point of incapacitation, and he was driven to alleviate it, or thought he might go mad in her presence.

A fork of lightning cracked open the sky, followed by a long roll of thunder and the first sheets of wind-driven rain. He had to act, and quickly.

The thieves would be coming from three different directions. He might have time to take out one, possibly two. While he was used to killing with his bare hands, and had above average strength, he doubted if even he could move fast enough to finish off all three before one of them reached her. She would have to take care of the third one herself, or at least buy him more time.

She refused to let go of him. "Don't leave me."

"I'm not leaving you." He picked up the pistol she had dropped. "Shoot anyone who comes near you. Not me," he added, more in an effort to make light of the situation than any real concern that she would. "And this time, try not to miss."

She bit her lip, looking as if she didn't believe that he would not abandon her, but in the end, she took the pistol from him and nodded.

"Be careful," she said.

Her words warmed him more than the intention behind them warranted. He was not used to any concern for his safety. What gave him pause, however, was the realization that she was not used to concern for hers, either.

He gave in to his demon's urgings and bent forward, brushing her upturned lips with his in a quick gesture of reassurance. "Everything will be fine. Trust me, Nieve."

But a part of him did not believe she would be able to do so. Inside, Nieve was as damaged and fragile as her missing son was likely to be.

As he emerged from behind the rock, he could not understand why his demon insisted that this delicate, tormented woman was his.

• • •

Nieve gripped the pistol with fear-frozen and clumsy fingers. She desperately wanted to believe that he would return for her, but she did not dare rely on the hope.

For protection, all she had was one bullet in a pistol with poor aim. She tracked Creed's progress across open land until he disappeared into a copse of cottonwood trees, worried because she could see him, and therefore so could their attackers.

The gunfire she expected never came.

The lightning in the sullen gray sky worsened. She counted the seconds between the flashes and accompanying bangs. Rifle fire was not the only threat to Creed. The bark on several of the trees he had vanished amongst bore long black scars from countless previous lightning strikes.

Another bolt shot from the heavens to strike the ground not far from her hiding place. The aftershock of electricity snapped at Nieve's hair, lifting it from her scalp, and the clap of thunder hurt her ears. The world sparked white then dampened to gray. A blast of rain swept over her, leaving her temporarily blind as well as deaf.

Then the rain passed, and her vision returned. As she wiped water from her face, she thought she saw movement to her right. She clutched the pistol to her chest, unsure what to do. It might have been Creed she saw, or nothing.

Or it might be whoever was shooting at them.

She was terrified now. Her chest ached from holding her breath. She did not want to die, but her imagination conjured up far worse scenarios than death. She had been afraid of Bear and the demon who had ruined her, and she feared Creed still, but until now, she had not known what all-encompassing terror really was.

Yet, deep inside her, she also found the solid core of determination that had set her on this path to find her son. All was not yet lost. If whoever approached was a threat, then she would be best served by letting him believe she was helpless. The pistol would only work at pointblank range. She had to let him get close to her. She hid the pistol in her lap, buried between the folds of her skirt.

Another flash of lightning and roar of thunder blinded and deafened her. When she could see again, a dark shape loomed over her. She caught a glimpse of a thin face with blond stubble on the jaw, and the brown canvas sleeve of his coat as he reached for her.

She knew at once it could not be Creed. This man was not large enough.

And Nieve stopped thinking. The pistol came up. As he bent over her, she pressed it into his side, closed her eyes, and fired.

The recoil knocked her hand back and up, and although she knew she had not missed, it seemed neither had she hit anything vital. Rough fingers grasped her wrist and yanked her to her feet. The man swore, his breath hot on her cheek, and then the flat of a palm slapped her face. She fell, dazed by the blow, and blinked against the blasts of rain as the blackened, angry heavens broke loose.

The toe of a boot caught her hard in the ribs, flipping her over. Nieve curled in a ball and blocked the pain from her conscious thoughts so that it could not overwhelm her. This was not the first time she'd been given a beating. All she could do was try to protect her weakest areas and hope it would not last long or be too severe.

She braced herself, but another blow never came.

Screams now drowned out the sound of the rain and the thunder as the head of the storm swept onward.

Terrible screams, accompanied by grinding, popping noises.

Nieve covered her ears and squeezed her eyes shut tight, not wanting to know what was happening because she had nowhere to run or hide from it except inside herself.

"Nieve!"

Someone was uttering her name. The voice was familiar, but also not. It ground out rough, like tumbling gravel, when it should have flowed smooth, like heated honey. She did not look to see who—or what—owned that voice. Some things were best not to know.

Then the voice changed, and the sound of her name became familiar and more welcome. She dared to sneak a look. Creed was beside her, touching her shoulder. Rain streamed from his face. His clothing hung off him in tatters, and he was covered in blood that sluiced down his chest and arms in pink rivulets.

But it was Creed.

"Did he hurt you?" he asked.

"I'm fine." She thought a rib might be cracked because it burned when she breathed, but when she probed at it with her fingers nothing shifted. She'd had cracked ribs before. They would heal.

All things considered, physically, she really was fine.

Creed took her by the elbows and helped her stand, blocking her view of whatever was behind him. "Don't look." He turned her around and nudged her in the opposite direction. "This way. We need to get to higher ground before the flooding starts."

She did not argue or ask questions. Even if she'd wanted to, she could not breathe well enough to be able to walk and talk at the same time. Dizziness was also a problem, and she had to hold onto him to steady herself.

After a few minutes, when it became obvious she could not move at the pace he wanted to set, he swept one arm beneath her knees and the other behind her shoulders and carried her. She crooked an elbow around his neck and held on.

He dashed through the stand of drooping cottonwood, unbothered by her added weight. The lightning had moved off at the head of the storm, leaving them awash in a deluge of the cold spring rain driving it.

On the other side of the trees, the ground rose to a small, flat plateau. A long shelter tilted sideways on broken pillar legs, one end in the air, the other on bended knees. The sign across its ancient and rusted roof read SAFEWAY. Beneath it sat two rows of decrepit, half-buried pumps, with cracked black hoses attached, unused for more than three hundred years. Beyond the pumps squatted a low building that had once been white but was now dreary with age. The glass in its front windows and doors was long gone. The holes had been boarded up, but the boards were rotted now and splintered by time.

Creed set her on her feet and punched a fist through the sagging planks nailed across the broken front doors, then peeled them off, piece by rotting piece, and tossed them aside. Once an opening large enough for them to pass through was cleared, he placed a hand on her back and nudged her inside.

Nieve had never entered one of these ruins before. Hundreds of years before, when the world was scoured by demon fire, any place like this that had stored flammables such as gas and diesel had gone up in balls of flame, leaving enormous craters in their stead. Very few remained standing. All of the ones that did were near, or in, the Godseeker Mountains, where they had been partially protected by the goddesses.

The interior of the building was dusty and dark, and it smelled as if something wild had been living inside, although not for a very long time. Nieve could make out straight rows of empty shelves forming center aisles, and odd, cupboard-like machines propped against two of the four walls. Other than that, the place had been gutted. There was a market for antiques from ruins such as this.

She shivered, not liking this ugly remnant of an era that was long gone from the world's history. All that could be said for the ruin was that its interior was dry, except for the puddles of water forming around her shoes because of her sopping clothes. She was soaked to the skin, but while cold, not unbearably so. Rain drummed against the roof and the sides of the building. Otherwise, the place was silent.

Creed's larger silhouette blocked the light from the doorway. He stripped the remains of his shirt off his arms and threw them away, outside, into the downpour. His trousers had lost all the buttons at the waistband, and were held up by a pair of stretched and frayed suspenders. The cotton seams had split at the thighs. The blood, for the most part, had washed away.

He had his back to her. The tattoo stretched from the small of his back, spread across his shoulders, then extended up his neck to cover the back of his skull. It glowed in the darkness, and appeared to undulate, as if restless and in possession of a life of its own. Its movement mesmerized her.

As Nieve stared at it, she tried to gather her thoughts. She knew she could not continue this way, where she was completely reliant on Creed for protection, because that protection was as much an illusion as his shifting tattoo. At some point she would need to take responsibility for her own safety. When she found Ash, she would be responsible for his, too.

She wanted Creed to understand that she was not a possession of his, and that she had at least made an attempt to defend herself.

"I shot him," she said to his back, breaking the silence.

"I know you did. But that pistol wasn't meant to kill a man so much as to discourage him. It's a weapon of last resort."

He sounded patient and understanding, somewhat distracted perhaps, but not at all disgusted by her helplessness.

"What happened to him?"

He remained very quiet, and did not turn his head to look at her when he spoke, but stared out the door, at the rain. "I'm an assassin. What do you think happened to him? And to his companions?"

Whatever he had done to them, it was bad enough to disturb him. She should not pursue this. And yet she could not stop herself. "I know you killed them. It's the manner in which you did it that I'm curious about."

He turned to her. Her eyes had adjusted to the dim light by then and she caught her breath, struck again by how beautiful he was with his golden skin and penetrating eyes.

And how much she should mistrust all of that beauty.

"Are you certain?" he asked. "Do you really want to know?" He did not give her time to respond. "I'm going to take a quick look around outside to make sure we're alone, then I'm going after my hross. Wait here for me."

Nieve watched him disappear into the pelting rain, both nervous and relieved at the same time. She did not care to be left alone, but neither was she anxious to remain in his company.

She folded her arms across her chest and hugged herself in an attempt to get warm and to ease her aching ribs. She knew what he had done, and how he had done it.

And she worried when he might turn demon on her, too.

. . .

If the thieves had more companions, they were gone. The area around the old ruin was empty.

Creed found an empty campsite and meager belongings that spoke of poverty and desperation, now battered by the pounding rain. They'd had to be new to thievery because the territory they staked was not well traveled enough to be profitable.

Unless they had been waiting for something—or someone—in particular, and he and Nieve had stumbled into their path through poor timing and misfortune.

There were no signs of anyone other than the three men he had already disposed of, so that was good news. By the time he found his hross a few miles up the trail, the rain had stopped and the sun shone bright. The flash flood along the ancient roadway had slowed to a mere trickle.

But Creed's uneasiness continued to grow, reaching enormous proportions. He could not recall ever before losing control of his demon to the point that it could shift form on its own. Until today he would have sworn it impossible.

Today proved him wrong.

He would not be so careless again. His mortal would not be ruled by his demon.

He had dispensed with the first two bandits and was tracking the third, already too late to keep him from reaching Nieve, but he'd known he would be. What Creed had not anticipated was the hot, visceral reaction of his demon when the thief put his hands on her.

It had torn the man to pieces.

And it put Creed in a difficult position. Spawn that were dangerous were to be turned over to the Godseekers, and he could not continue to pretend to himself that he was harmless. He would never have believed he was the type of man who reacted in anger, regardless of the situation, but when it came to Nieve, it seemed his demon took a different approach.

It was becoming unmanageable, and now it posed a different type of threat to Nieve — one he did not know how to circumvent.

After collecting his hross and changing out of the tattered remains of his damaged clothing, he returned to the spot where they had been waylaid so he could dispose of his victim's mutilated remains. He hauled them, piece by piece, into the trees and buried them under a pile of rock and brush. He had no wish for anyone to see what he had done and wonder about it. There were enough rumors about spawn circulating already. Wolven would take care of the other two bodies.

When that task was finished, he stood back and rubbed his neck. His tattoo itched and burned as he thought about what he should do, and what he had already done. The sun hung low in the sky now, and he did not want to make camp here.

He and Nieve would have to ride on for several more miles. He knew she was not in any immediate danger. His demon could sense it if she was. But it made him uneasy to think of how long he had left her alone, and he wondered if she would think he had indeed abandoned her, one more thing he had promised would not happen.

She did not trust him. Nor should she. He had proved that he could protect her from mortals, and had no doubt he could protect her from wolven, too, if the need should arise.

He did not know how to protect her from him.

• • •

Late in the afternoon, a spring rain began to fall, blowing in from the desert, gentle pitter patters of sound against the windows. Droplets merged, sliding in slow trickles down the glass.

Asher knelt on a kitchen chair and leaned against the window ledge so that he could watch it through the parted curtains. Airie loved the rain, and he loved Airie, so he figured it couldn't be all bad. She said the goddesses sent it as a gift to the world. It didn't speak to him the way it did to her though, no matter how hard he listened. And it wasn't that the rain didn't like him, exactly. It was more as if the goddesses hadn't decided yet whether or not he was okay. Therefore, he was content to watch their rain from indoors until they made up their minds.

Airie sat in a large rocking chair near the stove, her feet on the open oven door and hands folded on her stomach, her eyes already drifting closed. The baby kept Airie awake at night with her kicking, no matter how often Ash tried to tell her to stop. Right now the baby was sleeping, and Hunter, who had gone to help one of his sisters' husbands for the day, had told Ash to make sure Airie slept when she could.

While Ash watched the rain and Airie, he thought of his mother. And he knew it was time for him to start traveling again.

He hadn't done much of it since Airie banished the demons. They watched for anyone who entered the boundary, and they waited, hoping to follow them back to the mortal world. He knew the demon who searched for his mother had already found someone to summon him, and it wouldn't be long before the demon found his mother, too. When he did, he was going to be angry with her because she didn't want him anymore, and he couldn't make her.

The big man who watched out for her couldn't fight it alone. Hunter couldn't fight the half demons who were coming by himself either.

Ash slid belly first off the chair. Some people could only enter the boundary while they slept because that was when their demons took over. Ash didn't have that limitation. He and his demon got along fine. And traveling the boundary was a good way to cover more ground than he could in the mortal world. Time didn't work quite the same when he was inside it because the boundary divided the mortal world from an immortal one. While Ash couldn't cross through it to the immortal world, he could move back and forth between the boundary and this world with no trouble at all.

Except, of course, for the demons. And they couldn't see Ash if he didn't want them to.

He checked again to make sure Airie's baby was sleeping. If she woke up, she'd wake Airie, too, but she was curled in a ball, and he couldn't hear her thoughts, so he was okay. When she was awake she liked to talk to him, but she didn't know much of anything, and Ash found her boring.

Since they were both sound asleep, Ash decided it was safe to leave them alone.

The warm, cheerful kitchen disappeared. Rather than a

polished wood floor, he now stood on a bed of crushed rock. Above him, sharp-edged cliffs narrowed the sky to a thin, crooked band of flickering, red-and-orange ribbon.

Ash liked the boundary. He'd been coming here for as long as he could remember, especially when he needed to hide, and it made him feel safe. After Hunter and Airie found him and took him in, he'd had no real reason to visit. Besides, it seemed to upset them whenever he went missing.

Today, there was someone he wanted to meet. She'd been coming to the boundary for a few months now, and Ash always knew when she was here because she was afraid. It made her shine like a bright patch of light in a black night, and his demon could see her all the way from the mortal world.

So far, her demon had been hiding her from full demons and keeping her safe. It knew Ash wasn't any threat to her though, and that's why it didn't bother trying to hide her from him.

She was a few years older than Ash. Bare-legged, skinny, and dirty, with curly, nut-brown hair that looked like it hadn't been combed yet today, she'd nestled into a crack in the crumbly red cliffs.

Ash crept up beside her, getting as close as he dared before he allowed her to see him. She didn't cry out, or move, or make any sudden noise or disturbance that might attract unwanted attention, but her eyes widened at his abrupt appearance.

"You shouldn't be here," she whispered. "The boundary isn't safe."

Normally, Ash didn't let people know he could talk. Grownups asked too many questions that he didn't always think he should answer. He had something this girl needed to know though, and he wanted something from her in return.

"Demons can't see me," he said. "They have a hard time seeing you, too. But they won't if they find out our names, so we need to be careful. We can't say them out loud. If a demon has our name, and we owe it a favor, we won't be safe from it. Not here, and not even in the mortal world. Because you and I can cross here on our own, if it calls for us by name, we can be summoned."

The girl cupped her bony elbows in her hands and shrank farther back into the crevice. "I don't want to be summoned. I hate this place."

"You don't have to be afraid. Your demon protects you. You're safe enough here if you're careful," Ash added. He didn't want her to feel bad, or to be scared. "If you hate it so much, why do you come?"

"I'm supposed to find someone."

Ash already knew who, and that it had to be done. It was important that his mother get to the Borderlands. Airie couldn't travel because of the baby, and Hunter wouldn't travel without her. And Airie needed to be with Ash's mother if everything was going to turn out as it should.

It was also important that others like this girl find out they had nice people to turn to who weren't like the mean woman who used them.

"I'm here to help you," Ash said. "You'll find the woman you're looking for with no trouble at all once you know who she's with."

. . .

Stone wandered into camp shortly after darkness fell.

The younger children were bathed and already in bed. Thistle had found two scorpions to play with, and amused herself by using her demon talent to force them to fight each other. Imp hadn't yet returned from the boundary.

Willow, bent over a washbasin, scrubbed the last of the mud from the heavy rain off the children's clothing. She wiped the back of her hand across her forehead, pushing thick black hair out of her eyes as she tracked Stone's approach across the flat clearing.

He dropped a small canvas sack with a drawstring neck on the ground beside her.

She ignored the sack. "Where have you been?"

"Running some errands in Desert's End."

"You were asked to look after the children."

"Those scary little beasts?" Stone made a noise of disgust as he gestured in the direction of their sleeping forms. "They've looked after themselves for so long, they're like animals. I can't sleep when you aren't here to keep them leashed."

Willow did not argue the matter with him. She knew the children were wild. But they were hers and she loved them. Stone, however, she did not like at all. She needed him.

"All the more reason not to leave them unsupervised," she said. "It's taken a long time for them to become used to being around their own kind. They need an adult with them to see that they follow a routine, and make them feel secure. You have to earn their trust. If you can't do that, then maybe you should go try and steal another mining claim from mortals."

She threw the taunt in his face to see how he would react

to it. If he wanted to be part of the future she was building for them, then he would have to respect leadership. But she wondered how well might fare in a fight against the half demon assassin. If he beat him, it was possible he could also defeat the Demon Slayer.

If he lost, then she'd know for certain that he would have been of no use to her anyway.

Stone nudged the sack with his toe. It jingled. "Aren't you the least bit interested in what I found out in Desert's End?" he asked. "I spent some time in one of the saloons. You pick up all kinds of things in places like that."

She was interested, all the more so because a saloon was one of the businesses she dared not enter and he knew it. His ability to do so gave him a level of superiority over her that chafed, but she set her irritation aside because she did want to know what he had discovered.

She emptied the basin of dirty water onto the ground. "Tell me."

"There's a woman looking for slave traders." His expression grew sly. "It seems they come every year at this time, and they're overdue."

"A woman was looking for slavers? In a saloon?" Willow wondered if the woman was half demon, for her to be so bold.

"Quite the fight broke out, too." Stone grinned in remembrance. The lightening of his expression reminded Willow that really, despite his arrogance, he was no more than a boy. "An assassin came to her rescue. A big man. Bald."

Willow forgot her annoyance. "Did he have any tattoos?"

Stone crinkled his brow as if trying hard to recall and

seemed surprised that he could not find an answer. "I'm not sure about that. But there was no doubt he was spawn. I saw him again, just a few hours ago, down the trail. He's got the woman from the saloon with him. That's not even the best part," he added. "Some bandits took a few shots at him. I watched him shift to demon form and tear one of them into pieces."

The shifting surprised her. The news that the assassin now had a woman with him, however—one who was looking for slavers—gave her greater pause.

And made her very curious.

Willow gathered up the sopping mound of laundered clothing. Fortunately, it wouldn't take long for it to dry in the desert air. They'd have to go into hiding until the assassin passed them. As much as she'd like to, to see what might happen, she did not dare try to use Stone against him until she knew the full extent of the assassin's talents.

Imp materialized from out of nowhere. One second, the space at Willow's elbow was empty. The next, Imp stood in it as if she'd been beside Willow all along.

Stone stumbled back a few steps and swore at the girl. "Quit doing that, you little—"

"What luck did you have?" Willow asked Imp, interrupting Stone. As she did, she inserted herself between them, placing her back to him and her attention on the little girl, telling him without words who she found more important.

"I know where to find the woman you're looking for," Imp said. Her fingers worried the frayed seams of her skirt. She bit her bottom lip. "I mean, I know who she's with. A big bald man, with a tattoo on his back."

Willow absorbed the information, processing it so as to

understand what it meant. The woman the demon hunted for was the same one with the half demon assassin, and she was looking for slavers.

Willow's curiosity grew.

They'd hide until the assassin passed them, as she'd planned. But then, Willow thought she might follow him for a bit to see where he was headed.

Chapter Eight

For the better part of a week, they skirted the edges of the desert, staying close to the towns at the base of the Godseeker Mountains.

It was enough for Nieve that, at every place they stopped, Creed made inquiries as to the whereabouts of her son. Even though he had learned nothing, she could forgive him anything for that simple act of kindness. It kept her hope alive when she might otherwise have sunk into despair.

Creed also seemed genuinely concerned for her comfort, and went out of his way to see to it. Twice, they stayed in hotels and slept in real beds. At first Nieve had remained suspicious of his motives, wondering if she would have to repay him somehow. She hadn't forgotten the way he'd kissed her, as if he believed she belonged to him.

Or the way she'd responded, without any resistance at all.

After a few days, she began to entertain the possibility

that his kind thoughtfulness was genuine, and simply another facet of his already complicated personality. There was a simplicity to him that often lulled her into a reluctant sense of security.

Yet there was mercilessness in him, too. They had not spoken further of the attempted robbery or what had happened to the thieves. While he seemed in complete command of his demon abilities, she had seen evidence to the contrary. She could not figure him out at all.

She hadn't told him of the money she'd taken from Bear's house, and the pouch stitched to the casing inside the waist of her skirt. That was her safety precaution. She did not want to be left helpless and dependent ever again.

As they made their way toward the Borderlands, Nieve noticed an increase in fortifications protecting the towns they passed. Around the Godseeker Mountains, where she'd been raised, the goddesses' lingering presence had protected the people even after their departure. Demons could not enter. Walled cities and towns were neither necessary nor commonplace, and mining settlements sprawled throughout the mountains. The Godseekers maintained law and order.

The farther she and Creed moved into what was once demon territory, the more obvious it became to her that these communities, with no goddess protection, had been forced to rely heavily on ramparts. They'd found their growth restricted accordingly. To her, it seemed as if a lot of people were crammed in a very limited space.

It was late afternoon when they approached yet another small and fortified town. In the distance she could see that its palisades were strengthened by sturdy timbers, the posts sharpened to points along the top of the walls.

The day was hot. The hross, sensing food and water ahead, picked up its pace, and Nieve rocked in the saddle where she sat behind Creed. Both of her hands rested at his hips, her thumbs hooked in the buttoned suspender straps attached to his trousers, for lack of a better place to hold on.

"If demons could attack from the sky, would these walls really have kept them out?" Nieve asked.

"The walls weren't built as a defense against demons. They were meant to keep people out," Creed replied.

"I don't understand."

"Demons generally hunted alone, and at night. They'd go for easier prey, found out in the open, rather than try to attack people who were sequestered inside houses. Walls protected the residents by guaranteeing that there'd be easier prey outside." He pointed to a round watchtower on top of the wall, to one side of the front gates. "Guards stood on duty up there and shot anyone who tried to climb over the walls or ram through the closed gates before morning."

Nieve already knew how it would feel to stand on top of those walls and listen to the terrible screams of men being torn to pieces. She tried to imagine what it would have been like to be on the outside, under demon attack, and to have shelter so close but unattainable, all the while knowing what was coming.

Men could be every bit as monstrous as demons.

"The walls also kept women in," Creed continued. "Part of their purpose was to protect the innocent from the summons of demons."

"We didn't have walls around the village where I grew up," Nieve said. "Perhaps if we did, I wouldn't be where I am today."

The moment she uttered the words, a hot tide of guilt swept over her. It sounded as if she wished her son had never been born, and that was far from the truth. She'd never known how much love it was possible to feel for another person until she'd had him. She ached with longing for him, and from fear for his safety. And yet she could not help but be bitter about the hand fate had dealt her.

"I didn't mean to imply that women are weak," Creed said.

He had an uncanny way of picking up on her unguarded emotions. Without thinking about her actions, she leaned closer to him and rested her cheek against his broad back, seeking comfort through the physical contact. Heat from his tattoo blazed through his shirt.

At once, calm spread through her.

There was a long period of silence where nothing more was said. Nieve closed her eyes and listened to the thudding sounds the hross's great hooves made as they struck the packed sand and pebbled ground beneath them.

"How did you end up with Bear?" Creed asked.

For a moment she considered pretending she hadn't heard. Then she opted to tell him the truth. He already knew about Asher's father. She had nothing more to hide from him that was as terrible. If anything, the secrets she suspected Creed kept were far worse.

But she was a woman, and whether or not she was weak, judged far more harshly than a man in this world because of it. A band of pain tightened around her heart.

"My father paid him to take me after I told him I was pregnant by a demon," Nieve said. "I thought he would help me. Instead, he said I'd been ruined and that I no longer had any value to him, and that he couldn't stand the sight of me."

She sounded so matter-of-fact she could hardly believe that was her voice. This was the first time she'd told anyone her story, and even after so much time had passed she had difficulty forming the words. The sting of betrayal, and her incredulous disbelief that her doting father could turn against her so completely, remained a dull ache—not so much fresh as persistent, and undoubtedly permanent. She'd learned a harsh lesson about life. A woman, regardless of how privileged she'd been raised, could trust no one.

Creed's silence said he was thinking about what she had told him. Although curious as to what he thought, she refused to let his opinion matter.

"Even though my mother tried her best, because of what I am, she could never come to love me," Creed said at last. "For a lot of people, doing their best isn't enough no matter how hard they try. All we can do is understand and accept that the fault lies with them, not us, and be willing to forgive. No one is perfect or always right. We shouldn't judge them either."

Something snapped inside Nieve. Her hands tightened into fists where she held onto Creed, twisting the fabric of his clothing.

"My son is the most important person in the world to me," she said. "Ash isn't responsible for who, or what, his parents are. I'll never understand a mother's inability to love and protect her own child. Never. Your mother was *wrong*."

The fierceness of her outburst took them both by surprise. With a flash of awareness that burned deep, Nieve realized she was wrong, too. She had judged Creed for what he'd been born, and not his actions. He was unfailingly thoughtful and gentle with her. He had defended her. If he had been a simple assassin, and killed those thieves using mortal means, she would have thought nothing more of it. She hadn't thought twice of the manner in which he'd killed Bear, only that he'd done it.

He settled a hand on her thigh and gave it a light squeeze. While the chaste, simple gesture was no doubt intended to convey nothing more than compassion and understanding, it sent a blistering jolt of intense lust from where his fingers rested near her knee, straight to the juncture between her thighs. Nieve might have fallen from the saddle if she had not been holding on so tightly to Creed. In the back of her head, a voice screamed, *He's mine.*

It had nothing to do with his ability to use compulsion. It came from inside her. She could not have said what had triggered such an awareness either. They'd been together for almost a week, and this was not the first time he'd touched her this way. She could have had him any time she wanted. He had made that quite clear.

And she wanted him now, out of the blue, with an aching desire that left her lightheaded and breathless.

But another voice, equally loud, warned that she could not trust her own instincts while her son was still missing because all of her emotions were too extreme. It was as if, after a year of feeling nothing, a switch had been turned on and an avalanche of sensations triggered—but with every high there came an equal low. She could not be content to admire the beauty of the changing landscape as they passed through it. She had to bask in all of the glory the goddesses had brought to the world. She did not experience simple sadness—she drowned in the depths of despair.

She was more afraid of herself than Creed, and what this inundation of strong emotions might mean for her sanity.

And to her son, because she felt Asher slowly and inexorably slipping away.

He should be first in her thoughts.

Always.

She could not allow any distractions. Any division of purpose. If she did not think of Ash constantly, if he did not remain her priority, she might forget him again. The possibility terrified her.

Somewhere, her baby waited for her.

Creed had gone rigid in the saddle in front of her. The lazy, rolling motion of his body as he moved with the hross ceased. Tension radiated off him, as if he knew what she was thinking.

The thought of the two of them sitting so close, with her legs and arms around him for the next half hour, grew unbearable, even though they had been in this position for most of the day already. And indeed, for the better part of a week.

"I want to walk," she said.

She needed his help to dismount. Her skirt was an impediment, and the drop was a long one. Creed made no comment, only half turned, slid one arm around her waist, and swung her carefully to the ground. She smoothed her skirt over her hips.

He looked down at her for a moment. He did not try to ease or dismiss her nervousness. He also had to know that he couldn't have done so. Not with this sexual awareness so strong between them.

She was not innocent or virginal. And he was a demon.

He was very beautiful, she found herself thinking. He wore no hat, and right now his shirt sleeves were rolled to the elbow, yet the hot sun made no significant change to the warm golden coloring of his skin. She felt so pale and insignificant in comparison that she could scarcely understand what he found attractive about her, but that he found something was unmistakable. Two pale blue diamonds, set between thick black lashes, glittered as he gazed at her.

"When you get tired of walking," he said, "just say so and I'll trade places with you."

He urged the hross forward, keeping the impatient animal to a slow pace that Nieve had no difficulty maintaining. She trudged along the dusty, broken trail beside him with her thoughts in complete disarray.

And torn in two very different directions.

• • •

Creed could not spend the night in a hotel with Nieve as he'd planned. Not when his demon had been roused and every male instinct in him urged that he possess her. Whether she understood it or not, just now she had claimed him.

He's mine.

He had heard the thought as loudly as if she'd shouted it from the top of the town wall they approached.

But he would not be a demon. He had always controlled that side of himself, even in these past months when it had become stronger than he'd ever imagined possible. It frustrated and unnerved him to discover that Nieve, who was terrified of it, seemed to bring it out in him, in the worst ways and at the wrong times, when he would have done anything to protect her from it.

The town was within sight. Comfort beckoned. So did temptation. Creed brushed a droning hoverfly from the back of his neck, the tattoo itching and burning where she had touched it. He debated what was best to do. Being around strangers right now, when his demon was so restless and possessive of her, was not wise.

She might have claimed him, but she had chosen not to act on it. She might never do so, which he would do well to remember. She wanted her son. He wanted Willow. He had duties to consider, and his demon's fascination with Nieve sometimes made him forget them, or set them aside when he should not, because he'd stayed close to the Godseeker Mountains for her sake.

He could not continue this obsession with Nieve and her wishes.

On a whim, Creed set off from the main road toward the sprawling, red-soiled hills speckled with green clusters of shrubs that were bisected by a little-used side trail. He watched over Nieve closely as they traveled, worried that the heat and rougher terrain might prove too much for her, but she seemed far less restless and easier in her mind for the exercise. Walking had been a good decision.

For both of them.

A half hour later, and deeper into the hills, Creed saw that they were not natural hills at all, as he'd hoped they would not be, but ruins that had been burned out by demon fire in the days when the world had been razed, then abandoned to become buried by blowing sands and time. They would harbor dangerous sinkholes in their depths if the old buildings had rotted away, making it unwise for the newer settlement to build over them, but their location marked the presence of precious water aquifers and ancient reservoirs that the settlement could tap into.

Excitement prickled at the small of his back. These ruins were well worth exploring. Because the current town had not been built on top of them, but some distance apart, also indicated that there were things still buried here that the locals knew better than to disturb, either from experience or through folklore.

Deep craters, with colorful spring desert blooms tucked into their fissures and crannies, also suggested his hunch was correct. Old world towns such as this, located in strategic centers throughout demon territory, had once acted as a first line of defense against the initial waves of demon invasion. At their centers the ancients had built bunkers, where munitions were stored, while around the outer boundaries incendiary devices that activated when stepped on had been buried.

That was where these craters had come from. To Creed's eye, while they looked old and overgrown, they were not as old as the end of the world. Some of those buried explosives could well still be active. Hross, fortunately, had a natural instinct when it came to avoiding such dangers.

"You should ride from here on," Creed said to Nieve. "The ground is rough."

She took the hand he offered her, setting one dainty foot atop of his much larger boot where it rested in the stirrup, and allowed him to help her remount. She settled in the saddle and slid her arm around his waist, not leaning in as close as usual, but she had nothing to fear now that his demon had been distracted by the thought of adventure. It wasn't long before she relaxed against him.

"What are we doing here?" she asked.

"I want to see what's buried in these ruins, if anything."

He knew where to look, and what to look for. The first few ruins were unsafe. The hross refused to approach them, which meant the dangers from sinkholes and explosives was too great. The fifth ruin, based on its shape and location amidst the others, showed more promise as being what he was looking for.

He dismounted. Nieve watched from the safety of the back of the hross as he thrust his arm into a large crevice and scooped out handfuls of dirt and sand. When he put his hand back in for a third time, the tips of his fingers greeted empty space. After a few more minutes of digging, and chipping away at the debris using the spade he carried in one of his packs, he had carved a gaping hole large enough for him to pass through. He thrust his shoulder against the remaining blockage. It collapsed in a choking cloud of dust and he coughed as he yanked his neckerchief over his face.

Once the dust settled, he leaned through the hole to try and get a sense of how large the interior might be. His demon form had better eyesight in the dark and was almost indestructible, and exploring the ruin would give it a good workout, but he wanted to be inside before shifting so Nieve did not see him do it.

"Wait!" she called out.

He paused to see what she wanted.

She sat so poker-straight in the saddle that she looked like a doll strapped to the back of the enormous hross. Alarm filled her face.

"Do you even know what's inside? What if the structure

isn't safe?"

He grinned. "I'll be fine. I've done this before. If I can find a few artifacts, it's a good way to make extra cash."

"I have money," Nieve blurted out. Her fingers went to the waist of her skirt as if she planned to hand it over to him at once.

He'd known she had money. Men like Bear, who did not trust banks—or anything, for that matter—would have had a small fortune stashed away, and Nieve was not foolish. She would never have set out without some sort of means for funding her journey. It touched him to think that she would part with it, simply because she feared he might be harmed, when she needed it more than he did.

"Keep it," he said. He could not resist teasing her a little, and trying to put a smile into her somber, worried eyes. "If the sun sets before I return, you can keep the hross and the packs, too."

"At least until the first bandit I meet succeeds in taking them from me," she said.

Although undoubtedly true, he had to laugh at her droll observation. It gave him a glimpse into the girl she'd once been, and he liked what he was discovering. "Shoot them. But use the rifle in the boot behind you this time, not that tiny pistol." Then he added, with more seriousness, "But if you do have to leave here without me, for any reason, stay on the hross until you're back on the main road. The ground here isn't stable and the hross knows where to place its feet."

Creed eased the rest of the way through the doorway, more cautious of anything that might be hiding in crevices than of the ruin's stability.

Despite Nieve's concerns, the floor felt solid enough

beneath the soles of his boots. He quickly shed his clothes so that he would not ruin them when he shifted.

He loved the feel of the transformation—of the stretching muscles and loosening joints, the increase in power, and the way all his senses sharpened. Even though Nieve was outside, when he thought of her he could smell the warmth of the sun on her hair and the flowery scent she rubbed on her skin. He could feel the movements of air and the tiny vibrations of the earth as she fidgeted, restless, in the saddle, and when she breathed. It was little wonder that his demon had picked up on her physical desire for him when it was so attuned to her in this way.

It also picked up on her fear, and while anyone else's would have enflamed it, from Nieve, the effect was the opposite. She had no idea how completely she owned both him and his demon. He wondered what would happen when she figured it out.

And she would.

The interior of the ruin was completely black and it was difficult for his eyes to penetrate it at first, even in demon form.

Once his sight adjusted, he saw that the room where he stood was a jumble of broken joists and crumbling plaster from fallen walls. His demon form had much greater bulk and weight than a man. Although the floor creaked beneath him, it had been reinforced when originally constructed and remained stable enough.

He found a spiral stairwell behind a heavy steel door, also reinforced, at the far end of the room, where he'd expected one to be. These bunkers all followed a similar construction pattern, and appeared to be built at the same time and in great haste. The stairwell was wide, meant for moving large quantities of dangerous goods up and down, and he had no trouble fitting into it.

As he opened the door, emergency lighting over three centuries old flickered on. At the bottom of several long series of stairs, well below ground level, he passed through two more heavy doors. Their locks had been intended to keep mortals out, not demons, and he had no trouble snapping them off to gain entry. More pale yellow lighting came on, flooding the way forward as the stairwell behind him went black once again.

The storage room behind the final door was lined with row upon row of shelves, all filled with large wooden crates. Creed would have loved to take one of those crates with him but it wasn't practical, and exceedingly dangerous.

He pried the lid off one of the crates. Inside, he found layers of well-packed fragmentation grenades, deep green in color and with a smooth steel outer surface. Two of these would bring in enough money to pay for an entire year of any living expenses that traveling with Nieve could incur. As tempting as it was, taking too many would only invite unwanted attention that Creed might find difficult to deflect. Word would travel far of anyone attempting to sell such artifacts.

He took three, then replaced the lid on the crate. He knew where to find them again if he were ever back this way, and there was little chance that anyone else would discover the grenades. The ruins were too dangerous, and the fear of anything associated with demons—and the past—too high.

Upstairs, in the main room through which he'd entered, he shifted to mortal form and retrieved his clothing. A quick look around offered little else of value, except for a row of porcelain mugs on a shelf with a camouflage background and the words DEPARTMENT OF THE ARMY OF THE UNITED STATES OF AMERICA emblazoned on them. On a desk he found a manual, yellowed with age but well preserved otherwise. Its cover stated:

PROPERTY OF THE DEPARTMENT OF THE ARMY
UNITED STATES OF AMERICA
CONFIDENTIAL
HOW TO FIGHT DEMONS.

The world had lost that fight. Whoever had written this particular tome was not as well informed as he'd credited himself.

Creed left the manual where it was. He gathered up the hand grenades and several of the coffee mugs instead, then emerged into the fiery glow of a desert sunset.

He found Nieve right where he'd left her, he was only half surprised to discover. His demon would have known if she'd abandoned him, and while she'd been deeply unsettled by her claiming of him, she remained too naturally cautious to do anything reckless.

"We'll make camp here tonight," he said to her. "As long as we don't wander too far in the darkness, we couldn't ask for a safer refuge."

The element of danger in their surroundings would help serve to keep his demon instincts more focused on protecting her than in testing her desire for him. Tomorrow, he would take his demon in hand and remember his duties.

The diversion into the ruin had helped clear his head. Willow's trail around the Godseeker Mountains had grown cold. Creed thought that Freetown would be the likeliest place for him to hear rumors of her, and of any others like her. Once ruled by a priestess, it sat in the very center of demon territory. All trade routes across the desert intersected at its walls.

He placed the grenades into the coffee mugs to protect them from jostling, then inserted the mugs into his saddle bags. He cinched the binding straps tight.

Freetown would also be the best place for him to find answers for Nieve. If nothing about her son could be discovered there, then she would have to face an ugly truth.

She could continue looking, and not give up hope, but her search might take years, or be unending.

. . .

Nieve and Creed set up camp beneath the first glittering stars to dust the deepening blue and red of the evening sky.

She could not fully explain, even to herself, why she had suddenly told him of the money she carried, other than that she had not wanted him endangered because of her. If she were not with him, he could travel faster and cheaper. He would not feel so obliged to stop in towns he would normally pass by just so he could ask questions—that he had to believe to be pointless by now—on her behalf.

But that quiet, insistent voice in the back of her head continued to whisper, *He's mine.*

And she did not want to lose him, too.

He had built a small fire from the brush she had gathered, then made her a comfortable seat to curl up in so that she could be warm while she pondered the stars. With a soft word of thanks, she draped the blanket he handed her around her shoulders.

The lifeless ruins huddled around them, fencing them in. Even wildlife had abandoned this ancient site. Nothing stirred here other than a few feathered predators whose shadows skimmed silently in the dusky sky over their heads, and the occasional sigh of the wind through the grass.

This was the safest Nieve could remember feeling in a very long time. While her myriad and conflicting emotions had not gone away, right now they slumbered and left her in peace. Her eyelids drooped, too, but she was not yet ready to sleep.

Creed sat across the fire from her, his head bent, cleaning and polishing his weapons in what she'd come to understand was a nighttime ritual he found relaxing. As he worked, the flames caught the gold of his skin, and made his tattoo dance. She watched it in fascination.

"When I studied at the Temple of Immortal Right," he said, "I spent a lot of time in the library." He did not look up as he spoke. "It's filled with amazing books, most saved from the time before the demons destroyed the world. A few are memoirs written by the war's survivors, and others are handwritten reproductions of books that no longer exist in entirety. One of my favorite accounts is of old world airplanes that soared across the sky faster than a hross can run. Some accounts even state there were machines that could travel to the stars and the moon. Now that demons are gone and the skies are safe, maybe man can build such wonders again."

He had not acknowledged, in anything he had said or done, that he knew she desired him, and yet it simmered between them. By attempting to distract them both, he avoided the topic even now.

His thoughtfulness made her ashamed that she could not seem to get past what he was, even though she was the one in the wrong.

"Why do you do this?" she asked.

His head lifted so that he could look at her. His eyebrows went up in a question, as if his thoughts were miles away and he had not been speaking to her. Settling the gun he'd cleaned on the polishing cloth beside him he reached for another, as if absorbed in what he was doing.

She did not believe his attention was truly held by a mundane task that he'd carried out many times before, and could do in his sleep.

"Do what?" he asked.

"Treat me like I'm…" *Special. Beautiful. Valuable.* "Not able to take care of myself," she finished, her face flushing.

One of the good-natured smiles that so fascinated her about him tugged at his cheeks, creating creases at the corners of his mouth.

"I think you've proved to me, and to you, too, that you're more than capable of looking after yourself, at least within the limitations that the world has placed on you," Creed said. "Did you ever consider that I simply might like to do things for you? I liked doing them for my sister, too." His smile faded a little, then settled back in place. "I suppose, since she isn't here, I'm transferring the attention I'd normally give her onto you."

Nieve heard only one thing in his reply because the possibility that Creed might have a family had not occurred to her. "You have a sister?"

"A half-sister."

"Is she like you?" Nieve caught her breath, appalled by her daring to ask such a question, but at the same time curious as to the answer.

"You mean, is she unusually large and exceedingly handsome?" Creed's tone held amusement, but no trace of insult. "Not at all. She's rather small, with red-streaked, curly black hair. Her husband finds her attractive enough I suppose. But we shared a father, yes. Raven's mother turned her back on him when she became pregnant, even though the connection she had with him was very deep—and from what I gathered, mutual. My own mother, on the other hand, had no connection with him at all." He shrugged. "Or if she did I was never made aware of it."

Nieve rolled that information around in her mind. When she'd begun to suspect she was pregnant with Asher, the demon's summons had become easier for her to resist. After Asher was born, she hadn't felt it at all.

Now she did. Except it came from a different demon this time, and while she would not be tricked and manipulated again, she no longer believed it was Creed's deliberate intention to do so. He could not seem to help spreading the good nature that leached from him.

Nieve allowed it to lull her. She had never been talkative, but the urge to confide in him grew stronger. She wondered if he, too, would judge her for things beyond her control.

"He said I was his, but I never wanted to be." She tried not to shudder at the memories, but instead, forced herself to be honest about them. Physically, she had enjoyed the demon's attentions. He hadn't been cruel. Not to her. It was only after each encounter, when she was alone, that she'd burn with shame and fury for being unable to resist him, as if she'd betrayed someone she had no wish to hurt. "It wasn't difficult for me to choose my son over him. I knew what would happen if he found out I was pregnant."

Creed would know, too. Demons had not allowed spawn to live. While Nieve had been afraid of giving birth to a monster that would tear her to pieces, she'd been terrified for the baby's life and determined to protect it. Ash had been worth everything she'd endured.

Now, he was gone.

Creed's face gave little away as she watched him through the crackling play of the firelight. He stared up at the sky. The night was soft and still, and infinite. "A demon doesn't decide who belongs to him. The woman who's meant for him does her own choosing. So who do you think holds the real power in the relationship? What doesn't a demon want the woman he's chosen to know?"

"Are you saying I could have resisted a demon if I'd really wanted?" Nieve asked. That was what her father and Bear had both told her. Her stomach twisted. She'd somehow thought Creed's opinion would be different. She had not expected it to matter so much to her.

Creed leaned forward. His gaze, as it held hers, remained steady and gentle. Again, an almost incapacitating surge of raw desire for him crawled from inside her.

"Not at all," he said. "I'm saying you could if you had a strong enough reason to, and it seems you found one. I'm also saying that you don't belong to any demon. If there's a connection between you, then the demon belongs to you, not the opposite. Even immortals have laws they must abide by."

The jagged-edged lump in her throat made it painful to

speak, but Nieve managed to utter two quiet words around it. "Thank you."

"For what?"

"For all of the things you've done for me. For the little kindnesses you've shown me." Two tears tracked down either side of her nose, dampening her upper lip. She wiped them away with the back of her hand. "For trying to find my son for me when we both know it's most likely impossible. The trail is too cold."

Creed had stretched his long legs out in front of him beneath the white moon and stars, and the black backdrop of the sky. He shifted his gaze to stare at the tips of his boots. She had stated her worst fear out loud, and he was not able to correct her.

She was so very tired. Even her soul ached with a weariness that settled right to her bones. Her heart felt as if it were dead. But more than anything else, she was tired of her helplessness.

The shadows broadened and spread as the flames in the campfire lowered.

Creed got to his feet. "I'll get more brush." He paused, turning to her as if he'd forgotten something or had something important to say, before coming around the fire to where she sat. He crouched in front of her—a giant of a man—and cupped her face between his palms as carefully as if he were handling delicate, hand-blown crystal. He brushed one thumb through the dampness on her cheek.

"Nothing's ever impossible," he said. "Don't forget that half demon children tend to be remarkably resilient. We may have to set the search aside now and then, but I promise, we aren't going to stop looking."

Chapter Nine

Willow and the children had been trailing behind the assassin and the woman with him for the better part of a week.

Traveling mostly at night, it was now early morning, and Willow had made camp several miles from the main road they traveled The sun was still a few hours from rising, although the children, she knew, would sleep until noon.

They were good travelers and she had been able to cover considerable ground with them. Hardier than their fully mortal counterparts, the worst of the daytime heat did not trouble them. They could also walk through the darkest hours of the night.

Willow rolled over in her bedding, seeking a more comfortable position as she pondered her next move. The ground was hard, and she was becoming old enough for her body to mind it.

It was as Stone had said—the assassin was looking for the woman's son. He was not hunting for Willow at all. Or if he was, it was a half-hearted search at best.

She wondered why the assassin was so interested in finding this woman's boy when it was possible the child was also half demon. If so, the assassin's purpose in helping to find him would no doubt not be good for the child.

She tossed, waiting for sleep to return. If she followed the assassin much farther, his path would take her too far from her own. It was time to take the woman from him. In order to do that, she would have to make certain the assassin was dead. It was also time to put Stone's talents to the test.

Once they got to the Borderlands, she would call in the favor the demon owed her. She wanted her father's murder avenged, to prove to the world that she was the Demon Lord's true daughter and heir. She wanted what was hers, and would someday pass on to her children.

A soft, scuffing footfall alerted her to a small presence, and she looked up to see which of the children did not sleep.

Thistle approached, her golden curls tousled and partially covering her face, looking as if she'd been startled and was not yet completely awake. "Someone's watching us."

Willow flipped to her back and propped herself on her elbows, looking upward. "The man we've been following?"

"No." Thistle pushed the hair off her face. Her eyes took on a faraway look as she concentrated on something only she could see. "There are five of them. Three girls and two boys. They look to be Stone's age, or maybe a little older. Except for one of the boys. He's a lot younger than the others."

"Do you know what they want?" Willow asked.

"No. But I think they're hiding from us."

Willow was leery of having anyone she did not know,

particularly those with unknown abilities, so close to her and the children.

She rose from her blankets and trudged through the scrub and the trees in the direction Thistle indicated so she could confront them. She had no idea of their talents so she did not try to get close, but stopped a short distance from where Thistle said they were hiding.

"I know you're there," Willow called out. She kept her voice friendly but firm. She didn't want them to feel threatened. Not without reason. "Come out where I can see you. I want to know why you're spying on us."

With only a slight hesitation, a girl pushed her way free of the brambles of the bush where she'd been hiding.

Willow had no difficulty in summing up her appearance; dawn was not far off. Long, greedy fingers of light clawed at the shadows.

She looked to be about eighteen, undernourished, with dirty blond hair tied back in a sparse braid coiled and pinned at the nape of her neck in a manner that young married women often wore. Her clothing consisted of patches that covered more area than the original plaid fabric. She was also several months pregnant—something Thistle, little more than a child herself, might not have realized.

"I also know how many of you there are," Willow said. "I want the others out here where I can see them, too."

Although underfed and pregnant, and half Willow's age, the girl was no weakling. Her chin held steady and her eyes raked over the older woman, missing nothing in her scrutiny, either.

Her eyes returned to Willow's. "Not until I know that we have nothing to fear from you. We were here first."

They were not. Thistle would have known of their presence. The newcomers were following them, and Willow intended to know why before she offered them any assistance.

"I would think I'd have more to fear from you. You're the ones who are half demon." Willow tossed it out there, to see how the girl would respond.

"So are you, and the children with you." Pride filled the girl's face, but also indecision, and finally, desperation. "My companions and I have only just met up with each other in the past few weeks. The little one is my brother. All any of us want is a place to call home, where we aren't looked on as freaks."

Willow considered her again, but from a different perspective this time. These children, too, had been turned from their homes, and in recent months. Something about them had frightened their families and friends. She wondered what talents they had, and how strong they had grown.

"Tell me about yourself," Willow said.

"My name is Larch."

She was two years older than Stone and a great deal more clever. She was young, hungry, and undoubtedly sincere. She also had a pregnancy to consider. Although still in the early stages, the next few months would become increasingly difficult for her.

It turned out that the baby's father had been mortal, and when he discovered Larch was half demon, he'd turned her out. She had taken her younger brother with her when she fled. She defended her husband, however, and told Willow he had not known she was pregnant, as if that somehow excused his prejudice and cruelty.

Larch called out to the others. One by one they emerged from hiding, wary but willing to trust the girl who led them.

With the five newcomers, Willow's entourage would number thirteen. Fourteen, if she included herself. Despite the added burden of more mouths to feed, she saw the potential in having these newcomers join her. They could help care for the younger children. Stone was useless with them.

The future she'd envisioned brightened with the glow of the rising sun, and the promise that she might not need to rely so completely on the help of a demon, or Stone.

"You're welcome to join us," Willow said to the girl. "But each of you will be expected to earn your keep." War was coming. Even the littlest children, with the proper guidance, would be of use against mortals who had no natural defenses.

• • •

The day turned out to be a hot one.

They had left the Old World ruins behind them three days before. Tomorrow they would enter the desert, headed for Freetown, where they'd face the worst of the fast-approaching summer heat. Creed did not mind it, as high temperatures did not unduly affect him, but out of consideration for Nieve, they would do most of their traveling at night.

Right now, Creed was splitting kindling with the small hatchet he carried in his packs. He'd taken off his shirt while he worked beneath the increasing heat of the midafternoon sun, and sweat streamed down his bare back, only to evaporate beneath the scorching rays.

He swung the hatchet in rhythmic motions, his mind not on his task, but on Nieve. He watched her from the corner of his eye. She sat on the ground with her legs folded so that her skirt could be used as a workspace. A pile of clean clothing, which she'd washed in a stream that flowed nearby, sat next to her. She'd said she was going to do some mending, and she held one of his shirts, but her hands remained still.

His tattoo itched. That was how he knew she watched him, even without turning to look, and what she was thinking of. He bit back a smile of male satisfaction.

He lost the urge to smile, however, whenever he recalled the promise he had made to her.

We aren't going to stop looking.

He'd had no right to say such a thing, even if he had qualified it to state that their search for her son might have to wait. He was an assassin, in service to the Godseekers. While he could easily be convinced to walk away from them on Nieve's behalf, such a move would put her life in more danger, not less. The Godseekers would not forget his defection, any more than they had forgotten Blade's.

The difference was that Blade had never truly been one of the Godseekers' assassins while Creed had accepted his position—and their trust—willingly.

He had done so because he'd thought he could do more good by working with them. He still did. There were more innocent lives at stake here than Nieve's and her son's.

The Godseekers and their assassins would only tolerate the presence of half demons in the world if they knew they had an equal strength on their own side, and that such lines were being drawn—*us* against *them*—Creed was well aware.

He had no right to be making Nieve promises.

For that matter, and despite the tentative connection she was forging between them, he had no right to her. The life he'd chosen was not meant to include women or children. A woman like Nieve should settle down with a man who would make her the center of his entire world, and treat her as a goddess. She should be given more children to love and attend to, because it was obvious that she was meant to be a mother. Creed could no longer think of her as an innocent mouse. When it came to her son, she was as fierce as any brood kyson.

She also needed to be as fierce about every other part of her life. It was time she rejoined the land of the living. And Creed did not know how to help her do that.

He swung the hatchet with more force, splitting the chunk of wood into long, thick splinters that sprayed across the ground.

Nieve set aside the shirt she'd been holding. "Is all that firewood necessary, since we're planning to move on tomorrow?"

He looked at the pile of wood and the scattered chippings. She was right. They had enough wood. The tear she repaired in his shirtsleeve was of no matter. And the world around them was filled with wonderful things that she should feel free to explore, rather than focus on tasks he could as easily do himself.

Nearby was a ridge of sandstone, eroded by countless centuries. In its face, a number of crude holes had been carved. He'd wanted to examine those holes, but hadn't intended to take the time to do so.

He tossed the hatchet aside and beckoned for Nieve to follow him. "Come with me. I have something to show you."

They trudged side by side through flowering yellow brittlebush, the blossoms catching at the hem of Nieve's plain dress and bobbing as they passed. When they reached the ridge, Creed paused to search along the base, cautiously nudging aside scrub and patches of long grass, mindful of snakes and other small hazards.

"What are those holes?" Nieve asked, tipping her head back and shading her eyes so she could look up at the darkened holes.

"They're called cliff dwellings." Creed found the path he was looking for. It was actually a series of upward steps, worn but still passable. "These are a different type of ruin that predates the Old World by centuries. We'll climb as far as the first level, but I doubt if we'll be able to get any higher. The upper dwellings would have been accessed by ladders, and those are long gone."

The pathway of steps was uneven, and strewn with broken rock and hard clumps of sand where the softer stone face of the ridge above it had crumbled and caved in over time.

Creed reached back to help Nieve navigate over the worst of the debris. Without hesitation, she slid her slim palm into his. He found her willingness to accept his touch both disquieting and pleasing. She no longer feared him, at least not as much, which was both good and bad. While her trust made him happy, it might be best for her if she did not place too much faith in him. He wanted her.

The tension between them, that they both had been trying so steadfastly to ignore for the past three days, flared back to life. His heart rate picked up as his slumbering demon awakened. She could form other connections with men if she chose to. Once she accepted her connection with Creed, however, he could not. His demon would never permit it.

He would be hers forever, while she would be free to find someone else once she no longer needed him. And he had to ask himself why that should matter. He was an assassin. He'd never expected to belong to any woman anyway.

They continued to climb upward. The hot wind chased across Creed's bare shoulders, drying the sweat from his skin almost before it could form. Rather than withdraw her hand once they reached the first level, Nieve clutched his fingers and gazed around her in rapt fascination.

The small plateau where they stood had been carved from a natural fissure in the rocks, and held the remains of several round houses as well as hollowed-out cave dwellings. Even though the plateau was not all that high, the view of the sprawling desert below them was breathtaking.

Creed had seen such cliff dwellings before, and the remains of many more of these Old World wonders, and yet he never failed to be impressed by the ingenuity displayed by man in his quest for survival.

It was the effect time had on mortality, however, that the demon inside him found fascinating. Although born on this world, inside of time, and therefore as mortal as Creed, it could not seem to grasp that life here was finite. It had a beginning and an end. Civilizations, too, came and went, often leaving behind little to no knowledge of their existence.

His demon, although bound to this world through him, retained its immortal connections to the universe that gave it access to knowledge he could not always comprehend either. It had a tendency to react to certain things and situations in a way that Creed, if left alone, would not.

Right now it reacted to Nieve, and her awareness of Creed and their surroundings, in a way that he could not possibly ignore. She was very beautiful. That was undeniable.

But a beautiful face alone was far too common in this world, and subject to the ravages of time. Nieve had another, far more enticing, loveliness about her—one that went all the way to her soul and was eternal. She did not simply see beauty around her. She felt it. She drew it inside her. Then she released it so that others could experience it, through her eyes, and see things the way she saw them. That was what had once drawn a demon to her.

It was what beckoned Creed's to her now.

She crooked stray strands of hair from her face as she looked up at him, her face filled with wonder. "I had no idea places such as this existed. It's truly amazing."

The fragile trust for him that he read in her glorious green eyes sliced at his heart. He did not want to think of the future, and a time when she would choose a man other than him. His demon would never understand the need to let her go. Right here, right now, they belonged together. That was all that mattered.

He bent his head and covered her mouth with his. She made no objection, not even a half-hearted one that he would have had to take as denial.

Rather than simply accept his kiss, her lips parted.

She tasted of an equal desire for him that left him heady with hunger for her. The tip of her tongue brushed against his, a gentle exploration that had him hard, even though his intention had been to do no more than express his interest and willingness to her.

Both were evident enough between them. Too much so. He did not want to rush her, or make her feel as if she could not stop if she wished. He'd never used compulsion with women before, and he would not start now. Not with Nieve. Not even to give her an excuse, and for her to be able to say later that this was not what she'd truly wanted.

Creed also knew his own worth. She either wanted him as he was or she did not want him at all. The decision was hers.

He broke off the kiss, resting his forehead against hers.

"Anything that happens between us will always be your choice," he said to her. He still held her hand. He pressed her palm to his bare chest, placing it over his heart so she could feel how it pounded with longing.

Bemusement and trepidation flooded her lovely eyes. She bit the inside of her lip. Even if she could not have put it into words on her own, he knew what she was thinking. Whatever came next, she could not blame him for it. The consequences would be hers to own.

Creed did not dare draw so much as a breath.

Her free hand went to his hip. He drew her tight against him so she could slide it around to the small of his back. As the tips of her fingers came in contact with his tattoo, a searing heat shot through his torso.

She jerked her hand back and stumbled away from him. It took him a moment to realize that he was not the one in trouble, despite the sizzling pain of her touch.

Fire leaped from Nieve's outstretched, trembling palm.

Creed grabbed her wrist and smothered the flames between his own, much larger, hands. Then he examined her palm to see how badly she'd been burned.

The flesh of her palm was unmarked.

Her eyes had gone very wide. "How did you do that?"

Creed ran his thumb across her roughened, callused skin, giving his demon—and his heart—a few beats to recover. He frowned. A woman like Nieve should not have hands such as these. It pained him to think how she'd endured hardship and neglect simply because ignorant men like Bear and her father considered her damaged. She should have been treated as a person of infinite worth.

A goddess.

"I have no idea," he said when he could speak again.

But he did know. A demon offered its chosen mate a means of protecting herself from other demons. That offering was also a symbol of its claim on her.

Creed's demon had not crafted an amulet, as most did. It had created the tattoo Creed wore as an offering for its mate. And through it, it had given her fire for protection.

It became more and more obvious to Creed that the demon characteristics manifesting in half demons were unique to each individual—and were, for want of a better explanation, mutations. The possibilities inherent in such metamorphosing talents were endless.

And frightening.

Nieve eased her wrist from his grip, and the rightness of the moment between them passed.

He did not reach for her again. If possible, the abrupt eruption of demon fire through her hand had disconcerted him even more than her. He could not help but be thankful that she had not been harmed by accident through his ignorance. He no longer understood his own abilities, leaving him helpless and adrift, and unsure of his place in this changing world. He was not used to self-doubt. He had never seen himself as half demon.

He was an assassin. He wanted to help make a difference, to defend the rights of mortal and half demon alike. But how could he presume to judge others when he was becoming the very thing he'd been trained to fight?

He turned, his interest in the ruins gone, when a slight

movement and burst of unusual color between a tumble of rocks near his left foot caught his attention. Creed froze.

It was a juvenile sand swift, aggressive and mean-tempered, and far more dangerous than its more complacent adult counterpart. A fully grown sand swift could kill a man with a blow from its razor-sharp tongue. A juvenile used it to paralyze its prey so it could then feed on fresh meat at leisure. A single stroke against a victim's bare flesh was all it would take. The paralysis it caused was immediate and permanent.

"Don't move," he said to Nieve.

Years spent with a hard master guaranteed her instant obedience, especially when the harsh tone of Creed's voice conveyed the presence of danger.

Fortunately, she was on the far side of him and out of immediate harm's way. But he knew it would mean a slow death for her if anything should happen to him. The desert was filled with all sorts of unexpected dangers and this tiny, juvenile sand swift, no longer than the sole of his boot, was an excellent example that no one was exempt.

He had no weapons on him—another foolish, arrogant move on his part that they both might end up paying for. Once the sand swift tasted his scent and decided he was food, it would strike.

If he wished to save Nieve, Creed had no choice but to shift to his demon form.

Nothing happened when he attempted to summon it.

For the first time in his adult life that he could recall, Creed knew real panic and fear—not for himself, but for Nieve. She would be defenseless out here without him.

He had to do something.

He seized one of her hands and brought it to the tattoo

on his back, searing his skin as her palm caught on fire. The sand swift was moving now, too. Creed curled his body around Nieve's to protect her from attack, and grasping her wrist, aimed the fire she held in her palm at the creature to deflect the strike of its unfurling tongue. He then used the heel of his boot to crush the sand swift's body.

It squealed beneath his full weight as he bore down on it, its fat little body jerking a few times before finally falling motionless. Green, poisonous slime seeped from its mouth and through cracked, broken flesh.

Creed scraped the thick, sticky mess off the bottom of his contaminated boot as best he could. It would have to be burned now, and he did not have a spare pair. He could not walk barefoot into the desert. That meant they would need to return to one of the towns they had passed before continuing on.

He still clasped Nieve's wrist. Her whole body shook as he drew her against him. She pressed her flushed cheek to his chest and squeezed her eyes closed tight. He dropped his chin to the crown of her fair hair, his relief vast at the narrowness of their escape.

He had no idea why his demon had not responded to his summons. That had never happened before, and his head spun with possibilities before fastening on the most plausible. Nieve had not been the one in immediate danger, and his demon had instinctively reacted to the greater likelihood of her fear of it by withdrawing.

One other thing troubled Creed, possibly even more, and it had nothing to do with his fickle demon. He had used Nieve—who relied on him and needed him to defend her— as a weapon.

Chapter Ten

Above where Nieve crouched on the bank of the small, trickling stream, the sky deepened and the stars began to emerge as tiny speckles of light on a backdrop of endlessness.

She rinsed the tin plates from their supper in the clear, tepid water, keeping her head down and her eyes fixed on her task. No matter which way she turned, always, her internal compass brought her back to wherever Creed was. Right now she knew without looking that he stood near the fire and watched her.

Her desire for him had not abated. If anything, since she had touched him and her hands burst into flame, her longing had grown. And yet, while she knew he felt the same desire for her that she did for him, and even though he was demon, he had not acted upon it.

She could not remember the last time something she wanted so desperately was hers for the taking. All she had to do was give Creed some indication that she was willing.

She closed her eyes. She was afraid to discover he had not been truthful with her, and it was not as he'd said, and that she was not the one who would claim him. She was not the same woman who had once managed to extricate herself from the lure of a demon. She could never do so again.

For an entire year, she had forgotten the most important person in the world to her. What did that say about her, and her strength of will? What if she allowed herself to be distracted by this irresistible attraction to Creed, and in so doing, she forgot her son again?

"Is something the matter?"

The concern in Creed's voice washed over her. With a start, she realized she had been kneeling at the water's edge and staring into its ripples for quite some time. It was almost completely dark now.

She glanced over her shoulder, to tell him nothing was wrong, but the words died in her throat. Wearing nothing but a well-worn pair of denim trousers that strained across the heavy muscles of his thighs, light gleaming off his gold skin, he had not moved from his position beside the fire. He'd burned his boots. Even his feet were well-formed and magnificent. She had never seen a man, or demon for that matter, quite so perfect as this, and it struck her that the beauty she saw was shining from within him, and not merely a glittering surface illusion.

Asher's father had not been beautiful in this way. Not as Creed was. He'd been like a wormy apple, sleek-skinned and smooth on the outside, nice to look at, but so riddled and rotten underneath that it had made her feel tainted to have him touch her. Because of that, she had believed both her father and Bear when they said she was ruined.

Creed did not make her feel ruined, but as if she were precious—not only to him, but to the world.

It stunned her when she thought of how she might have lost him today. He always seemed so larger than life to her, so invincible, that it was too easy to forget he could be as fragile and mortal as she.

The fire that had burned in her hands rekindled in the cradle of her stomach. Its source sprang from Creed, and extended to her through this connection between them, spreading to her thighs and her chest so that she could hardly stand or breathe.

Somehow, she managed both. Before she had put more than a single thought into her actions, she was on her feet and walking toward him.

He did not move, but watched her approach, heat in his eyes, letting her come to him.

Then she was standing before him. With trembling, tentative fingers, she reached out and pressed their tips to his naked chest. A pulse leaped in his throat, but he did not reach for her. She stepped closer. When she slid her arms around him, fire did not flare from her palms as it had at the ruins. It ignited like an explosion of fireworks inside her.

The same heated reaction emanated from him. He took hold of her elbows, staring down at her face with such intensity and naked longing on his that she had to lower her eyes.

"If we begin this," he said, giving her fair warning, "I won't stop. Not unless you ask it of me."

"You told me that any connection between me and a demon is through my choice, not his," she said. "Does that include this connection I'm feeling to you?"

His jaw worked, but his gaze did not waver from hers. "It does."

"And I can end it whenever I wish?"

"You can."

"Will you promise me something, then?"

"Anything. As long as it's in my power to give it to you."

"Do you promise never to allow me to forget my son? Or to let me give up on finding him?"

"No," Creed said, and her heart stopped beating. She wilted in his arms so he had to tighten his hold. "Look at me," he commanded her. When she did, his gaze had softened. "Those choices are also yours. I promise never to be the cause of you forgetting or giving up."

She could ask nothing else of him. Not without giving more than she was willing—or able to—in return.

"Then I choose you," she said, so low that she wondered at first if he'd even heard, because he still did not move.

Then he pulled her into his arms and lowered his mouth to cover hers. The kiss was deep, and as he parted her lips with his, he thrust the tip of his tongue between them so that she gasped with pleasure at the taste of him. Her hands wandered, uninhibited, over sleek, naked skin, sliding lower until she'd pushed the length of her fingers beneath the waistband of his trousers to stroke the hard, lean curves of his hips.

His hands cupped her face as he continued to kiss her, then he eased them down the length of her throat to slip the loosened bodice of her dress from her shoulders. The roughness of his palms as they scratched over her flesh, and his thumbs caressing her collarbone, made her shiver with need for him.

He kissed the corner of her mouth, then the point of her jaw beside her ear, and trailed hot kisses along the path his hands had traced.

The bodice of her dress slipped to her waist as she fumbled with the buttons of his trousers. She had never undressed a man. It took her longer than she'd expected because he watched her. He scooped her into his arms and carried her to the bedding he'd unrolled beside the fire. As he lowered her onto the blankets, he kicked off the trousers that had settled around his thighs so that he was completely naked. Nieve caught her lip with her teeth. He unfastened the rest of her dress and lifted her hips so that he could ease off the remainder of her clothing.

He lay beside her, his fingers trailing along her cheek as he scrutinized her face. "I don't believe I've ever seen a woman as lovely as you are," he said, his voice husky with wonder and thick with desire.

She'd once been beautiful, but did not believe that was true anymore. Time and a hard life had not been kind to her. She made no effort with her appearance. She had silvery stretch marks from her pregnancy on an otherwise flat belly because Asher had been a large baby.

Still, Creed made her feel as if she were somehow amazing, and when she looked into the brilliant depths of his eyes, she knew he meant every word and that his compliments for her were sincere. To him, she was beautiful.

His fingers moved to the swell of her breast, testing its weight, and he looked to her with a question in his eyes before he bent his head to take the nipple between his teeth. He flicked his tongue across its tip and Nieve arched her back, pleasure searing through her, her reservations forgotten. He was stiff and hard, and she cupped him with her hand. He groaned encouragement as she twirled the tip of her finger in the liquid at his head.

She was not used to the freedom of doing as she pleased.

"What would you like me to do?" she whispered into the curve of his shoulder.

He raised himself on one elbow and smiled down at her. "This is not about what one of us would like the other to do," he said. "We're both to do what brings pleasure, as long as neither of us protests. And for what it's worth," he added, "I'm unlikely to protest." His widening smile teased one from her in return. Then his tone turned more serious and the smile faded. "Are you?"

"No," Nieve said.

"Then tell me you want this, and me," Creed said. "I would never use compulsion on you. Not for my own gain. I don't think I could."

It was as if he'd splashed cold water on her. Her reservations returned. He had been good to her, and kind. She could not treat him otherwise. "I don't want to use compulsion on you either."

He seemed confused for a moment. Then his expression cleared. His eyes softened and he pressed a kiss to the top of her breast, where the swell began.

"Any connection you feel between us has nothing to do with compulsion. I'm yours because it was meant to be that way. Whether or not you want me is your decision to make."

That did not feel right to Nieve either. "I'd rather you wanted me by your own choice," she said.

Creed took her hand, which she'd removed, and returned it to him, pressing her fingers around his hard length as he answered her. "Even if I were compelled, which I'm not, I don't think I could want you any more than I do right now. My choice is made."

Dampness pooled between her thighs as she curled closer to him. He had said they could each do what brought them pleasure. She wished to prolong these moments before reality returned and the world intruded once more.

She wished to explore him.

She got to her knees, pushing him to his back beneath her, and straddled his hips. She watched his eyes darken with amusement and interest in the flickering light of the campfire, and he rested his hands on her thighs. Somewhere, far off in the night, she heard wolven howling as they gathered to hunt, but the noise did not alarm her when Creed was near. They avoided him as if they sensed the demon in him, and no wolven would take on a demon. Not even when hunting in numbers greater than usual.

She had nothing to fear when she was with Creed. With him, she did not need to be invisible. She bent to kiss him. As she did her braid of hair fell from over her shoulder to drape across his chest, pale against the gold of his skin. He picked up the long length of braid and wound it around his wrist so that she could not lift her head, her lips caught against his. With his free hand, he stroked his palm over the curve of her buttocks. His erection pressed heavily into her stomach. She moved her hips forward and back, creating friction against it, and the soft moan he emitted left her panting with a need of her own.

"I want you inside me," she said, surprising them both. She was not normally this explicit. So direct.

Creed froze, but only for a second. He let go of her braid and went to lift her so they would trade places, with her on the bottom, and she grabbed hold of his wrists to stop him.

"No. I want to be here." She raised his hands so that they were above his head.

She lifted her hips in order to slide a hand between their sweat-slickened bodies and guided his erection to the opening between her thighs, then stopped with the tip barely pressed into her heat. She eased him inside her, but barely an inch, before forcing him to withdraw. She did it again, and again, until his jaw clenched with the effort it took him to remain so uninvolved. Although he'd curled his hands into tight balls, he did not move them from where she'd positioned them above his head.

"Have I done something so awful," he said through gritted teeth, his voice filled with good-natured frustration, "that you're trying to kill me for it?"

She stopped. Sat back on his thighs. Her eyebrows went up as she looked at him. She could not quite believe that she dared to play such a game with a giant of a man like this, who was restrained only by the force of his own good will.

And yet she dared also to tease him.

"Are you protesting?"

"No," he said hastily. "No, not at all. But it's only fair to warn you that I do plan to get even."

Nieve leaned forward to place a kiss on his chest. As she did, she ran her tongue across his nipple, then blew a soft breath on it. A shudder ran the entire length of his body.

"I'll be looking forward to it," she said.

"I have to live through this, first."

She could wait no longer. This time, she took him inside her completely. And then she began to move in slow, easy motions, up and down, reaching to take his hands with hers and drawing them down so that he was once again free to touch her.

He was gentler with her than she'd expected him to be, particularly after she'd toyed with him for so long. He had his palms on either side of her breasts, stroking them with his thumbs, and held her steady as he thrust upward to match the rhythm she had set.

Pleasure seared through her, building in hot waves until she could no longer contain it. With soft, tiny cries she could not quite stifle, her inner muscles clenched tightly around him as she came.

Creed was not so restrained. As she collapsed on top of him, her cheek pressed against his throat, he climaxed with an arched stiffening of his body and a loud groan of relief that made Nieve smile.

They stayed as they were for a long time after, feeling the combined pounding of their hearts as they each enjoyed the warm presence of the other.

And Nieve knew it was as he'd said. He was hers.

Yet there remained a cold, empty place in her heart that Creed could not fill.

• • •

With one arm draped across her waist, Creed watched over Nieve as she slept next to him. The fire had burned low, but the brilliant, cloudless heavens shone bright.

They had not bothered to dress. She lay on her stomach, smooth skin pale against his darker, golden-toned flesh, with her face turned toward him and her hands tucked beneath her cheek. She looked innocent and content, and happier than Creed had yet seen her, although he wasn't certain of her feelings.

Normally he was quite good at reading people. Not so with Nieve. She guarded her emotions as tightly as she was able and he tried to be respectful of her reticence. Consequently, he had not expected her to be so demanding in bed. So sensual. She was not at all what he had first thought her to be.

She was not what she thought herself to be either.

Pleasure and pain ate at his insides. Never before in his life could he remember wanting something so much that he knew would never be his. He would enjoy her company while he could. He would be good to her. And when the time came, he would let her go.

She made a small noise. A tiny frown furrowed her beautiful brow. He ran the tip of his finger across it, to smooth it away, and she averted her face from the slight touch as if she found it unwelcome.

She was dreaming. Whatever it was, it robbed her of the peace she'd been projecting only a few short moments ago.

Creed debated waking her, but before he could make up his mind, her eyes opened. She stared at him without recognition, her expression alarmed, and then it cleared so fast at first he thought he'd been mistaken.

She did not go back to sleep. She said nothing, only shifted closer to nestle against him, tucking her head beneath his chin. His heart flipped crazily at the intimate gesture of trust.

Her earlier happiness had leached away. He wanted to know what had disturbed her, and if it was something he could somehow resolve. If possible, he would take all of her worries away.

But while Nieve might trust him with her body, she

trusted no one with her thoughts and fears. One evening of intimacy would not be enough to earn him those privileges.

"You were dreaming," he said.

The warmth of her breath drifted across his skin with her response. "Was I? I don't remember."

She'd been dreaming of the demon who had once possessed her. That was the only reason he could think of for her to lie to him right now. He pressed a kiss to the crown of her head and tightened the arm he held around her. He would not ask her to speak of one lover with another. He harbored no jealousy in that regard, particularly since she did not recall the other one with fondness.

He wanted to distract her.

"Tell me of your happiest memory," he said.

"This is it. Right now." She trailed her hand over his hip, from his waist to his thigh, the touch light and possessive. Distracting. "Tell me of yours."

"That's hardly fair," he said, amused. "How could I choose anything other than this moment, now?"

"Tell me something from your childhood."

His breath quickened, his thoughts scattering beneath the seductive movements of her fingers. He wanted her again. He could sense that she wanted him, too, but whether or not to distract him from his questions, he was less certain.

More than the physical connection, he discovered he yearned for a deeper, longer lasting intimacy with her.

"I was a model child," he said. "Obedient and quiet."

"And a liar, too, I'm sure," Nieve said, "because I don't picture you as obedient. Or quiet, for that matter. You talk far too much."

That made him laugh outright. He had always been friendly

and affable. People tended to respond to him in kind. Not Nieve.

"I had no one to obey, so that point's debatable. And I suppose I do talk a lot, at least compared to you."

"Tell me of your sister. Would I like her? Would she like me?"

At one time he would have said no without hesitation. Nieve, however, was more complicated than he'd first thought. She did not lack courage, but confidence in her own abilities.

"I really couldn't say for certain if you'd like each other," Creed said. The two women were such opposites. "Raven was always in trouble. When she was younger, she had no idea of the way in which boys—and often, grown men—were drawn to her. She had no control over her allure, and no understanding of why it was necessary for her to gain it. I spent a lot of time fighting before she learned how to take care of herself."

"And now?"

Creed smiled, his memories of Raven warm and dear. "She still doesn't have to. I can't imagine there are too many men brave enough to get within a hundred feet of her these days. Not once they've met Blade. Not if they wish to live."

"He's half demon, too, then," Nieve said.

"No." Creed tried to find the right words to describe Blade. "He's a man who does what needs doing. Even demons fear him, as well they should. Raven is no doubt the only person in the world who has no reason to. Except, maybe, for the Demon Slayer, who considers him a friend."

"Do you miss her?"

"More than you can imagine." But less so lately, he discovered, faintly surprised that he did not think of her as much. "She's happy and safe with someone who loves her, and that's all that matters to me."

He watched her roll his words around in her head.

"I wondered why you were so insistent about offering me help when we first met. You were alone, and needed someone to care for, and then you found me."

She spoke with quiet and enlightened understanding, as if she had found the missing piece of a puzzle that had stymied her. He started to argue, and tell her it was nothing like that at all, but found he could not deny it. Not entirely. Nieve did need him.

Uneasily, he realized he liked it too much that she did. "You didn't want my help," he reminded her. "You tried to shoot me."

"And you abandoned me because I did. But still, you came back."

He said nothing. He'd not gone back because of her.

Her hand paused at his waist, arrested by what she must have heard in his silence. "I wasn't the reason you were in Desert's End that night, was I?" she said.

"No," he admitted.

"You weren't coming back for me."

He wished he could tell her otherwise, but he was not going to lie to her. "I would have, eventually. In the meantime, I made certain that you weren't completely defenseless. I spoke to the sheriff about you. But there are changes coming to the world that take priority over anything else I might want. I told you I have a job to do, and that it would have to come first."

Nieve let her hand drop limply between them. "You'd already found something to care for before you ever met me, then. That means I'm a burden for you."

"No." Creed tangled his fingers in her hair and settled a

kiss on her forehead. "You're not a burden. Never. Having you with me makes no real difference to the things I need to do, other than that you're a good travel companion."

He was not lying to her, simply not being completely truthful. She was not a burden to him. He had made promises to her, and raised expectations he should not have done, but were little enough, really, that he would do so again.

But he could not keep her with him forever. He could not spend his days overseeing her happiness as he would like, or allow his feelings for her to interfere with his commitments to the changes that would be coming.

The best way to protect her, and others like her who could not defend themselves, was to make the world safe for them all.

. . .

"Willow!"

She heard her name being bellowed from some far off, distant place, rousing her from a deep, exhausted sleep, her heart hammering in her chest.

It took her a moment to understand what emotion it was she was feeling. The anger she heard in that summons would have made the Demon Lord himself tremble.

She listened for the sound to repeat, but all around her, the night remained silent and undisturbed except for the usual stirring of nocturnal creatures.

She and the children had made camp earlier than usual this evening. The newcomers, although strong enough to carry on at the same pace as the little ones, had been too close to starvation and Willow wanted them to be at their best long before they reached the Borderlands.

Thistle slept peacefully beside Willow, her chest rising and falling in deep, even breaths, which meant there were no half demons nearby. The girl would have been the first to sound the alarm.

And then Willow heard her name roared again, this time followed by an imperious command. *"Come to me!"*

Despite her efforts to suppress it, the unfamiliar sensation of fear mounted. The command did not come from the mortal world, but the demon boundary. He tried to summon her. *Her.* And, while the tug on her to obey him was so irresistible as to be painful, she could not answer it.

She could not cross into the boundary.

Neither could she let him discover that he held the least bit of power over her. She did not know how he had gotten it, but he had.

She did not know what had so enraged him either. Her mind raced, seeking some sort of solution that would afford her, and the children, the greatest protection.

It came to her in a flash of awareness. Rather than let him discover she could not cross to the boundary, she would make him believe that she was simply too strong for him to command. She would summon him here instead, even though it was night, and he would be near full strength.

He needed her. She counted on that for protection.

She eased from her bedding, careful not to awaken the others, and slipped off into the night. When she reached a small valley where the topsoil and vegetation had been well worn away by the wind, nearly a mile from the camp, she stopped.

The night was cold. Willow did not mind it so much, but

the heat from the circle of fire she was about to raise would be welcome.

Within moments, she had a fiery circle in place. A second after that, the demon surged into its center. Willow kept the circle deliberately small so that she would have greater control over it, and of him.

He wore man form, but not even its physical beauty could hide the demon ugliness that percolated beneath the surface. He came to the very edge of the flames so that they licked at his skin. He neither burned nor backed away from them, but he did not pass through them either.

She was not certain that she could stop him if he tried. With sickening clarity, Willow understood she'd gotten herself ensnared in something a great deal more complicated and dangerous than expected.

She scrambled through her memories, and her past encounters with him, trying to figure out her mistake.

He stared at her for a long time without speaking.

"When I call you by name, you are to obey me," he finally said.

And she knew. She had given her name to him.

How foolish of her to respond willingly to a demon's demand, even one so seemingly insignificant.

Now that she knew how he had called her, the sickening sensation of fear abated. She dared not show such an emotion to a demon—or to openly defy one when it had a hold on her. Better to brazen this out, and let him think that he did not command her at all. "What do you want?"

The demon pushed his face close to the fluttering flames that distorted his features, and cast shadows across the ground more reflective of his demon form than the one he now wore.

Willow fought an instinctive urge to give ground.

"I want the payment you owe me. I want what's *mine*." His hands curled into fists. "And I want the spawn with her dead."

Understanding dawned. The demon was jealous. The assassin had tried to claim the woman he sought.

Willow had little doubt he'd succeeded. She wondered if she could return the balance of power to her favor. She had to give the demon something more, and of significant value.

Something the woman would relinquish the assassin for.

"The woman is searching for a small child she says is her son," Willow said, thinking as fast as she could. The wind picked up, making the tips of the flames bow toward her. "He seems important to her. What would you give me in return for the boy's name?"

The demon's bearing grew cunning. "Why would I want his name?"

"You tried to summon me with mine. Could this child, if he's yours, be able to refuse you as I just did?" Willow asked. "If you had him, you'd have all the control over his mother you want."

And he'd still need Willow to bring her to him. Even with the son in his possession, he could not get to the mother.

She watched the demon struggle to think past his anger. She did not want him thinking too hard.

"Very well, you don't want his name. However, the assassin wasn't part of our agreement either. And since it seems the woman you want so badly has taken a new lover, finding her for you is a waste of my time." Willow began to release her hold on the circle of fire.

"Wait." He came close to the fire. It sparked in his eyes, which had gone blood red. "Get me the name."

Chapter Eleven

Creed tied his hross in front of a shop in one of the many tiny desert outposts that scattered the edges of demon territory.

They had been traveling for several days already, and he needed those new boots to replace the ones he'd been forced to burn. His feet were wrapped in strips of tarpaulin that he'd cut from his tent's rain barrier.

He'd need a new one of those, too.

He also had two grenades in his pockets that he planned to try and sell. A man had to be careful. If the person he offered them to didn't want to meet his price, or couldn't buy them for some reason, word would be out that he had them. They had already been set on by thieves once. He did not want to subject Nieve to that again if it could be avoided. He wished for her to see him as mortal, not demon.

She might as well wait for him in a tea shop where he would not need to hide her presence. This was a place for women to sit while their men conducted business elsewhere in town. Her fearfulness surfaced in unguarded moments and kept his demon on edge, making it difficult for Creed to move around unobserved.

He escorted her up the stairs to the tearoom, his hand a light touch on her elbow. Inside, the room was bright and cheery. The walls were white stucco, the floor a rich, terracotta tile. Wide beams crisscrossing the low ceiling carried hanging baskets of flowers. The tables and chairs were handcrafted from mesquite, solid and plain.

She chose a table by the window so she could watch the street. He ordered her a pot of tea and some biscuits at the counter. From the corner of his eye, he watched her remove her bonnet and set it on the chair beside her.

She looked very pretty, all white-blond hair and luminous eyes, and Creed had not yet recovered from a hunger for her that had multiplied over the past few nights. The thought of being away from her, even for a short while, with evening approaching, unsettled his demon even more. Once he took care of his errands, he would see about finding them a room for the night.

"Aren't you having anything?" Nieve asked when he did not join her.

"I will when I come back. I have some things to do first," he replied. "I won't be long. Wait for me here."

He left Nieve in the tearoom and walked the short distance to the town's one hotel, where he booked them a room and deposited their belongings.

His next stop was the general mercantile. He bought his boots and asked a few questions that the clerk had no answers for, and immediately forgot being asked.

Since they'd moved farther from the shadows of the

Godseeker Mountains, and into former demon territory, the tales of spawn had become less prevalent, and of Willow specifically, almost nonexistent. Most of the stories Creed had been hearing were secondhand and obvious rumor.

Tales of slavers, however, were not. They passed through these parts on a regular basis, and even though Creed believed any trail leading to Nieve's son was long dead, he would never take the hope of someday finding him away from her. He'd continue to stop in each town and ask questions.

This outpost's sheriff was not at the jail. A young deputy was on duty instead. His friendly smile flattened when Creed introduced himself and asked if he knew anything about slavers in the area who dealt in children.

The deputy rested a long leg on the sheriff's desk as he lounged in his boss's chair. Creed made himself amiable. The farther he moved from the Godseeker Mountains, the less cooperative law keepers became. Many towns had formed their own systems of justice in the years since the goddesses' departure and did not yet see the need to incorporate others.

"You're a long way from home, assassin," the deputy said. "We don't get many of you in our town. If you're hunting slavers, you're out of luck. The sheriff locked the gates on the last ones to try and come here to do business. That was when we still had a demon roaming the area."

Creed thanked him. He then moved on to the local saloon, his next usual place to flush out information.

The farther into the desert a man went, the earlier in the afternoon business was conducted. When demons had ruled here, people tended not to travel the streets after dark.

Even though night was still well away when he walked

into the saloon, the crowd was thin. He made his way to the bar, asked his questions, and received the same answer he'd gotten at the sheriff's office.

As he started to leave, already thinking of Nieve and whether or not they would stay in town for the night or move on, he noticed a young man sitting alone, not far from the door. Brown hair hung to the collar of a plain shirt that had cuffs too short for his long arms and bony wrists.

The boy hadn't been there when Creed entered. He was certain of it. But the boy also had a familiar look to him. Creed was good with faces, but he could not recall where he had seen him before. He didn't like that either. His memory was good.

The boy rose from the table, stepping into his path and blocking his exit in a manner that Creed would never have tolerated from an older, more experienced man. As it was, it did not make his demon feel friendly. Nor could he seem to read this boy's intentions.

Creed waited for him to speak.

"Are you buying or selling?" the boy asked.

That question was not one Creed had expected. "I beg your pardon?"

"You've been asking about slavers who deal in children. Is that because you're interested in buying them? Because I have several to sell."

He had Creed's complete attention now. "If I say yes, I'd want to know where you got them. Can you prove that you have a legal right to sell them? Do you have papers?"

The boy's face became sly. "No papers, but I do have the right. They're brothers and sisters who don't add much value to the family business. They won't be missed."

94   Dᴇᴍᴏɴ Cʀᴇᴇᴅ

This type of exchange was hardly a rare one. Plenty of families had too many mouths to feed. Creed was about to explain that there had been a misunderstanding when it occurred to him that perhaps he was the one who had misunderstood.

Something about the boy didn't ring true to Creed. He had the look of a farmer, but did not seem to be local. His accent wasn't quite right. His hands had a particular kind of gritty stain to them that spoke of time spent in the mines, not behind a plow. The bartender was taking no notice of their conversation either, and he would have displayed more interest in what was happening if he knew the boy personally. He might even have tried to warn him that he was dealing with an assassin because Creed knew he'd been pegged as one the minute he walked through the door. Bartenders paid attention to that sort of thing.

Still, Creed was about to brush the boy off, and tell him he was not interested, when he thought of the children the boy claimed to be selling. And he became curious as to where they'd come from. Or if they even existed.

"How many are you offering for sale?" Creed asked. "And are they boys or girls?"

"Two boys and a girl."

Creed was now very curious as to what the boy's game was.

"I'd want to see them first," he said. Nieve was waiting for him, but she'd be safe enough where she was for a while longer. He did not want her involved in this.

The boy shrugged as if that was more or less what he'd expected to hear. "Follow me."

He led Creed through the streets, and once past the

gates, a short distance from town.

· · ·

Nieve tried to remember the last time she'd been in a tearoom. It had occurred in what seemed like another life, and to a different woman.

She sipped her drink and ate one of the biscuits Creed had ordered for her. Her overwhelming desire for him had not dissipated over the past few days. As another night approached, it began to consume her thoughts.

He did not seem to care who was in control when they were in bed together. Rather he was fascinated by, and indulgent of, her assertiveness, as if he understood her fear of being compelled and dominated.

She could not get enough of him. For that reason, neither could she believe that she was not being compelled in some way. In her heart a part of her did not quite trust him.

The plump, friendly waitress returned several times to make certain she had everything she needed before finally leaving her in peace, but Nieve could tell by the interest lurking in her cheerful brown eyes, and her hovering manner, that she'd return before long. Nieve did not want to answer a stranger's questions, no matter how kindly meant they might be, or to have to think too hard about anything. She stared into the delicate cup she held, swirling the leaves that had settled at the bottom.

The bell above the door tinkled, disrupting and scattering her thoughts. A young girl, perhaps twelve years old, with lovely, honey-brown curls and blue eyes that looked almost purple, came into the tearoom.

"Excuse me," the girl said to the waitress. "Are you hiring?"

Nieve watched the exchange, idly at first, then with more interest.

The waitress was sympathetic but firm. "I'm sorry, darling. No. But if you're hungry, I can give you something to eat."

"Thank you." The girl smiled at her, and the waitress blinked several times as if enchanted. Nieve could understand her reaction. There was something about the girl that drew a person in and made them want to take care of her.

"Go have a seat and I'll bring you something from the kitchen," the waitress said.

The girl looked around the almost empty room. Her shy gaze fell on Nieve, then shifted away, as if she were too embarrassed to make eye contact.

Nieve could not sit there and do nothing. The sight of a young, hungry girl in outgrown clothing slapped her with the reminder that she was a mother. The child reeked of hardship and neglect. Kindness killed no one.

"Would you like to join me?" Nieve said to her.

The girl nodded. She came over and edged into a chair, perching on the seat as if ready to run at the first sign of danger, and Nieve's heart melted.

"My name is Nieve," she said. "What's yours?"

"Thistle."

The waitress brought Thistle a large mug of hot kyson milk and a plate of cookies. The girl thanked her, and the older woman patted her shoulder before leaving them alone. Nieve pretended not to notice as the girl slid some of the cookies into her pocket.

"Where are you from?" Nieve asked.

The girl took a drink of her milk. She held the mug carefully in both hands, as if warming them, although the day was far from cold. "I don't really remember. I've moved around a lot."

"You can't be here by yourself." Nieve could not see how that would be possible. The girl was too pretty, and too close to womanhood, to be roaming desert towns alone. Nieve wondered if Creed could help her somehow. Her hand went to the bulge in the seam of her skirt. She had money. If Creed would do nothing, she could give some of it to her.

The girl cast a furtive look around her. "I'm not alone. I have brothers and sisters with me."

That was why she had put the cookies in her pocket rather than eat them all, even though she was hungry. Nieve could see it in her pinched face, pretty as it was. She had other mouths to feed.

Nieve nudged the plate with the remaining biscuits on it toward her. "Why don't you take these for them?" she said. "I've had enough."

The biscuits disappeared with the cookies. The girl leaned across the table. Those purple eyes embraced Nieve with gratitude. "Do you have any children?" she asked.

Nieve's heart constricted. "A son."

"What's his name?"

"Asher." Nieve cleared her throat, which had gone dry and sore. "I call him Ash for short."

"My little sister is sick," Thistle whispered. "Our mother disappeared a few weeks ago. I'm the oldest and I don't know what to do for her. Could you help me?"

Nieve could hardly refuse. Only the thought of Creed,

and what he might say, kept her from agreeing at once.

"How old is she? Does she have a fever?" Nieve asked.

"She's three." Worry pinched Thistle's forehead. "I don't think she has a fever. She just won't eat. More than anything, I think she misses our mother."

Nieve thought about Ash. What if he were the one who was ill, and missing his mother, and no one would offer him anything—even a little bit of money and comfort that could easily be spared?

Creed would understand that she had to offer her help.

"Where is she?" Nieve asked.

"Not far. Just a few minutes' walk outside of town."

Nieve glanced out of the window, but saw no sign of Creed. She didn't know how much longer he would be, but when he returned, if she was not yet back he would only have to wait a short while. She would explain the situation to him. He'd understand that she could not abandon a child in distress. She would make certain the child was not ill, and perhaps leave a little money with Thistle to help ease her conscience.

Nieve gave the waitress a message for Creed, saying that she had not gone far and would return shortly. Then she took Thistle's hand and allowed her to lead the way.

The direction they took led them off the main road and deeper into the desert. The walk was farther than Thistle had implied, and the terrain difficult to navigate on foot. Broken chunks of granite, and red-and-yellow-blossomed prickly pear cacti, littered uneven hillsides overgrown with bear grass.

Just when she began to think she should turn back, and questioned the wisdom of having come in the first place, they came around the bottom of a knoll to find a clustered stand of singleleaf ash.

From out of the trees a woman appeared. Tall and slender, with waist-length black hair, she was older than Nieve, and might have been quite beautiful if not for the coldness in her eyes that spoke of an ugliness inside her. Thick tresses of her hair lifted in the dry wind, twisting like angry serpents.

Nieve wondered if this icy woman was the mother who had abandoned Thistle and her siblings. If so, she looked nothing like her daughter. It was difficult to imagine her as caring for any child, let alone one who was ill.

Thistle tugged on her hand, urging her forward, although reluctance made Nieve drag her heels.

"I brought her," Thistle said to the woman. "Her name is Nieve. Her son's name is Asher. Ash, for short."

"Asher," the woman repeated, as if committing it to memory.

"Is this your mother?" Nieve said to Thistle. She hoped the girl would say no, and that this was a misunderstanding of some sort. She did not want to believe she had been duped with such ease.

"Thank you, Thistle," the woman interrupted before the girl could offer any explanations. "You can let go of her now."

As Thistle released Nieve's hand and went to stand beside the other woman, Nieve's protective instincts toward her thinned. An icy chill spread outward from the pit of her stomach to gnaw at her extremities. The younger girl's calm, peaceful demeanor never altered. That alone, from the very beginning, should have alerted Nieve that things weren't what they seemed. She'd been coerced into coming here—

manipulated against her will—by a fresh-faced child.

She looked at Thistle with new eyes, and could scarcely credit the fact that she had been tricked by someone so young and innocent. She could not begin to imagine what the motivation behind the deceit had been. If it was money they wanted, Thistle could have compelled her to hand it over back at the tearoom.

"The girl is half demon," Nieve said. A part of her hoped to be contradicted, although she knew she was right.

The black-haired woman rested a slender hand on the girl's shoulder. "So am I. So is the assassin you're traveling with."

Caution increased the chill Nieve was feeling. This was not about her at all, then. It was Creed the woman wanted.

She did not acknowledge the comment that Creed was half demon. He did not reveal that to anyone. In fact, he denied it. "If you wished to speak with him, all you had to do was approach him. There was no need for this subterfuge. He's no threat to you," Nieve said.

"He's a half demon masquerading as an assassin. That makes him a threat to us all because he's not being honest with anyone." The woman's thoughtful contemplation of Nieve held a hint of contempt. "Perhaps you should ask him if he's being honest with you about his search for your son. Did you know he was turning half demons, including children, over to the Godseekers for judgment?" She smoothed a hand over Thistle's curly head. The girl's expression remained serene, yet was so frightening now that Nieve could not catch her breath.

"You've seen firsthand how persuasive we can be when we want something. Haven't you wondered what the assassin could possibly gain from helping you find your son?"

· · ·

Creed trudged over the rough terrain with the boy, well aware that this was some sort of trap. Not a professional one by any means, but intriguing enough to keep him engaged in the game—although glad it did not involve Nieve.

The boy's name was Stone, and Creed still could not shake the sensation that he'd seen him before. There was no doubt he was spawn, but he did not use compulsion. Of that much Creed was certain. The surface had barely been scratched regarding emerging half demon abilities, however. Creed remained cautious as to what this boy's might be, but hardly concerned.

He was more interested in their surroundings. The hills they maneuvered were, in fact, more remnants of Old World buildings, hidden by time and reclaimed by nature. Stone did not try to climb them, which was wise, but skirted their base.

Creed had been somewhat distracted as he'd examined the ruins until they came around the base of one grassy knoll and approached a scraggly copse of ash.

Then he saw Willow. The trap—and the game—took on a higher level of sophistication, because standing behind her was Nieve.

Creed dared not look at Nieve. His demon could sense the confusion and fear in her, although it remained more watchful than hostile. Creed hoped that meant any danger to her was not immediate.

He pinned his attention to Willow. The last time he'd seen her, she'd commanded a feral, mutated child to tear out a man's throat. He hated to think of what such a creature could do to delicate, defenseless Nieve.

"Every assassin and Godseeker in the Godseeker Mountains is looking for you," Creed said. "You're very popular with them."

Willow smiled as if the thought entertained her, which no doubt it did. The news could hardly come as a surprise. "Men do love me."

"You understand, of course, that I have to take you into custody for judgment," Creed continued.

That seemed to amuse her even more, and she shot a sidelong glance at Nieve. "Of course."

"There's no point in involving others. You're the one I'm after. Let the woman go. If you do, your young friend here," Creed gestured to Stone, who had remained in a watchful position beside him, "is free to go, too."

"I'm not interested in going anywhere," Stone said.

"Perhaps Nieve is." Creed finally looked at her. She was frightened, but something more, too.

"I'm not going anywhere either," Nieve said.

"I didn't invite her here to let her leave so soon." The demon in Willow appeared to enjoy the escalation of tension. "There's someone who's anxious to see her again. It seems he misses her. I think he thought she was dead. Imagine how pleased he'll be to see her looking so well." She smiled at Creed. "And so well cared for."

She had summoned the demon who had fathered Nieve's son back into this world, and placed him in a position where he could reach Nieve again. Creed saw the initial confusion, then the spark of panic in Nieve's eyes as she figured it out.

This was one spawn that Creed would not bother taking

back to the Godseekers for justice. He'd kill Willow himself.

"You're starting to make me angry," Creed said. "You aren't going to like it."

"Because you'll shift to a demon form?" Willow tapped her chin with the index fingers of her clasped hands. "You're wrong. I think I might like to see that. Besides," she added, "You're likely going to need it. I got the distinct impression that the mortal's demon lover isn't at all happy with you. You took something he claims is his. And I wonder what this demon might do if he finds out he also has a son?" Willow's eyes remained fixed on Creed, not Nieve, as if testing how far she could push him. Or, perhaps, she did not see Nieve as a threat. "I'm sure he'd like to know where he is, too. If he knew about him, of course. But how do you suppose he'd find out such a thing? Who do you think would be cruel enough to tell him?"

Nieve, who'd been standing meek and submissive, hurled herself at Willow, catching everyone by surprise. She had her hands in Willow's hair before anyone could think to move.

If she had gone after a mortal, Creed might have let her be, but Willow was of demon heritage. Creed, however, was farthest away and not fast enough to come to Nieve's defense. Willow struck her, knocking her back a few staggering steps. Nieve emitted a small sound that was more impotent frustration than pain.

Creed, although he had weapons on him, reached for none of them. He reacted to Nieve's distress in blind anger, as a half demon would, not an assassin, and he started for Willow.

The boy, Stone, stepped into Creed's path and swung a fist at the side of Creed's head. Creed dodged it so that the blow landed on his shoulder, but even so, he reeled from its unexpected and formidable force. He was a big man, much larger than Stone, who was not full grown, and yet the blow hurt.

Then he saw that the fist at the end of the boy's arm was not mortal but demon, and felt the sting as blood flowed from the wound on his shoulder where demon claws had torn his flesh.

Creed swung his own fist. It hit Stone in the jaw, and by rights, should almost have killed him. At the very least, it should have knocked him unconscious.

Instead, the boy's jaw had shifted and hardened on impact so that Creed hit the hard bone plating of a demon, and not the mortal flesh he'd anticipated. A blossoming, mind-numbing pain shot up his arm, and Creed suspected he had broken several knuckles.

The boy's demon talent was far more impressive than it first seemed. His shifting was instinctive, and a pre-emptive response to danger.

Creed, as enraged as his demon now, prepared to unleash his own demon form.

And for the second time when he'd needed it of late, his demon did not respond when he commanded it to shift.

Chapter Twelve

Stone struck Creed another hard blow, this time to the chin.

Creed felt the dampness of blood trickling from the corner of his mouth where he'd bitten the inside of his cheek, but no pain.

Adrenaline took care of that.

He scrubbed at the blood with the back of his hand as he assessed his next moves. The skin across the top of his knuckles had split open and was also bleeding. His eyes and his tattoo blazed with heat.

He threw a few more quick punches that Stone didn't bother to avoid. Every time Creed swung at him, the part of his body Creed connected with shifted to demon.

But Creed was no longer swinging hard, he was testing. Looking for weaknesses. He knew where his own were—in the chinks between the bone plating that allowed for freedom of movement and a greater agility in the demon form. He wondered if Stone would have the same chinks between his bone plates, or if his demon ability to shift individual parts of his body covered even those natural vulnerabilities.

In case it did, Creed mentally ran through his other options. Stone had unique demon defenses, and could not be hurt, at least not by Creed, but he was a clumsy fighter with no tactics. He telegraphed every move. His fists were easy enough for Creed to avoid.

So Creed decided to make him work for the blows he did manage to land, because while he tired the boy out, he had another plan to put into action.

Not all fights were won using simple brute force.

He danced on the balls of his feet in the fighting stance he'd been taught, and as he bobbed and weaved, he brought them both closer to the base of the ruins.

Stone was breathing more heavily now, although he remained untroubled by Creed's efforts to dodge him. He was not intelligent, Creed discovered with relief. He was a typical young bully, used to winning against opponents who did not know how to fight either, or who were simply intimidated by his greater strength and abilities.

Creed did not try to lead him up the side of one of the hilly ruins, which would have been an obvious ploy even to Stone, but instead searched for a depression in the ground that indicated an old world foundation — and modern day sinkhole — beneath it.

He found one of the depressions he was looking for. It took him a bit longer to work Stone into position, drawing him close before backing away. Once Stone was where Creed thought the center was on top of the depression, he reached into his pocket for one of the grenades he'd been planning to sell at the outpost.

He fumbled with the pin, yanking it free, and lobbed it underhand so that it rolled to Stone's feet. He didn't dare move out of range too quickly because he didn't want Stone to pursue him and also escape.

It became apparent that Stone had never seen one of the old world explosives before, which was what Creed had hoped, because he stooped and picked it up, and held it. He looked at Creed with a sneer of contempt, as if about to hurl an insult at him in return, or brag about his invincibility. Then his hand shifted shape.

His expression changed with the shift, moving from arrogant, to confused, to angry understanding. He let go of the grenade, but it was already too late.

Creed dropped to the ground and covered his head with his arms as it detonated, rocking the earth. Debris, thick chunks of soil and rock, rained down around him and he worried for Nieve, hoping she was far enough out of range to be safe. The blast was loud enough to set his ears ringing, but other than that he seemed fine. He uncovered his head. Where Stone had stood was a large hole about ten feet in diameter.

He started to rise. Then the ground beneath him began to tilt. His whole body teetered, tipping downward, and before he could roll to safety, he was sliding headfirst into a deep black abyss.

He tumbled once, a single somersault done in freefall, and slammed painfully against what had once been a floor joist in an old world building. It was twisted and broken, the jagged steel edges sharp, and Creed lost flesh off his leg even as he snagged onto the beam with one arm. His lower body swung back and forth like a pendulum, dead weight that threatened to pull him loose, before he managed to steady himself.

He looked down. Below him was nothing but masses of broken beams, fallen walls, and blackness. Puffs of stale air and ancient dust made him cough, and his grip slipped an inch. Some of these old sinkholes could be as many as four stories deep, if not more, and lined with concrete and bedrock. Even in demon form, if Stone had tumbled to the bottom of this pit he would be lucky to survive.

Nieve was the only one Creed worried for. Willow would not think twice about handing her over to a demon. He would not let that happen.

He got one leg over the joist and hauled the rest of his body up. The joist where he perched was solidly wedged between two broken pieces of flooring. He fumbled for the second grenade he carried, pulled the pin, and after a three second count, he let it drop into the dark hole. The explosion rocked the joist, which swayed but held steady.

He balanced precariously on his hands and knees and stared at the tiny patch of sky high above him, waiting for the dust to settle. He had to get out of here. Nieve was not yet out of danger. His irrational mortal fear for her mingled with the colder, results-oriented thoughts of his demon until he could not disengage the two sides of his nature. The back of his shirt grew too tight. He heard it rip, felt it tear, then the seams parted across the shoulders. As his demon form emerged, its greater weight dislodged the joist.

One end began to tip downward, toward the abyss below.

. . .

With a sense of detached horror, Nieve watched the ground swallow Creed whole. The day had taken on a nightmare quality for her. She had no idea what to do next. What she could do to help him.

Or what would happen to her.

She started forward, the need to do something irresistible, but Willow seized her arm in cruel fingers that dug deep into her flesh to hold her back.

"It's too dangerous," Willow said, with unmistakable disdain, "and I need you alive." She called to Thistle, who had come out of her hiding place amongst the ash trees when the explosion went off for a better look. "Hold her hand. I want to make certain that the assassin's dead."

Nieve heard Willow utter the word *dead*, but it made no sense when used in relation to Creed. He was invincible. She replayed what she had seen over and over in her mind. *Creed lying on the ground, covering his head. The earth tilting. Him sliding headfirst into a crumbling hole.*

He was as mortal as she.

Heat tingled behind her eyelids. Creed was not dead. He would never leave her with Willow, who planned to give her back to the demon who had once taken everything from her.

She watched as Willow walked toward the wide hole, testing the ground with each step to see if it was stable. Nieve remained where she was, her hand clasped in Thistle's. The girl smiled at her, and Nieve found herself smiling back, although it felt odd and distorted, as if the corners of her mouth had been drawn back by invisible fingers.

It was a horrifying and familiar sensation. Nieve felt like a puppet on a string, helpless to take control of her own body. The girl had a gift for compulsion, already even greater than

Creed's. It did not bear contemplating how strong her gift would be when she reached adulthood.

The ground rumbled again. Willow stopped, tilted her head to the side as if assessing the risk, then turned away.

"It's not safe," she said to Thistle. "I already have what I came for. We're leaving."

"What about Stone?" the girl asked, but Nieve knew the question was empty, and merely something Thistle thought was required of her.

The child had no soul.

"Stone should have been more careful," Willow said. "Even if either one of them survived, it will be difficult to escape from that hole. If the ground is too weak to support my weight, it would never hold one of them."

Another tremor shook the earth.

And then, even as Willow finished speaking, a giant figure emerged from the rubble and shot skyward on widespread, leathery wings beating so hard that Nieve had to shield her eyes against blasts of blowing dirt.

The demon shot over their heads as if testing its wings for the very first time. Then it swooped downward with alarming speed, aiming at Nieve and Thistle, who held Nieve's hand.

Nieve flinched as those enormous wings pounded the air, and outstretched, taloned feet reached for her. Even though she knew the demon had to be Creed, she did not believe him able to control his natural instincts while in that form.

She could not find the breath to scream. Instead she reacted out of maternal instinct and fear, and threw her body in front of the younger girl to protect her by enfolding her in her arms.

The pain of those sharp talons tearing into her flesh did not come. A flash of bright red ignited the inside of her tightly squeezed eyelids. She cracked them open and turned her face skyward to see a ball of glowing red and gold fire arcing through the air. It caught the demon Creed low in the chest, beneath one of his wings, bowling him over. He tumbled from the sky, shifting to mortal form as he fell, and although he hit the ground feet first, his forward momentum drove him to his knees. He got a foot beneath him and half rose so that he was crouched and panting, with the fingertips of one hand on the earth to steady him and the palm of the other pressed against his ribs.

With lightning-fast reflexes, he rolled out of the way as another ball of fire skimmed across his shoulders. His shirt was gone, his trousers were torn, and his feet were bare. His face was battered and bleeding, and he had long tears on the upper part of one arm.

But he was alive.

The compulsion that had held Nieve transfixed to Thistle crumbled as the girl looked to Willow with the first hint of uncertainty she'd exhibited thus far. Nieve shook free of her hold and rushed toward Creed.

"Get back!" he shouted at her, but she did not stop. Demon or not, she would take her chances with him.

She did the only thing she could think of to help him. She slapped her hand to the tattoo on his naked back.

Creed did not waste more time by arguing with her. He seized hold of her free hand and brought her around so that he partially shielded her, and the next flame Willow shot at them was met with a flash of fire in return. Showers of red and gold, glittering sparks rained down around Creed and Nieve when the two bursts connected. Within seconds a blazing fortress of fire encased them, holding Willow's flames back.

Creed, however, was weakening. The fire Nieve drew out of him might flow through her, but he was the one whose energy was being expended. Still on one knee, droplets of sweat rolled off his face. He breathed in heavy, panting gasps.

Nieve also found it increasingly difficult to inhale. The fire around them was burning up all of the air. Her lungs might as well have been filled with boiling water. The heat bit at her skin until she too was sweating. It pooled between her breasts and soaked through her dress.

They could not keep this protective wall up for much longer.

"If she's feeling as badly as I do right now," Creed said, his head dropping so that his chin approached his chest, "then she's no longer a threat. We'll have to risk that she's used up most of her strength."

He let go of Nieve's hand. She slid her other palm from the shimmering and undulating tattoo on his back, and the sparkling wall of flame that had encompassed them disappeared.

The hills and trees around them echoed nothing but silence. Willow and Thistle were also gone.

Nieve helped Creed to his feet and tucked herself beneath his arm to steady him. The early evening air, although not cold, was cool and fresh enough to be welcome as she breathed deep gulps to soothe the inside of her enflamed and screaming lungs.

All she could think of, and feel, was how glad she was that he was alive. But she also thought, in a darker part of her head, of how he had looked when he'd plummeted toward her in demon form, with talons extended and reaching for her.

Creed considered his bare feet.

"I'll need another pair of new boots," he said, as if that was his biggest regret from all that had transpired. Then he looked at Nieve. "What are you doing here? Why didn't you stay where I left you?"

She told him about Thistle. Creed said nothing about how easily she'd been fooled by a child, but instead, tightened his arm around her.

"Let's get out of here. I don't think she'll be back. Not today. And I don't have the energy to pursue her right now."

They began to walk.

His face was bleeding from the beating he'd received. One of his eyes was partially swollen shut. He wheezed when he breathed, so Nieve thought it likely he'd cracked a few ribs, or possibly even broken them. And yet he looked like he'd just had the best time of his life.

He noticed the way she was looking at him, and the way her lips trembled at the sight of him so battered, and he grinned. Good humor oozed from him.

"I'll heal in a day or two. I'm more concerned with how to explain this at a hotel. I don't think I can find enough energy to conceal it."

"We can tell people we were robbed. To look at you, that's a story anyone would believe."

"I can't have people thinking I was robbed. I'm an assassin."

A spurt of anger that all of this was a joke to him coursed through her. She hated that he'd been hurt, and that it was her fault, at least in part.

"You're a terrible assassin," she said. "You didn't use your best weapon."

His smile remained easy despite her petty attempt to provoke him. "I used two hand grenades. Assassin weapons don't come much better than that."

Those were not his best weapon. His demon form was. It was the only reason he was alive. She did not know how to say it, and wasn't sure that it was a subject she cared to discuss, because even though it meant he was alive, she did not like that side of him.

She did not want to be possessed by a demon again.

Any demon.

. . .

Ash trailed along behind Airie as she did her shopping in Cottonwood Fall. It was about a half hour's ride from the ranch, and Hunter didn't like Airie going without him, but she got that stubborn look on her face that warned him she'd do as she pleased.

Hunter told Ash it was one of those times when a man had to pick his battles, and he was saving up for a rainy day. Ash wasn't sure what he meant, except that Airie got her own way and he got to go to town with her.

Then Hunter said Ash was to keep an eye on Airie for him.

So that was what he was doing, but really, Hunter shouldn't be worrying about watching over Airie and instead, needed to pay more attention to what people were saying.

Because Ash heard a lot of whispered talk about spawn. All he had to do was make himself inconspicuous and wander a little away from Airie's side.

They entered the general mercantile. Ash liked the smell of this store. It was a combination of sun-dried goods, wooden barrels, and spices and herbs.

Five barrels had been unloaded into one corner, near the front of the store. Ash liked to observe the things happening around him in private, so while Airie headed for the flour bin at the back, he wormed his way in between those barrels.

One contained sauerkraut. Its sharp, tangy scent bit the inside of his nose and made his eyes water. A cat prowled along an overhead rafter, its muscles bunched as it hunted mikken— tiny rodents with long tails, sharp teeth and flexible bodies that could squeeze into surprisingly small spaces. One crawled over Ash's foot, paused to look at him as if startled by his presence, then scurried away to disappear into a crack in the wall.

As Ash waited for Airie to finish her shopping, it wasn't rumors of spawn that he heard. Instead, clear as a bell, he heard a half demon girl ask his mother for her son's name.

And his mother, who didn't know any better, gave it to her. Asher hunkered a little deeper into the small fortress of barrels.

That meant the mean woman now had it, too.

• • •

They were in their hotel room.

Creed had wanted to move on and get as far away from town as they could, but even though she knew it was foolish, Nieve had refused. Walls could hardly protect them, yet she felt safer inside.

She had taken matters into her own hands. Once they'd

gotten to their room she'd ordered cleaning cloths, as well as the pitchers of warm water that now sat on the floor next to a small fire spitting in the hearth.

Creed lounged in a chair by the window, one leg stretched out, an occasional table beside him. She dipped a cloth in a basin of tepid water, wrung it out, and dabbed at the cuts on his face. He remained motionless beneath her ministrations, his characteristic good humor dampened as he pondered recent events aloud. Nieve listened, but her own head was tired and filled with too many questions. Most had to do with all of the things that could have gone wrong. Or worse than they had.

"She's burned entire villages. She destroyed a wagon train. She could have summoned a demon, yet she didn't. Why not?" Creed asked.

Nieve did not want to think of demons. It was too painful for her to connect the winged creature that had shot from the ground to this man. "She said she had what she wanted."

Creed slid an arm around her hips and she leaned into him. "What she wanted was you," he said. "I'm curious to know why she would obey a demon in the first place. Or why she would risk angering him by accepting defeat so easily and walking away when she'd had you, then lost you."

Nieve bit her lip. She had no idea either, but was glad all the same.

"I know I promised you that we'd search for your son," Creed continued, "but I also told you there'd be times when we had to set the search aside for other matters. I think right now we need to get to the Borderlands as quickly as possible. The sooner I enlist the Demon Slayer, the better. I can't continue hunting half demons on my own. There are far too many, and with unknown abilities."

Willow's words returned to taunt Nieve. *Did you know he was turning half demons, including children, over to the Godseekers for judgment?*

She did not want to think about the terrible things Willow had said, and the accusations that had been leveled against Creed. He had never lied to her.

But she had to prepare herself to hear the truth he had not told her either, especially if it was not going to be to her liking. She had known all along that hunting half demons was what Creed did. She also knew he'd been investigating the disappearance of children. She simply hadn't considered what it might mean if those missing children were also half demon, and that his duty to the Godseekers would then extend to passing judgment on them for something in which they could not be held accountable.

"I didn't realize the half demons you hunt include children," Nieve said, testing the waters.

He took too long to answer her. When he did, he did not deny it. A part of her heart shriveled and turned to dust.

"Their age doesn't matter," Creed said. "Whether or not they are damaged, or too demon in nature, is what's most important."

"You think Asher won't pass Godseeker judgment. That if he's survived the slave trade it's because he's too demon." Her lips had gone numb, the words falling from them like the tiny droplets of blood still seeping from the cut above Creed's blackened eye. She wasn't certain which hurt her worse — the thought of her child suffering abuse, or that even if rescued, he would be deemed dangerous and condemned for it. Unshed tears blurred her vision. None of this was his fault.

He was a child.

Creed caught Nieve's hand. She clutched the bloodied cloth in her clenched fist and realized she'd been wiping his cuts and bruises with too much force.

"If he's survived it means he's resourceful. There's nothing wrong with that," Creed said. "What do you remember of him?"

"He's adorable," Nieve replied. She could not bear to speak of him in the past tense. "Affectionate. He always knows when I'm troubled and brings me little things, pretty rocks and flowers, or unusual objects, to distract me. He can make himself go unnoticed for hours at a time, which is no doubt the reason Bear let him stay with me as long as he did."

"The young girl who lured you to Willow," Creed persisted. His one open eye was steady on her face. "Was she also adorable? Persuasive? Could she make herself go unnoticed?" Nieve jerked her arm, trying to free her hand from his, but he refused to release it. His fingers tightened and his voice hardened, demanding that she listen to him and acknowledge what he was saying. "I'm half demon, too, Nieve. I know what drives us. There's a good chance your son is everything you say he is, and that his mortality outweighs the demon instincts in him. But no one can know for certain if that's true, or what slavery has done to him. I can't even say that my own mortality outweighs my demon anymore. So how do you think that makes me feel about my duties? How careful do you think I'm going to be when I employ them? Do you believe this is somehow easy for me?"

She'd never stopped to think that perhaps he was conflicted over his duties. Willow had accused him of betraying both half demons and Godseekers by lying to them. Nieve, who had come to know him, knew this was untrue. He was doing his best, and what he believed was best for everyone, in a world that was changing in unexpected and often fearsome ways.

But she would not stand back and allow his best to bring harm to her son. An alternative presented itself, one she was not quite ready to contemplate. If she had to give up her search for Ash right now in order to keep him safe from both Creed and his demon father, then she would. But if she gave it up, she could not stay with Creed. It would be too much as if she had chosen him over her own child, and she could not live with herself if she did that. Sooner or later she would hate him for it, too.

Their search for Ash together had ended. As soon as she could, she would take the money she had hidden in her clothing and leave Creed. Then she would need to find a place where she could hide from Willow. Once the danger to Ash had passed, she would pick up her search again.

The thought of parting from Creed caused a sharp, shooting pain to erupt beneath her ribs, but she, too, wanted Willow stopped. She did not want her bringing Asher's father back into this world. It was best if Creed continued with the task he'd originally been given and forgot he'd ever heard of her or her son.

"No," Nieve said. "I don't think what's happening will be easy for anyone."

"First thing in the morning, at the break of day, we'll set off for the Borderlands," Creed said.

He let go of her hand and she rinsed out the cloth in fresh water, then with more gentleness, continued to dab at his injured face.

Chapter Thirteen

Ash heard his name and sat up in bed.

It echoed in his head like the ringing of a loud mental bell. He held his breath, expecting any second to end up in the boundary, hiding from demons, but that didn't happen.

Everything was shrouded in dark. Through the plain cotton curtains, the moon rode low in the black night sky and did not give off much light. Hunter and Airie were asleep. Ash listened to their breathing — Hunter's deep and relaxed, Airie's lighter and more restless. The baby was awake but quiet, giving Airie a few moments' peace.

Ash would like to go back to sleep, too, but Imp was hiding in the barn and she was scared.

He slid out from beneath his blankets and crept down the stairs, the treads smooth and cool beneath his bare feet. He let himself out through the kitchen door, lifting the heavy bar that locked it with a bit of a struggle because he was small, and had to stretch on his toes to get it free. That took him a few minutes. His natural instinct was to take a shortcut through the boundary, but that path was too dangerous now that the woman who summoned demons knew his name.

The yard looked much different at night. A hross snorted in the paddock, bumping against the wooden railing. Shadows and moonlight made things seem bigger and more threatening than they were during the day, but Ash had walked through the demon boundary too many times to be afraid of a few noises in a mortal night.

He scampered across the yard and cracked the barn door open just wide enough for him to squeeze through. He didn't want to startle the girl hiding in the hay loft. She was already frightened enough.

"Hello?" he called out, not very loud, only enough so that she'd know it was him in case she couldn't see in the dark as well as he could. He didn't expect her to answer. It didn't matter. He already knew where she was, and he knew this barn as well as he knew his own bedroom, even at night.

The floor was wooden, and scattered with loose bits of hay that caught between his toes as he crossed the wide open space to the ladder that led to the hay loft above. In a stall in the corner a mare due to foal any day kicked at the side of the barn, not liking being disturbed.

He climbed the ladder and found her hiding in a narrow tunnel he'd made between the musty mounds of last summer's hay. She had the same tangled hair he remembered, although the scraped knees were new. She'd drawn them up to her chin.

"You shouldn't have answered," she whispered when he crawled through the tunnel to join her. "I only wanted to find a good place to hide. I figured if you were safe here, I would be, too."

That was why she'd spoken his name. She'd wanted to find him, not try to summon him.

"You know my name," Ash said.

"So does Willow, so you have to stay out of the boundary. She plans to give your name to a demon."

Ash wasn't too worried. Not for himself. "If a demon summons me to the boundary, all you have to do is summon me back."

She looked uncertain. "How am I supposed to know if a demon summons you?"

"That's why you've got to go back," he said. He took her hand. It was skinny and rough, and he felt bad because his was not and he had people who loved and looked after him. He gave her fingers a squeeze. "But you won't have to stay with the mean woman forever."

His mother would take care of Imp. So would Airie. Then she'd know what it was really like to be loved.

· · ·

The night was cool and the hotel quiet. Two large sliding windows that led onto a narrow balcony had been left open to let in fresh air. Long, gossamer, wraithlike curtains fluttered to either side of them.

Creed lay in the moon-fed darkness with Nieve in his arms, spooned against him. Her hair was damp from the bath she'd had earlier, silky soft and smelling of flowery soap. Feminine and delicate. He listened to her quiet breathing and thanked the goddesses that she was safe. But Willow had gotten something from her, something she believed more important even than Nieve, and it worried him that he did not know what it was, or might be.

Although the injuries he'd received were already healing, they also kept him awake. The demon fire burn on his chest was taking more time, and that troubled him, too, but not because of the pain.

Creed had seen the look of fear in Nieve's eyes when he'd approached her in demon form, dropping from the sky, intending to carry her off to safety, and the way she had turned from him.

Not only had she turned away, she had tried to protect a half demon, who wished her nothing but harm, from him. And his demon, focused entirely on Nieve and with no concept of time, had responded to her immediate fear and not the impending danger, as it should. It had begun to shift in midair, which was when the fire had struck him. That fire also saved his life, because it had startled his demon enough to interrupt the spontaneous shift.

Creed did not delude himself. A part of Nieve would always fear him for what he was. Even after the danger had passed, and she'd called him a terrible assassin because he hadn't used his greatest weapon against Stone, she had not been able to articulate what that weapon was.

To her, he was a demon.

He could not even deny it with honesty. Not anymore. He did not have it under control, as he'd always believed. It had given her fire as a means of protecting herself, but she could only use it through him, which robbed her of freedom. That was no true gift.

More was at stake here than Creed's feelings for Nieve, or his demon's possessiveness of her. If he could not regain command of it, and have his mortal side once again in complete control, all of his well-placed plans would disintegrate. What he valued most would be lost to him. He did not want to choose one side, demon or mortal, over the other.

He wanted justice for all.

When they got to the Borderlands and the Demon Slayer, he would see to Nieve's future. He would again promise to search for her son. Then he would leave her, and he would pursue that justice.

The bed was thick and comfortable, and quite large, but Creed was a big man who took up his fair share of the space and he must have made some movement or noise to disturb her. Perhaps she simply sensed his somber mood, which was so out of character for him.

She stirred, turning toward him, her wide, beautiful eyes drifting open to focus on him. They held no fear now, only languid desire, and Creed's somber mood diminished.

"What are you thinking about?" she asked.

The question began as something light and teasing, as if she already anticipated the answer he would give. Or perhaps it was simply the one she wanted to elicit from him so that she would not need to delve deeper into who—what—he was.

Creed found that second possibility unbearable.

"Other than your son, if you could have anything you wanted, what would it be?" he asked in return.

Often when he asked Nieve such questions, she gave him responses that were cautious and incomplete, as if she did not dare speak them aloud for fear they might somehow evaporate. This time, her answer was swift and undoubtedly heartfelt. It was completely honest in that it reflected dreams that had already gone astray for her.

"A home," she said, her tone wistful. "A dozen more children to love. A world where they can all be happy and safe and know that I'll do whatever it takes to protect them."

She did not say she wanted him, too, but he could feel that she did. He also knew she believed it impossible. He did not fit into her dreams.

Which was fair enough. Her dreams did not fit into his life.

"What about you?" she asked. "What do you want?"

"I want you to have everything you dream of," he said.

She frowned as if his answer was trite and insulting. "Let's say I have those things. What would you want then?"

"I meant what I said." He did. It was what he'd been thinking of before she awakened. "I want a world where you and your children are safe, but where everyone else is, too."

"But what about for yourself?" Nieve tucked her hand beneath her cheek and inserted one knee between his thighs, then answered her own question. "You've always put duty first. You've never given any thought to what you might want."

"Not true," he said. "I think about what I want constantly. I'm thinking about it right now."

He bent to kiss her forehead, then her lips. She arched against him, her breasts pressing tight to his naked chest, and returned his kiss on a sharp inhale of desire that made him instantly hard with need. Her fingers toyed with the edges of his tattoo, making it burn, but in an intoxicating way that only increased his hunger for her.

"That's not what I meant," she said when he lifted his head, although a smile curved her mouth upward.

"Nevertheless, when you first woke up, you asked

me what I was thinking about." He ran a finger from the underside of her chin to the tip of one breast. "This is it." It simply wasn't the only thing. But right now, in this moment, it was all that mattered to him.

She slid cool fingers around the curve of his neck, pressing against him, and ran the tip of her tongue along the crease of his clavicle. The jolt of that delicate touch seared his chest to his groin. While he did not want to rush her, but to allow her to set the pace that gave her the most pleasure, he could not think past how ready he was to be deep inside her.

Nieve pushed at his hips, edging him onto his back, and straddled his thighs. The sheet that had covered them fell away to tangle around his legs. He cupped her breasts in his hands and she sighed, a sound of unrestrained enjoyment that brought his tattoo alive. It was not that Nieve was not passionate. She very much was. But always, she held a part of herself back and Creed grew more determined to break past that reserve. He kissed first one breast, then the other, as his erection nudged at her folds.

She leaned forward, pinning his thickened shaft with the flat of her stomach. The slight movements she made created a friction against his sensitive skin that left him having to fight to stay calm. She took one of his nipples between her teeth, tugging it gently, licking the nib with her tongue until he lost all ability to think. She switched to his other nipple. As she did, she reached down and took him in her hand. She stroked her palm up and down, over and over, increasing the pressure with each downward movement and rubbing her thumb in the dampness of its head until he was ready to explode. He slid his own hand between them, dipping the tip of one finger inside her and caressing her folds until she was panting with need. She guided his shaft to her opening as he clutched at the soft flesh of her bottom with both hands.

"I want you," she said.

He lifted her off him, half expecting her to protest, and rolled with her so that she was beneath him.

She was so soft and beautiful in the dim light, with her pale hair glowing against the pillows and her green eyes dark pools of desire fixed on his face. He positioned himself and thrust slowly inside her. She closed her eyes and tipped her head back, exposing her throat, and Creed kissed it.

He moved without hurry at first, then harder and deeper, until she cried out as she came. Creed came, too, his mouth against hers, stifling their sounds.

He stayed inside her, listening to her breathing return to normal, resting on his elbows so that he could watch her face in the dark as she relaxed.

She stroked her hand up his back. His tattoo flared where she touched it. Inside him, his demon growled its contentment. The sting from the burns on his chest was long gone.

"I think I enjoy you too much." Nieve sounded bemused, as if the observation somehow had a profound meaning that he was not meant to know.

Creed nuzzled a kiss in the sensitive spot behind her ear, burying his face in her hair as he withdrew with reluctance and settled beside her, one arm thrown across her. He tucked the sheets back into place so that they were cocooned together in the bed.

"Impossible," he said. "How could you possibly enjoy me too much when I can't seem to get enough of you?"

He wanted her to know she was important to him. That

this meant more to him than a simple act of physical release, even if their time together was not to be permanent. He would not have her feeling as if she were nothing more than his whore. And he could not begin to explain to her all of the emotions she elicited in him, or the fullness she generated in his heart.

He settled for the simplest. "I love you," he said.

There was no need for her to say the words back to him, but he had not expected no response from her at all. She nestled deeper against him, her hand on his naked hip and her knee between his thighs, as she liked to sleep.

He brushed her hair from her face, tucking it behind her ear, and tried not to read too much into her silence. She had no real experience with being loved by a man.

It took him a long time to fall asleep.

In the morning, when he awoke, she was gone.

Chapter Fourteen

Nieve huddled in the tiny, fenced-in kitchen garden, waiting for the tea shop to open, her meager belongings in a pack in her arms. She had stolen a gun and ammunition from Creed. That was all she dared take for fear she might wake him.

She planned to cut off her hair and pass herself off as a young boy. She was thin enough. Once Creed left town she would buy the right clothing and a pair of scissors, and when she was a few miles from town, too, she would take on an identity that would give her greater freedom of movement. She should have thought of it from the very beginning, thus avoiding his company altogether.

Right now she needed a place to hide. Yesterday, the friendly waitress had been the only person in the shop. The town was small, and out of the way, and Nieve thought it unlikely the shop had any other staff. She hoped the waitress would provide her with sanctuary until she was certain Creed was long gone.

She had not wanted to hear his words of love when she could not return them, and covered her ears as if that might somehow stop them from replaying, over and over, in her head. A deep sense of bereavement, equal to the loss she continued to feel over her son, filled her.

Under different circumstances she thought she could have loved Creed. Now, she did not know if she could ever love him the way she wanted to, and he deserved. Asher had been gone from her for more than a year, but the loss remained as raw as it had been the day she regained her memory of him. Grief had frozen her fragile heart, and she truly feared that if she opened it up to Creed, and then lost him, too, it might shatter completely. One person could not contain so much sorrow, and she was not very big to begin with.

Creed would not change his mind when it came to duty and justice. He didn't need her and Asher did. Her son was important to no one but her. Even if she never found him, she could never set aside her search for him. Not even this soul-twisting pain that tore her in two different directions and warned her she was making an irrevocable mistake. How could she live with herself if she did not do all that she could for her child?

It was still dark out, but she knew from years of cooking for Bear that the kitchen stove would need to be lit early. The biscuits she had eaten yesterday were fresh made.

A light came on in an upstairs window of the tiny shop. A few minutes later, the light went out. Shortly after that, the kitchen interior filled with a warm glow. Through the window that overlooked the garden, Nieve could see a stout shadow puttering around the room.

She crept to the window for a better look, wanting to make certain the person inside was the woman she was waiting for.

The woman was bent over the open oven, her back to Nieve, tossing in sticks of honey mesquite from the pile stacked neatly in a nearby rack. She reached for the cast iron match holder on the wall, sparking one of the long wooden matches by dragging it down the holder's striker plate. It was the waitress, as Nieve had hoped. She set the burning match to the kindling in the stove, and the kindling caught on fire.

Nieve could not look away from those dancing flames. She remembered the way the fire had grown in Willow's hands. She thought of how it had felt in her own hands, how empowering it was, when Creed had forced it through her.

Except he had not forced it through her. She had drawn it from him. Fire was her weapon, not his, and now he would be without it. He would need to exercise extra vigilance against Willow if their paths should cross again, which they would eventually, because Creed's duty involved bringing her to justice.

Nieve rapped lightly on the dusty window with her knuckles, leaving several long smears in the thin layer of dirt.

The woman inside lifted her head, startled by the noise. She did not go to the door. Instead, she crossed the room and eased the window open a crack so she could see who was outside in the predawn hours of the morning.

She recognized Nieve at once.

"Oh, my dear," she said, concern edging into the immediate and welcoming friendliness of her manner. "Did your young man not find you? He didn't come back here, so I assumed you met up elsewhere and were together."

At first, Nieve didn't fully comprehend her meaning. Then she remembered that she had left the tea shop yesterday in Thistle's company, and that she'd given the woman a message for Creed on her way out. That message had gone undelivered, because neither she nor Creed had gone back.

"No," Nieve said. The lie slipped far too easily from her. "I have no idea what's happened to him. He must have gone on without me."

The woman made a small sound of pity. "He seemed so concerned for you," she said. "I'm sure it's a misunderstanding of some kind and he'll be back."

"I don't think so," Nieve said. "His money ran out. So did his interest in me. I was one more expense he no longer needed." Guilt plucked at her. She was not painting a flattering image of Creed. She tried to improve it, for the sake of her conscience. "He knows my father is searching for me, and it won't be long before he comes for me. I need a place to wait until he does. I promise I won't be any trouble to you. I'm a good cook," she added. "I'm good with pastries."

"I'm sorry. I don't have any work for you," the woman said. "I wish I did." She sounded genuinely sympathetic, but resolute in her refusal. "I have barely enough to feed myself."

"I'm not looking for paid work," Nieve assured her. "I need somewhere to wait. That's all. And I'm happy to help out in return for it."

The woman continued to hesitate. "There was odd goings on last night, out by the ruins. Your young man wouldn't have gotten involved with anything like that, would he?"

She was afraid of demons, Nieve realized. They had not

been gone long enough for people to overcome the fear that they might someday return. Since a demon hunted her, Nieve could not claim that such fears were groundless.

"I wouldn't know anything about that," she said, adding more lies to those she'd already uttered. "I spent the night looking after the girl who came into your shop, and her sick little sister, until their brother returned."

Nieve was ashamed of herself for preying on this woman's good heart. But she was desperate.

The woman came to a decision. She withdrew from the window. A few seconds later, she opened the back door and beckoned for Nieve to come inside.

· · ·

Her name was Pistil and she ran the tea shop while her husband worked kyson for one of the many ranches around the Godseeker Mountains.

She put Nieve to work rolling pastry and supervised until she was satisfied Nieve knew what she was doing.

Several hours later, as Nieve was taking the last pie from the oven in the now sweltering kitchen, she heard heavy footsteps enter the dining area of the shop, then a low, friendly, familiar voice.

She almost dropped the hot, fragrant pie she held in her hands. A curl of steam spewed from the vent cut into the pastry's light crust. She had been so careful. She could not understand how he had found her.

Perhaps he was hungry, and did not know she here. Her heart vacillated between terror at discovery and a profound relief if she were. She set the pie carefully on a long counter, listening to the quiet voices out front, and wondered which it might be.

She had told so many lies.

She eased her pack off a chair and headed for the back door. She had one hand on the latch when a presence behind her warned that she was too late.

"Where are you headed this time?" Creed asked.

Behind him, Pistil hovered as if she had no idea what had just happened. Nieve's eyes went to Creed's tense expression. He was furious beneath all of that warm friendliness he projected.

And he had used compulsion on the woman to get what he wanted, because Pistil did not seem to take any notice of his blackened eye or the cuts on his face. If she had, she would never have helped him, Nieve was certain, because without the compulsion, he looked very dangerous.

She said nothing in response to his question. There was little that could be said.

"Pistil tells me you're waiting for your father," Creed said. "I told her if that's what you truly want, then I'll return you to him myself."

"If you want my advice," Pistil added, her anxious eyes on Nieve, "you'll give your young man another chance. He doesn't have to take you back. It's generous of him to offer to do so."

"Very generous," Nieve said.

Creed took her bag from her hands. He then thanked Pistil with a graciousness that left the woman red-faced and smiling, and no doubt convinced that she'd done a great thing. Nieve, too, smiled at Pistil. This was hardly her fault. She could not fight the will of a demon.

No one knew that better than Nieve.

Creed took Nieve by the elbow and guided her through the front room. Only two tables had occupants. He took some coins from a pocket of his trousers and set them on the counter near the till as they passed.

Outside, without a word, he lifted her onto his hross's back. Nieve looked down at him as he placed one hand on the saddle horn and his foot in the stirrup and prepared to mount.

"How did you find me?" she asked. "How did you know where to look?"

He swung up behind her so that he could sit with his arms around her, as if afraid she might leap from the back of the hross, even though it was impossible for her unless she was willing to risk breaking a limb, or even her neck.

"It was easy enough," he said. "I went to the one place in town where I knew you'd already felt safe."

Nieve had no rebuttal for that. He'd been correct in his prediction. So instead, she fell silent.

It was still early in the day. She hadn't slept, instead lying awake for most of the night in order to make her plans for escape, and now, exhaustion settled bone-deep into her extremities. In the past, Creed would have taken pity on her and allowed her a short rest.

Instead, they rode on for a few hours. He finally stopped at the bank of a shallow spring bubbling up through a bed of rocks so that the hross could have water.

He then set up a shelter from the heat of the sun where they could sit out the remainder of the day. Now that they were entering the worst part of the desert, they would be forced to travel in the evenings and early morning hours.

As he worked, not once did he speak to her. Nieve found this silence from him unnerving. He was not normally a quiet man.

"I'm sorry," Creed finally said to her, once they were both settled in the shade. He'd unfastened his shirt so that it exposed a broad spread of smooth, golden chest. She kept her gaze fixed on it. It was easier than meeting the accusation in his eyes. "I should have understood that you wouldn't be able to wait in order to search for your son. I made you a promise and I intend to keep it. But you have to understand that my work is also too important to set aside, and I've done that already for too long."

The understanding in the apology surprised her and made her feel guilty. That soon turned to a slow-burning anger. She was not sorry for putting her son first. She would do it again.

"I'm a mother," Nieve said, as if that explained every-thing, because to her it did.

"Yes, you are." Creed regarded her thoughtfully, but without the smile he usually reserved for her. "I understand how important finding your son is to you. But there are other children out there who have no one to search for them. No one who cares. And there are a lot of innocent people in danger because of what's coming, and they can't defend themselves. As long as you're with me, at least you have some freedom of movement."

"No, I don't," Nieve said. "You don't understand anything about me. When I'm with you I have no freedom at all. You're all I can think of. You consume all my thoughts. You make me forget how important my son is to me." Her throat ached. "You make me a bad mother. I forgot my son once. I'll never forget him again."

His mouth tightened. The fractured chips of blue in his eyes reflected the color of the endless sky.

Nieve could not look away.

"I've never asked you to forget him," he said. "I don't expect you to. I'm asking you to understand that I have my own priorities, and I can't forget them either." He stretched out on the ground so that his head and shoulders remained beneath the shelter, but his legs and boots extended into the sun. "I'll make you a new promise, and this one, I swear to you I'll keep. I'm going to the Borderlands. I came looking for you today only because I was certain I knew where you were. If you hadn't been there I'd have left you behind, and if you run off again, I won't look for you again. You're on your own."

He folded his hands across his chest and closed his eyes. There was nothing considerate or lover-like in his manner. He had said his piece. As far as he was concerned, the conversation was finished.

Despite the blistering heat, Nieve felt very cold.

And more alone than she could ever remember.

$$\cdots$$

Imp had gone missing.

By late afternoon the next day, when she was still not back, Willow decided she would wait a few more hours, but if the girl had not returned by then, they'd be forced to move on without her.

Stone had not yet made an appearance either. Willow could only assume he had not survived, and she would need to change her plans.

The assassin's shift to a full demon form had disconcerted her. She'd not known it was so...complete. His use of fire had been equally unexpected. When she tried to draw fire from the boundary in retaliation, the demon had attempted to follow its path. She had been forced to craft fireballs, using short bursts of flame, instead of forming a steady circle in which to trap the assassin.

She'd had no choice but to abandon the woman.

That, in turn, had infuriated the demon. Willow had ignored his summonses, which had gotten progressively angrier throughout the night. He had not fallen silent until morning dawned, and then, that silence became heavy and ominous.

Willow needed to reclaim the woman.

Thistle said the Godseeker assassin had spent the night in the nearby town. This morning, he'd headed into the desert. She'd asked a few questions that confirmed the mortal whore had been seen leaving with him.

For the next few days, until her strength returned, Willow would be frustratingly helpless.

While she waited for Imp's reappearance, she decided to turn her attention to the newcomers. Willow was not yet certain that Larch and her friends fully embraced their immortal heritages, as they should. They'd spent too many years hiding their differences from mortals, and behaving as if they were somehow inferior, when in fact they were better.

They needed to learn to take what was theirs.

Willow had planned a small test to see how they'd react. Thistle had reached another level with her talents and Willow was anxious to explore it. If the newcomers did not respond to the test as they should, then they would be on their own once again.

She and Larch, along with one of the new boys and Thistle, walked into town shortly before the end of the work day.

The group entered the small mercantile. Willow sent the boy to the back of the store to collect the heavier dry goods she needed. She, Thistle, and Larch stayed at the front, near the door, examining jars of baked beans and slices of smoked meats.

The robust woman with bad teeth behind the long counter was friendly enough at first. She rested plump, brown, sun-wrinkled elbows on the counter. A large mole with three long hairs sprouting from it graced the corner of her mouth.

"Did you hear a disturbance late yesterday afternoon?" she asked. "There was an explosion, and the sky lit up like the demon wars. Some of the men went out to check on it this morning, and one of the sinkholes had caved in."

"No," Willow said. "We didn't hear anything."

A shadow darted across the open door. A tiny face peered around the framework. Then, as she'd asked him to do, one of her feral children slipped inside. He scurried forward to hide in the folds of her skirt.

By mortal standards he was misshapen and monstrous. He had been born in a partial demon form, and survived for years in the mountains by living like an animal in the wild. His skin was gold, not red, and hard as rock. Two useless humps, where wings should have been stored, twisted his back. His long hands and feet were clawed, and yet his face was breathtakingly beautiful. He trusted no one but Willow, although Larch had been making overtures—no doubt because he was a small child, and she was pregnant. Larch had no idea what form her own baby would take when it was born. It might be no different than this. Willow wanted her to understand it, and be prepared to love it no matter what.

The mole-faced mortal woman, who was not nearly as beautiful as this child, gasped at the sight of him. A hand went to her slack-jawed mouth. "What is that?"

Willow lifted him into her arms. He clung to her like a burdock. "This is a child," she said. "You've no doubt seen them before."

"Not like that." The woman's face lost all friendliness. Her lip curled. One hand dropped out of sight beneath the counter. "I don't want his kind in here."

"What is his kind?" Willow asked.

"He's a spawn."

"He's a child," Willow repeated. She turned to Larch and the boy who had come forward from the back of the store with his arms full of goods. She set the child on the floor. He darted outside and would make his way back to camp on his own. "Take what we need. I'll be along shortly."

Larch hesitated, looked as if she had something to say, then nodded. She motioned for the older boy to precede her out the door.

"Stop right there!"

The mortal woman withdrew her hand from beneath the counter. In it, she held a long-barreled pistol. Willow knew that many such weapons had been adapted to fire round balls of lead, which were cheaper than bullets and easier to make by hand. Their cost effectiveness came at the expense of accuracy, but the pistol would not have to shoot at any great distance.

"Thistle," Willow said.

The girl, who had been standing close to the counter, smiled at the woman.

The woman's eyes grew round. The pistol in her hand wavered. The weapon swung back and forth at first, as if it couldn't make up its mind, and then with more dedication until the barrel turned to press tight against its owner's own temple. Beads of moisture formed at the woman's hairline. Her whole body trembled. Fear crept into her expression.

"I don't want any trouble," she said.

"Then you should be kinder to children."

Willow turned away. The pistol went off behind her with a loud, percussive report that would soon bring other townspeople to investigate. She heard the thump as the woman's heavy body slid to the floor.

Larch, who had paused in the doorway, made a small sound in the back of her throat that she quickly stifled. Without a word, she turned and left.

Willow wanted to burn the store to the ground, but her fight with the assassin and her fear of raising the demon left her without the use of her talents. She felt impotent. As if she were a slave in this world once again.

And that made her angry.

It took her a few moments to spark a fire by mortal means, but the building was old, and dry, and caught within seconds. She waited until the flames licked up the walls and entered the rafters.

Then Willow, too, left the store.

As she stepped across the threshold, she bumped into someone deliberately blocking her path. He was covered in dirt, and somewhat worse for wear, but nevertheless familiar.

His face was twisted with hate.

"I want the assassin dead," Stone said.

. . .

It had taken an hour after finding Nieve before Creed's heart stopped pumping blood at adrenaline-fueled speed, leaving him lightheaded and incapable of rational thought.

Even his sister Raven had not instilled worry in him to this level because he had always known she could take care of herself far better than most ordinary women.

But he had been terrified for Nieve who, while far from ordinary in his eyes, was defenseless without him. He had thought Willow had somehow coerced her again.

Then he'd realized she'd run from him. Hurt that she would trust him so little settled in. She'd abandoned him with complete disregard for how he would feel to awaken and find her gone.

A part of him had wished to hurt her in return.

As he lay under the shade of the shelter he'd erected, with her so motionless and silent, and as far from him as she could manage without sitting in the sun, he thought it likely he had accomplished that much.

He deeply regretted the things he'd said. He would not have left her behind. He would never leave her in danger. The need to hurt her had been unworthy of him, and unfair to her. She could no more help her maternal instincts than he could fight his demon ones. And his demon continued to want her.

They were about to spend almost a month in each

other's company, and cross an expanse of land that would soon be more treacherous as the summer months settled in. They could not do so in angry silence.

He had not been the one to begin a physical intimacy between them. She had claimed him, whereas despite his demon's insistence to the contrary, he had no true claim on her. That was not how it worked. He did not read her as well as he read other people. It frustrated him and made him uncertain, two more emotions he was not used to experiencing. While his profession of love could not be unsaid, or her rebuff of it undone, if she should ever want it again, next time she would have to earn it.

Late in the day, as they were getting ready to move on, Creed happened to glance at the horizon and saw a red glow where the town they had left behind should be. His jaw tightened.

"Is that fire?" Nieve asked, seeing what had caught his attention.

"Yes."

"Are we going back?"

By the time they did, there would be nothing he could do. It had taken them several hours to travel this far. It would take that long, or longer, to return, especially if darkness caught them.

Or something else did.

"No," Creed said. He swung the saddle to the hross's back and began to tighten the straps. "We ride on."

Chapter Fifteen

Summer had arrived, and still, there was no sign of his mother.

It was just past lunch and Ash was supposed to be down for a nap so that Airie could get some rest, too. Instead he was chasing kittens in the hay loft, burrowing between the fresh bales of new-cut hay and trying not to think about what might be keeping his mother, while Hunter mucked out the stalls below. One of Hunter's many brothers-in-law came into the barn.

His name was Tremor. He was a big man, and hard, who believed children should be seen and not heard. Whenever he came to visit, Ash usually made sure he was neither. He wedged himself between two of the bales and peered through the cracks in the floorboards. Sparkles of dust and tiny bits of dried grass swirled in the air as the warm, musty scent of hross flesh drifted up to him, along with the men's voices.

Tremor was not a man to waste words. He got straight to the point.

"We've got trouble," he said.

Hunter leaned on his pitchfork. The inside of the barn was hot, even with the doors open wide, and he'd taken off his shirt. Ash could see the long, ragged scars riddling the sweat-dampened skin of his chest and back. Hunter used to fight demons, Ash knew. He'd seen him do it.

And Hunter always won.

He wiped the sweat off his face with the crook of his elbow. "What kind of trouble?"

"The kind that's starting to cause panic over the notion of Airie, and how she's carrying another spawn."

Hunter went still in a way that Ash knew meant danger, and got a big knot in his stomach. He'd never fully understood how people could be so afraid of Airie, and mean to her, but they were. At the same time, he knew if she was backed into a corner, she'd do whatever she had to in order to protect her family.

So would Hunter, and he wasn't going to let this go.

"That's my baby she's carrying," he said. "Anyone who says anything different can say it to me."

"Try and see this from their point of view. There've been rumors of spawn in the Godseeker Mountains ever since the demons disappeared. There's no doubt that Airie's not mortal. All anyone has to do is spend five minutes with her to know that, so what could she be if not spawn? And people say that boy with you is one of them, too, so they have to believe that those other rumors are true." Tremor held up a hand. "Don't get all hostile with me. I'm just the messenger. But this isn't only a problem for you. It affects the whole family, and your sisters aren't nearly as used to dealing with danger as you are. They've got children to look after, too. There's a little concern that people may try to come at you through them if they can't get to Airie."

"Is it my sisters who are concerned, or their husbands?" Hunter asked.

Tremor was straightforward. "Maybe a bit of both. And maybe their husbands think their brother should be more concerned about them."

Hunter was angry now, but also frustrated. Ash could tell.

"I looked out for them for years. When I was killing demons, I kept that part of my life away from them. When I was ready to leave it behind, I came home. Don't tell me I'm not concerned about them."

"Then prove it," Tremor said. "What are you going to do about it?"

Hunter threw the pitchfork across the barn with such force that the tines stuck in the wall. The long handle quivered.

"I'm going to make a trip into town and see what the situation is for myself." He grabbed his shirt off a railing and jammed his arms into the sleeves. "Not one word of this to Airie," he said. "I don't want her worried."

After both men had left, Ash hunkered down between the bales and rested his chin on his crossed hands.

Things were about to get bad.

• • •

After countless days spent crossing the desert during the worst of the heat, the last dusty, rundown, empty town was now several weeks behind Creed and Nieve.

They were no longer forced to travel at night. The sun shone bright above them, countermanded by a cool breeze whiffling through the grasslands.

The main road into Cottonwood Fall was well established and bustling with travelers. The town itself, although small in comparison to the towns of the Godseeker Mountains, radiated prosperity.

Even though the Borderlands sat at the farthest edges of demon territory, a high wall surrounded Cottonwood Fall. The road Creed and Nieve followed led to its gates, which were thrown wide in a welcome to all.

Creed suspected that the days of those gates being open to everyone would be numbered once the Demon Slayer knew of the threat that was coming.

Willow was only the beginning. More half demons would emerge, not all of them friendly.

Nor evil. That, too, was important to remember.

When they rode through the gates Creed asked for directions to the town stables. From there, once his hross was settled, he asked about a hotel. The town had three, none far from the stables, and he decided to check them all before making a final decision. They still had a few hours before dinner would be served and he wanted to find a place where Nieve would be safe.

They set out on foot to find a room. Creed carried the larger packs on his back. He gave Nieve possession of the smaller, lighter ones, but only because it kept his hands free. They moved, unnoticed, through the streets. He wished to remain as unobtrusive as possible.

Closer to the desert, the towns tended to be coated

in a layer of dust that was impossible to prevent and cast everything in the same shades of browns, reds, and grays. Here, shop fronts were clean and well maintained, with signs of fresh paint, as well as numerous trees and flowering shrubbery. They passed a mercantile and a bank, two more signs of wealth. Creed thought an assassin could make a good living in a place such as this. Now that trade routes could expand, more protection would be required—except this time, against mortal bandits and not demons.

And against spawn. The time for denial was long past. These people had no idea what was coming their way. Once Willow was inside their walls, they were lost. He had to find the Demon Slayer and deliver both the Godseekers' message, and a warning.

"It's a very pretty place," Nieve said, looking around.

For the first time since they'd abandoned the search for her son, interest filled her beautiful eyes. Life had begun to return to her face. It both heartened Creed and brought him to despair. He could not expose her to any more violence. He wished for her to be able to return to the type of life she'd been born into, where she was loved and protected, and hoped that someday she would know such happiness again.

But he was half demon. That would always be there, between them. She could not forget it. Neither could he. Denying it would not make it less present or true.

She also believed he had let her down in regards to her missing son. That was true, too.

A commotion erupted at the gates. Creed was too far away to see exactly what the problem was, but he guessed it might have something to do with the sand swift someone was trying to ride into town. What in the world would a sand swift be doing in this part of the world, where hross made for better and more plentiful mounts?

The rider was fair-haired and tall, not heavily muscled like Creed, but not thin either, and to Creed, who picked up on such things, he seemed angry. He drove the sand swift through the small group of protesters, ignoring their complaints, and proceeded into the town. He turned in the opposite direction from where Creed and Nieve stood and was gone from sight within seconds.

Creed had a bad feeling about who the man was and why he was creating a ruckus. He was torn between following him to find out what was up and in getting Nieve settled into a hotel room first.

Curiosity won out.

"Stay close to me," he said to her.

They walked back the way they had come, with Nieve almost running to keep up with his longer stride, and Creed wished he could carry some of her bags for her, but did not dare. Something was up.

When they turned the street corner, Creed saw the sand swift alone, untethered, outside of what was commonly known as a gentlemen's club. Its agitation was plain in the shifting colors of its scaly hide from green, to gold, to purple, and the dangerous flick of its long, sandpapery tongue. The sand swift acted as a door keeper for its rider, who had obviously gone inside the club. No one would go in or come out while it stood in the way.

No one but Creed.

Nieve began to fall farther behind him. Creed stopped to see what was wrong, and if she needed help, because she never complained and would not ask for it if she did. He saw her stoop to pick up a rock. Then he remembered she had a healthy wariness of the creatures, and how he had told her to strike it on the nose.

"I won't let it hurt you," he said.

She allowed the rock to drop.

The trust in her eyes never failed to warm him. It had taken a long time for him to earn it from her. The thought of losing it again made him more cautious about safety than he might have been in the past. He eased past the sand swift, positioning his body between it and Nieve. The sand swift cast him one long, considering look as if wondering how he might taste, but other than that, chose to leave him alone. Creed dropped his packs on a long bench beside the front door, then added Nieve's to the pile. The sand swift's presence alone would be enough to keep them secure.

He pushed open the door. The interior of the room was well lit by west-facing windows designed to capture the last light of the day. The tables were spaced well apart for private conversations. Several booths at the back had curtains for additional privacy. Two were open and unoccupied. The remaining two booths had their curtains drawn.

The sand swift's blond-headed owner sat alone at a table in the very center of the room, near the bar, although he held the undivided attention of the other five men present. His clothing was dirt-stained and sweaty. The only person more out of place in the club would be Nieve, except no one had noticed her presence.

The blond man addressed the waiter, who looked as if the pressed and well-starched high collar of his white linen dress shirt were strangling him.

"I don't suppose you could give me a definition for spawn?" the blond man asked. His question was loud and clearly intended for everyone to overhear.

"No, sir. I'm afraid I can't." The waiter, ill at ease, set a small silver teapot and a china cup on the table and tucked the tray he carried under his arm. "Is there anything else I can get for you?"

"Why don't I give you a definition you can use?" the man persisted. He lifted the teapot and poured a stream of amber-colored liquid into the delicate cup. "A spawn is half demon and half mortal." He set the teapot down. "I guess we'd have to come up with another definition for anyone who's any different than that. Wouldn't you agree?"

"Yes, sir." The waiter brushed his fingers over the pristine red tablecloth as if wiping away crumbs that Creed doubted were there.

"So if you, or anyone else here, could come up with something else to call my wife, and say it in the right tone of voice when you speak of her, I'd deeply appreciate it." The man's gaze had gone hard as steel. "Otherwise, we're going to have a problem. And I don't like problems."

Creed decided it might be time to intervene. He wished to speak privately with the Demon Slayer, not become involved in a public altercation on his behalf. He wove his way through the tables with Nieve following close behind him and good humor spreading in his wake.

He pulled out a chair at the man's table and held it for Nieve, then sat down between her and the other man. The spectators in the room relaxed as they returned to their own business. The waiter vanished, taking advantage of the diversion Creed had created even if he was uncertain of its precise nature.

The man's eyes narrowed in a way that said he didn't like not having noticed Creed. He would like it even less when he realized Nieve was there, too, but Creed was not about to draw the other man's attention to her until he knew for certain who he was.

"Would you be the Demon Slayer?" Creed asked.

The man assessed him from head to toe. When he finished, it was obvious that he was not pleased with what he found. Creed was not a man easily overlooked, and that he had done so meant something unusual was up. "That depends on who wants to know."

Creed increased the level of amiability. "The Slayer and I have a mutual friend named Blade. He sends his regards."

"And why would Blade send someone to the Slayer rather than come here himself?"

Creed smiled, wide and friendly, and repeated the man's own words. "That depends on who wants to know."

The man hesitated. He assessed Creed carefully. He looked directly at Nieve, then met Creed's eyes as he spoke. "Stop trying to influence my thoughts and perhaps we can talk." He smiled in return when he saw Creed's surprise, although there was little amiability in his. "I never claimed my wife is one hundred percent mortal."

"No," Creed agreed. "Because she's half goddess, and not mortal at all."

The man examined Creed for several long seconds more. He leaned across the table and extended his hand. "Hunter."

"Creed." He shook the offered hand. "This is Nieve."

Hunter nodded to her, but did not offer to shake her hand, which relieved Creed. He was unsure how his demon would respond to another man touching her.

Hunter addressed him. "Tell me why Blade, of all people, would send a half demon to speak with the Demon Slayer."

Creed was unsurprised that the Demon Slayer had figured out what he was, although he did find it unsettling. "Blade said to give you his regards if I should ever meet up with you. The message comes from me."

Hunter pushed his untouched tea toward Nieve. "Why don't you have this?" he said to her. "Would you like me to order you something to eat?"

The gesture pleased Creed as much as it startled Nieve, who was not used to being acknowledged. She looked to him for help, uncertain how to respond.

He pressed her fingers, which were clenched together in her lap, under the table. How sad it was, he thought, that she had to seek confirmation in order to accept a kind act.

"Drink the tea if you want it," he said. Then, to Hunter, "I'll get her something to eat later. This isn't really a place where she can enjoy it, and I can only do so much to keep attention away from her."

"But thank you for the offer," Nieve added, her smile for Hunter breathtakingly sweet. Light caught the brilliant green of her eyes and turned them to gold-fractured emeralds.

Creed watched with a possessive jealousy at how the transformation caught Hunter off guard. It was her smile that a man truly noticed. When combined with the unusual white-blond hair and the gemstone green of her eyes, it made her truly stunning in appearance.

Despite the unwelcome sensations of jealousy, it said a lot to him about Hunter's character that he had been kind to Nieve before noticing how beautiful she was, not after, and it made Creed trust him even more than his natural instincts were already assuring him that he could.

But Hunter was frowning, as if puzzled by something.

"Have we met before?" he asked Nieve.

"I don't think so." She looked again to Creed, as if wondering if she might be wrong, and needing confirmation that she was not.

"She's never been farther west than the farmlands around the Godseeker Mountains before now," Creed said. "I can't imagine how you'd ever have met."

Hunter shrugged, then returned to his original inquiry. "How do you know Blade?"

"He married my half-sister."

Hunter's jaw slackened. "I don't believe you."

"I assure you, it's true." Creed gave him a moment to overcome his surprise, amused by his reaction to the news. The two men were, indeed, close friends. "I'm guessing from the conversation you were having when we came in that you've already heard the rumors about half demons in the Godseeker Mountains." Hunter said nothing, so Creed went on. "The rumors are also true. A woman named Willow has destroyed entire villages filled with innocent people using demon fire. The Godseekers want her stopped."

"The Godseekers and I don't have a warm friendship. Where do you fit into this?" Hunter asked.

"I'm an assassin," Creed said. "I serve the Godseekers." At least he thought he still did. He was uncertain what the future held for him now, or if he would be welcome when he returned to them. He spoke from the heart. "I protect the innocent, all of them, regardless of birthright. Not every half demon is bad, any more than all mortals are good. The bloodlines, however, are far more complex and historic than the Godseekers realize."

"I know. Spawn have been around for years. Possibly centuries." Hunter looked at Nieve. Red crept past his collar as he remembered that a lady was present. "Beg your pardon," he corrected himself. "*Half demons*."

"Many of them aren't half-blooded demons. Not even a quarter. I have no idea what to call them," Creed said. "Some have demon talents, others don't. Either way, the world has a problem. While I don't believe Willow has much true demon blood in her, there's no doubt in my mind that she has all of their instincts. And I've seen her raise demons."

Hunter's hand, resting on the table, curled into a fist. He bounced his knuckles up and down, staring out a window for a long time. Life in the room returned to normal around them, their presence at its center now largely ignored. The waiter did not return, although it was possible he was afraid to, and not that he had forgotten.

"The Godseekers will have to handle it as best they can. I can't help you," Hunter said.

At first, Creed thought he must have misheard. "You're the Demon Slayer. Your wife is the daughter of two immortals. The two of you have been credited with driving demons from the mortal world. I would have thought you'd be anxious to find some sort of solution to this problem."

"That life is over for me," Hunter said. "For Airie, too. We came here to get away from it. I want her to have a home here. I don't want her to be seen as anything other than the special woman she is. I'll do whatever I have to in order to protect her, and what I can for Cottonwood Fall. The Godseekers will have to find someone else to fight spawn for them. I have a family to care for." He stood. "Be sure to tell Blade how happy I am for him." He met Creed's eyes. His own were hard with resolve. "Your sister must be an amazing woman. Blade deserves happiness. He's a good man to have as your friend. Between the two of you, I'm sure you can give the Godseekers more help than I can."

"So you won't help? Not even for Blade's sake? Is he a better friend to you than you are to him?" Creed asked.

Hunter's jaw worked. "Tell him that Airie's pregnant and I have my family to think of. He'll understand."

He walked away, leaving Creed sitting with Nieve in the middle of a gentlemen's club, wondering who he could possibly turn to now.

Chapter Sixteen

As Nieve finished her tea, she wondered what Creed would decide to do next.

It felt odd to be sitting with him in the cigar-smoke-filled air of a gentlemen's club and have no one take note of it. Under normal conditions they would hardly make an inconspicuous pair. Creed's size alone was enough to capture attention. Days in the desert had not influenced the delicate gold coloring of his skin. His smooth scalp emphasized the startling beauty of his face. She rather enjoyed how he rendered her invisible to others, even when he did not intend to, because he was so much more striking than she.

She mourned the distance between them that she had created and could not seem to circumvent. A part of her remained frozen, unable to accept what he was willing to offer. He was as kind and thoughtful as ever. But the intimacy was gone, and he had not tried to rekindle it. She had been stupid to run from him and she did not know how to make things right again.

He sat, lost in thought and staring into space, a frown puckering his brow. She wished she could do or say something to help him, but she had no useful skills or ideas.

"You can't blame Hunter for putting his family first," she said at last, when the silence seemed as if it might linger forever.

"I don't blame him," Creed said. He pushed at the teapot with one finger, edging it across the tablecloth. "I'm worried for him and his wife. Cottonwood Fall sees them as being the same as Willow and her young companions, and as good as he might be at fighting demons, not even the Demon Slayer can stop a bullet." Creed's frown deepened. "I'm not convinced he can stop half demons either. I don't think he's ever faced any before. I've fought both demons and half demons, and they aren't the same thing at all. Regardless of her immortal blood, his wife is pregnant and won't be much help to him." His gaze met hers. "He thinks he's left demon slaying behind him. What kind of man would I be if I walked away now and left him to fight this alone when he's so obviously unprepared? What of the sacrifices I expected you to make when I brought you here with me? Was all that for nothing? Where is the justice in any of this?"

Creed had just been handed defeat and yet his thoughts were not of the impact on him, but of worry for others. While he might have demon in him, its ferocity came from protectiveness and not a thirst for blood. Gentleness was by far the more dominant side of Creed's nature.

In that instant, Nieve saw him with a hot and blinding clarity that melted the final shards of ice encasing her heart. It allowed her to feel the enormity of a love for him that she wished she had the words to express. He was so much more than a demon or mortal. He was a man, with strong ideas of what was honorable and right and fair. He expected no reward for the things he did other than that he be able to live with himself afterward. She could not quite absorb how a man such as this, who was larger than life, could ever want a timid woman like her, but he did.

Impulsively, Nieve placed a hand over his. It looked very small and insignificant in comparison, and made her think of how they also compared as people.

He was a far better person than she. The day he had arrived at Bear's ranch had been the luckiest day of her life, and yet from the first moment she met him, she had done her best to throw that away. Nieve looked into his eyes. They were very blue against the silky, brushed-gold luster of his skin. As well as strong, and larger than life, he was indescribably beautiful. Her pulse fluttered to life as he smoothed his thumb along the soft flesh on the underside of her wrist.

She wanted him. She wanted his love. And she would tell him tonight, when they were alone, how much she loved him, too. When he could, he would find her son for her. She should never have doubted that. She should not have given up hope.

But right now, he had to help Hunter.

"Then don't walk away," she said. "Go after him."

Creed flipped his hand over so that he could link his fingers with hers. He squeezed them. "Thank you for understanding," he said, which made no sense at all to her, but the rift between them narrowed ever so slightly as he rose from the table.

She followed him from the gentlemen's club.

Outside, their packs were where they had left them. The sand swift, too, remained in the same place as before, although Nieve noted with relief that its color had stabilized to a steady and peaceable green.

Creed's thoughtful frown settled back in place at the sight of the solitary sand swift. "Where could Hunter have gone?"

"He went into that club determined to make a point. Now he'll want someone to enforce it," Nieve said.

Creed looked at her. Admiration warmed the startling blueness of eyes that contrasted starkly with the gold of his skin. "You're right. He'll have gone to the sheriff." He looked up and down the street. Traffic flowed to their left, giving the sand swift a wide birth. "Come on."

It did not take long for them to find the jail. The building was false-fronted and weathered, and looked very much the same as many of the others she and Creed had seen in their travels.

A crowd had already formed in front of it, neither ugly nor benign, but it would take very little to shift its mood. She could see in the way he kept her close to him and how his head continually turned that Creed sensed it, too. The tattoo that peeped above the collar of his shirt came to life in a way she knew meant the demon in him was also restless and wary, and protective of her.

She was much smaller than he, and therefore saw things from a different angle. She looked around, curious but unafraid in a way she would not have been a few short months ago, all because Creed was with her.

A slight movement to their left stirred the shadows

against the side of the bank, where the scorching rays of the sun did not quite stretch. Nieve pressed the palm of her hand against Creed's broad back to draw his attention to it, but he was distracted by a scuffle at the front of the crowd, near the entrance to the jail.

The tattoo burned hot beneath her hand, a sure sign of danger. Creed stopped. His head turned. Nieve felt the change in him as his demon fully awakened. Her own heart beat faster, but not from any fear of him. Something was wrong and now Creed knew it, too.

"I don't understand," he said, scanning the shadows. Frustration thickened his voice. "I don't see any danger. There's nothing unusual. And yet it's here. I can feel it."

"Perhaps something's happening inside the jail," Nieve suggested, but before Creed could reply, someone threw a rock.

Protected as she was by Creed and compulsion, whoever had thrown the rock could not have seen her. It was no doubt aimed at a window of the bank they stood in front of and not at her in particular. Nieve saw it coming out of the corner of her eye, but could not move fast enough to avoid it. It hit her hard in the temple, above her left eye. She collapsed against Creed, who caught her beneath her arms so that she did not fall.

A dull, bellowing roar filled her ears with heavy puffs of air, like the sounds an enraged kyson made as it got ready to charge. She clung to Creed, her face against his chest, both her hands flat on the tattoo on his back as she willed him not to change form here, of all places. The pain in her temple where the rock had struck her ebbed away and all was forgotten, except for the need to keep him from shifting so that people would not see his demon emerge.

The skin of her palms tingled, then burned, and within seconds, her arms were engulfed to the shoulder in flames.

"What in the name of the goddesses…?" Creed began, pulling away for a better look, but not releasing her.

They had the attention of the crowd now. People turned from the jail, a few heads at a time, then in greater numbers, to focus on Creed and Nieve with an incredulous and pervasive shock that did not bode well.

Nieve dropped her hands from Creed's back and the scorching hot tattoo that burned beneath her touch. The flames that licked up her arms died away. She wiped at the trickle of blood from the small cut on her forehead with her fingertips. They came away damp and red, but only slightly so.

"I'm fine," she said to Creed, a little afraid of what he'd do next, not for herself, but for others. "It was nothing more than an accident."

Hunter had come to the door of the jail. He spoke a few words to the sheriff, who nodded, then he pushed his way through the onlookers until he reached them.

"You should have told me that she's sp…half demon," he said to Creed, his voice low and hard.

"She's not."

Hunter had the good sense not to call Creed a liar. Instead, he gave a sharp jerk of his head in the direction they had come from. "Let's get out of here before people begin to ask questions you won't want to answer. Follow me."

They walked at a normal pace back to the sand swift and their belongings. Not fast, but not leisurely either.

"You can't stay in town now," Hunter said. "You'll have

to come home with me." He did not sound happy about it.

Why would he, Nieve thought. He had enough problems of his own.

He and Creed began to fasten their packs to the sand swift's back.

• • •

Hidden by tall grass and a deep hollow in the otherwise flat land, Willow watched as the assassin and the mortal woman rode through the town gates in the company of the Demon Slayer.

The lone road they followed took a circuitous route around the fortified walls, then snaked off in a single linear direction. Sprawling ranches, with miles of grazing between them, dimpled the landscape along the length of that road until it disappeared from sight.

One of those ranches hid the half demon Airie. The Demon Slayer would be riding to join her. Willow needed to draw the men back here, separating them from Airie and the mortal.

She waited as distance and the fields of swaying grass swallowed the three travelers from view.

Willow narrowed her eyes in thought. Far to the east, against the horizon, a craggy mountain range scraped a blazing sky. The sun had just passed its zenith, and it was still hours before night.

The town was busy during the day but it would quiet around sunset. Mortals feared the dark, because that was when demons had once terrorized the world. Only murderers and thieves would be about, and it was unlikely even they would stray far from the town walls. An attack after the sun went down would create chaos and confusion, and the Godseeker assassin would be bound by duty to investigate. He would not bring the mortal woman into danger with him. Neither would he leave her behind unprotected, which meant someone would need to remain with her.

Since the assassin had gone straight to the Demon Slayer for help, and they had ridden off together, Willow thought it likely that the Slayer would also be convinced to help defend his home town. He had come to the defense of Freetown when the demons had tried to burn it to the ground.

Willow counted on the women being left to fend for themselves in a place that would seem to be safest.

She had left the children at an encampment a mile down the trail, in the opposite direction from the Demon Slayer and his companions. Larch, whose pregnancy was more advanced now, had forced them to move at an increasingly slow pace that chafed at first, but had given the children time to develop their talents and for Willow to study their weaknesses.

Imp and Larch were both too gentle. While Imp would go missing at the first sign of trouble, Larch with her blossoming motherly instincts could be trusted to look out for the younger ones.

Stone's erratic behavior had become both aggressive and myopic. All he could think of was fighting the assassin again. He could not conceive of a future beyond that. While he would not have been Willow's first choice, she planned to place him in charge of the attack on the town.

Thistle had developed a liking for compelling others into committing deeds that generated havoc and fear.

She had little success against the other children anymore, because as soon as they'd understood what she was doing their demons deflected her compulsion away from them. She needed a new outlet for her aggression. Willow would place her with Larch. Thistle could then use compulsion to keep the mortals occupied while Stone fought the assassin. At the same time, she could help Larch protect the children.

The older boys were typical teenagers. They liked to destroy things, and she knew just what they should target. Willow had always found that smashing a temple built to honor the goddesses caused the greatest outrage among mortals. It never failed to astonish her because from what she could recall of them before their departure, they had been self-centered, pleasure-seeking whores. No different from demons.

Once the boys began their desecration of the temple, she would set the town's walls ablaze with demon fire. And after she made certain the women were alone, she would pay them a visit.

That meant she needed a demon to help her.

It had been several months. She had no idea how cooperative the demon would be, or even if he was the one who would respond. But if she were going to summon him, or any demon, she had to do it now, before darkness fell and it gained greater strength.

She scorched a wide area of earth using short spurts of fire so that the circle she made would not spread to the surrounding miles of rippling grasslands.

She crafted the circle. Then, full of caution, she reached into the boundary.

He came at once.

"Well, well." His arms banded across his bare chest. The cold of his eyes seared her skin, but not so much as the thin smile pressed on his lips. "I never thought to hear from you again. I've missed you."

"I had nothing for you until now."

"You had the woman I asked for."

"Who was taken from me again by a half demon who was stronger than I expected," Willow said.

"I could have helped you keep her."

He would have taken her and left, and Willow would have had an angry, half demon assassin to deal with, as well as an unfulfilled promise she could never claim.

Willow played with the fire in her hands, sparking the flames back and forth between her fingertips. She did not want to use up too much of her strength. As it was, when she summoned him again later that evening, she would not have the control over him that she should.

"I have something for you now." She snapped her hand shut. "I have the boy's name."

• • •

The Borderlands were nothing at all like the mountains Creed and Nieve had left far behind them.

The road to Hunter's homestead was little more than twin, well-worn wagon ruts that cut through miles of grassland. The ruts veered off at various points to lead to other ranches along the route. To one side, Creed saw dark, humped masses that indicated scattered kyson herds grazing.

Back in the Old World days, this land had been heavily settled. Those original cities had been some of the first to be destroyed by the arrival of demons. Now this vast, rich-soiled land was filled with emptiness.

And also opportunity, Creed thought, looking around him at all the potential. *For the right type of man.*

But it would burn just as easily today, if not more so, because of the endless miles of fertile grasslands.

As they rode, Creed told Hunter as much as he knew of Willow, and who she had with her, which was little enough.

"Her companions are young but dangerous, and will do as she says. She seems to be gathering children who've been abandoned by parents and families who fear them, and is raising them to be demons," he finished.

"Not demons," Nieve spoke up from behind him. Her hands bunched in the waist of his shirt. "That little girl at the tea shop thinks of Willow as her mother. Don't you see what she's doing? She's teaching them to prepare for the future, and how to survive, just as you say your sister Raven and her companion are teaching others."

Hunter looked at Creed, his eyebrows raised in an unspoken query, as if seeking confirmation of Nieve's assessment.

"It's no doubt true," Creed agreed, although he could hardly imagine a less motherly woman than Willow. Since his own had not been overwhelmingly maternal, he was not in the best position to judge. Nieve's opinion was as good as any, and most likely better than his. "There's one more thing."

"There always is." Hunter sighed as if he knew what was coming.

"Willow is following us. She has no compassion for anyone weaker than she is. She'll burn Cottonwood Fall to the ground. She'll kill everyone in it. And she'll want the

Godseekers to know that she defeated the Demon Slayer."

He watched Hunter work it all out in his head. He slouched in his saddle, allowing the sand swift to make its own way. Its tongue flicked out to curl around a small gray bird hidden in the grass at the side of the trail.

"I don't want Airie to know these are children we'll be fighting. Not while she's got two of her own to think about. She has enough to worry over as it is," Hunter said.

Creed wondered if he truly understood the complexity of the situation. The dangers. These were not normal children. "I was hoping she could help."

"She's due any day now. How do you propose she fight demons?" Hunter asked. "I have to help put her shoes on."

"She has no demon talents to protect her?"

"She has plenty. None of them change the fact that she's nine months pregnant. With my baby," Hunter added. "She's not to be involved."

"I guess it's up to you and me, then," Creed said. "I hope your demon slaying abilities haven't gotten too rusty." He regretted the words as soon as he uttered them. Nieve's fingers tightened when he made reference to slaying, and she sat a bit straighter in the saddle as if attempting to put distance between them.

Hunter was quiet for a few moments more. "These aren't demons," he said. "I don't respond to sp...half demons in quite the same way." He looked at Nieve, although his words were addressed to Creed. "I didn't react when she began shooting fire back in town."

"She's not half demon," Creed told him for the second time. He hesitated. He could not get past the strangeness of openly discussing something he had spent so many years denying. "The fire comes from me."

A large gate was in sight now, straight ahead of them, looming over the horizon. Beyond the gate could be seen a scattering of tidy buildings, and an enormous wooden-railed paddock that held a few head of restless young hross. A tiny figure sat on the top railing, watching their approach.

"I see." Hunter shifted the reins from one hand to the other, thinking. "What other talents do you have?"

"I'm friendly," Creed said. "Everyone likes me."

"I'd rather they feared you. Anything else?"

"I can shift to full demon form."

"That talent I can use." Hunter eyed him. "And you can manipulate demon fire. That should come in handy, too."

"No," Creed said. "Fire is Nieve's protection, not mine. She claims it through me."

"Then we've got a problem," Hunter said. "Our only defenses are mortal weapons and I don't—"

He interrupted his own words, nudging the sand swift to pick up speed as the small figure on the railing made a dangerous leap to the ground.

The tiny figure—a young boy, Creed could see— stumbled over his feet, righted himself, and came hurtling up the trail toward them with his little legs churning and his arms pumping hard.

Behind Creed, Nieve sucked in a sharp breath. She would have thrown herself off the hross if Creed hadn't caught her arm and lowered her, with greater caution, from the saddle to the ground. As soon as her feet touched the dirt she, too, began to run.

Creed could not imagine what had possessed her. Then, with a heavy weight compressing his ribs, he noted the boy's blond head and his age, and feared that Nieve had made a false assumption. It was only natural that she would see her son's face in every boy who was the right age and coloring. Confusion and disappointment were bound to occur. He couldn't protect her from emotions.

"I'm sorry," Creed began, beginning to explain her behavior to Hunter, "but Nieve lost her son and I'm afraid—"

His voice trailed off. Something was wrong. Hunter's expression had gone grim. Nieve was in tears. The boy had his arms tight around her neck, and was not fighting off the kisses she showered on his beaming face.

Nieve had made no mistake. She knew who this boy she held was. It was equally plain that he recognized her, too.

A woman had come to the door of the log house to stand on the long verandah running its width. She was tall, with long black hair that fell to her hips, and with the exception of Nieve, was without a doubt the most beautiful woman Creed had ever seen. She was also heavily pregnant.

This had to be Airie. He had always thought of her in terms of her demon blood. That she was half goddess, too, was equally obvious. Kindness radiated from her.

At the moment, so did concern. She surveyed the scene in the yard. She saw Hunter and Creed. She saw Nieve on her knees in the dirt with the little boy in her arms. She turned to Hunter with a hint of panic in her eyes.

"What's going on?" Airie asked.

But she knew. Creed could see it in the way the panic spread to her face, and how her hands fluttered to her breast.

Hunter slid from the sand swift's back, one hand on its reins to keep it under control as it reacted to the woman's distress.

"I think we all need to talk," he said.

Creed, too, dismounted. He started for Nieve, reaching out to place a hand on her shoulder and get her attention.

Nieve, however, flinched away from his touch. She swung the child out of his range, placing her body between them, as if she thought Creed intended to harm him in some way. Fear flared in her eyes when she looked up at Creed, then a fierce, angry, determined protectiveness. "Stay away from him!"

Along the connection between them, already tenuous and strained for weeks now, Creed felt a searing pain.

Chapter Seventeen

Somehow, Creed set the hurt aside. They had more important matters to settle than Nieve's rejection of him.

The boy broke and ran.

Nieve would have pursued him if Creed had not caught hold of her wrist to stop her. She lashed out, a small fist pummeling him with all her strength as she fought to free herself.

The threat of tears he saw in her eyes, and the fear that her son was being taken from her again, were the fists that struck him the hardest. His chest ached to think that she did not trust him.

Creed swallowed hard and refused to release her. He could hardly unleash this mad, desperate woman on a confused child. She'd not get the reaction from her son she was hoping for. He'd let her wear herself out before he tried to reason with her, although he doubted if anything would make her listen right now. She had found her son. She was not about to let him go again without a fight, and it was Creed she chose to vent her frustrations on.

When she finally showed signs of tiring, he drew her to him and held her. By now, the boy had disappeared into the barn.

"Let him go," Creed said into her ear. "Give him some space. He'll be back when he's ready. Until then we have a lot of things to discuss."

Hunter had an arm around his wife, but it was Nieve he addressed. "Creed is right. Scratch is fine. He won't go very far."

"His name is *Asher*."

Nieve's chest heaved as she renewed her efforts to gain her freedom, pushing at Creed's arms in an attempt to break his hold, but he did not relent. Neither did he try to calm her distress, but allowed her to come to terms with her emotions on her own. She had waited a long time for this moment. She'd begun to believe it might never come.

He was not above using her love for her son against her.

"Stop thinking of yourself and what you want, and have some regard for what he must be going through right now," Creed said. "He hasn't seen you in over a year. He barely knows you. Let him come to you when he's ready."

"Bastard," Nieve whispered. But she stopped struggling and leaned against him, pressing her cheek to his chest, closing her eyes as if drained. He tightened his hold on her, wishing there was more he could do, but it was too soon to make her promises he might not be able to keep.

Airie had remained silent throughout. She looked anxious now, and tired, and Creed knew that upsetting her was no way to win Hunter's support, but far worse was coming. Willow would not be too far behind them.

Hunter rested a hand on his wife's swollen belly as if to reassure himself that both she and the baby were safe. "Let's go inside."

The log house was well-constructed and spoke of generations of hard work and affluence. The Demon Slayer's family had not been idle in the centuries since the demon occupation began.

They gathered at the long kitchen table. Hunter pulled back a chair next to the window for Nieve so that she could watch the barn for signs of her son, a thoughtful gesture that Creed silently thanked him for and that Hunter acknowledged with a brief nod.

In return, as Creed took a seat beside Nieve, he allowed Hunter to tell Airie what he wanted her to know of the events that had transpired in town without interruption. It did not include any stories of children.

As it turned out, he did not need to tell her. She'd already heard the rumors. And she'd drawn her own conclusions.

"There won't be as many mixed blood demons as you think," Airie said to Creed. Of the four of them, they were the two people who knew exactly what it was they were facing. What their instincts would be. "If the mother is part demon, the demon in her won't willingly tolerate carrying a child of mixed blood to full term. The baby is unlikely to survive unless its demon side is stronger than hers."

Creed watched from the corner of his eye as Hunter turned that information over in his head. He saw when understanding hit him, and he cast his wife a sharp look.

"You should have told me," he said to her. "That's what's been keeping you awake at nights, isn't it?"

"Not at all," she assured him. "Ours is a little more active than most babies, but she has two full immortals for protection. My parents will allow nothing to happen to her."

Hunter was not appeased. It was clear he did not like that his wife had kept something from him. Creed was about to step in, wanting the conversation focused back on the danger that was coming, but Nieve interrupted first.

"A baby born to a mortal mother who survives the birth can't possibly be a monster, can he?" She looked at Creed, and he felt the hope blossoming in her. "Your mother survived and you aren't a monster," she said to him. "Neither is your—" She caught herself before she said *sister*, and the stricken look on her face told him she had not intended to reveal any secrets.

He smiled at her, and her fingers inched across the table to touch his before she placed both hands in her lap.

Airie picked up on the affirmation Nieve was seeking and answered her with compassion. "Scratch—Asher," she corrected herself, " —isn't one, either. He's sweet and gentle. But he's still a little boy. His demon talents are already strong and they're going to grow. Are you prepared to deal with that side of him? Are you certain you know what that means?" She looked to Creed for support.

Because he did understand what it meant. His own mother had not been able to deal with the fact he was half demon, even though he knew in his heart that she had tried her best. But Nieve was different. She was a lot stronger than she seemed.

"Nieve will do fine with him," Creed said, but he did not smile at her again. He could not. He did not want to see surprise or gratitude in her eyes. She should have trusted him in this. He had never asked for anything from her but that.

"What about you?" Airie asked him.

Another knife twisted in Creed. Airie thought he was the boy's father, and worried about what that also meant. Demons did not share well, particularly the affections of the women they chose.

"The boy isn't mine," he replied. For that matter, neither was Nieve. He'd been mistaken. She had not claimed him. She had no room in her heart for anyone but her son. "The demon that Willow has been relying on must be his father. That's the reason she's following us. He's helped her only because he wants Nieve back. Count on it."

"Of course a demon is involved," Hunter said. "Because half demons alone wouldn't be trouble enough." Although his outward demeanor remained calm and steady, Creed sensed his simmering anger and did not blame him for it. "It can't enter the mortal world completely."

"What if it has some physical connection to this world?" Creed asked. "Could it enter the mortal world then?"

Hunter and Airie exchanged a look that Creed hoped Nieve could not interpret. Any physical connection to the world that this demon had would involve either her or her son.

"I don't know," Airie admitted. "But I sent them away once. I can do it again. They can't bear the touch of goddess rain on their flesh."

"But goddess rain obviously has no effect on half demons, or they'd be gone, too." Hunter's expression soured. "Is there anything else I should know?" he asked Creed.

"I think that's everything."

"It doesn't matter what the demon wants," Airie said to Creed. "Not if Nieve doesn't want him, too."

Compassion spilled from her eyes so that Creed had to look away. He had no time for self-pity right now. Airie turned to Nieve, who was sitting quietly, her attention fixed on the window and the barn rather than the conversation at hand. She thought only of Ash, Creed knew.

"*Do* you want this demon? Have you claimed him already?" Airie asked her. "No one here will judge you for it."

"No." The faraway expression of longing in Nieve's green eyes faded as she responded to the question with unwavering resolution. A delicate pink brushed her cheeks. "All I want is my son."

Creed had known this from the beginning, so he couldn't explain why her words cut him. He did not begrudge her the return of her child.

He resented that his time with her was now almost over because Nieve no longer needed him. Airie and Hunter would let no harm come to either her or her son if she stayed in this area. She had some money. He would leave more for her. He still had one last grenade taken from the ruin that he could sell.

Airie smiled at her husband, who was not at all appeased by her unconcerned manner. "A single demon, I can handle," she assured him. "I have my father and mother to help protect me and our baby. And since the demon has no true claim on Nieve, it's the least of our worries. The people in Cottonwood Fall are in far more danger. You should go."

"How far behind you do you think this Willow is?" Hunter asked Creed.

Nieve suddenly stood. She reached for Creed, who was beside her, and steadied herself against his shoulder.

Her eyes remained riveted on the window. Creed peered through the gleaming glass, wondering what had alarmed her, and saw a dull orange smear in the distance. Black smoke billowed skyward.

The time for talk was over. Willow was already here.

And it did not bode well for Cottonwood Fall.

Hunter, too, turned to look. His expression darkened, if possible. Creed could well understand why he and Blade were good friends. Ruthlessness emanated from them both.

"It seems the matter has been decided for me," Hunter said. "It looks as if I'll be helping the Godseekers, after all."

While Creed would be happy to have his help no matter how grudgingly offered, Nieve was his bigger worry. He did not like leaving her unprotected.

Yet he had a duty. He had to go.

"Stay here with the women," he said to Hunter. "I'll go alone."

"No," Airie and Nieve said together.

Nieve fell silent. Her eyes, green and anxious, remained on Creed. When he looked at her, she turned away. Disappointment scorched him. She had her son. She no longer wanted him.

Airie reached for one of Hunter's hands, taking it between hers. "You can't stand back and let the town burn. If fire is Willow's talent, and summoning demons, then I have better protection than Cottonwood Fall. They need the two of you more than we do."

"If it were just you, I wouldn't worry at all," Hunter said. He dragged his fingers through his blond hair. "But what about the baby?"

Airie placed his palm on her round stomach. "See? All's quiet. No contractions or anything. The baby's not coming anytime soon."

Hunter stood there, his hand on their baby, for several long moments. Then he nodded.

"Very well," he said, and Airie smiled.

Envy sideswiped Creed at the obvious affection they had for each other. This was how it should be between a man and a woman.

The men started for the door. Creed paused at the foot of the front steps and looked back, because Nieve had followed him.

She stood a few steps above him on the verandah, her fingers working the worn fabric of her skirt into pleats as she gathered her thoughts. Dusk heightened the paleness of her hair and the depth of her lustrous eyes. She looked as if she had something she wanted to say but could not find the right words, or perhaps did not want them overheard by Airie and Hunter.

"I don't want you in danger," she finally said.

His heart untwisted. The hold she had on him was frayed, but not yet completely severed. She simply could not decipher her emotions. Or more likely, was not used to doing so—which was understandable under the circumstances, and given her past.

Perhaps that was for the best. He had no right to add to her worries. Not when she had found the one thing that meant the world to her and gave her hope for the future. More than anything else, Creed wished for her to have happiness in her life.

"You forget who I am," he said. "What I am. I'm not the one who'll be in danger."

He left her standing there, and went to ready his hross and his weapons.

Chapter Eighteen

Nieve watched as the men rode off. Soon they were nothing more than two black, moving masses in the lengthening twilight. When they disappeared entirely, swallowed by the tall grasses to either side of the road and a dip in the land, she returned to the kitchen.

Airie had lit the lanterns and set a kettle of water on the stove to boil. Nieve resumed her position by the window.

She knew Creed was right when he told her she needed to give Asher time. She should take comfort in the fact that her son recognized her. It was more than she could have hoped for, given his age.

He had grown so big though, and it caused an enormous ache in her heart to see the proof of everything she had missed in his life. As she looked around Airie's bright and beautiful kitchen, and thought of all that Airie was, Nieve could also not help but think she did not have anything of equal value to offer him.

Except her love. The enormity of that could not be surpassed by anyone else. She had crossed the world to find him. She had crawled through the depths of depression and fought off mountains of fear and despair. She would not give him up again. She would provide for him as best she could, and what she could not offer, she would make up for by teaching him that material possessions did not matter. She'd once had them all. They had not imparted anything of true worth. The most valuable lessons had been taught to her by life and its hardships. She wanted Asher to grow into a good and decent person. She could teach him morals and ethics as well as anyone else, including Airie and Hunter.

But even though she resented the place Airie had taken in Asher's young heart, Nieve was also grateful that he had been loved.

The black, cast iron kettle on top of the stove began a slow whistle. Nieve started to rise from her chair. "Let me get that for you."

Airie motioned for her to remain seated. A smile stretched across her stunning, perfect features, blindsiding Nieve, and for the first time ever, she felt as if she truly were plain and could never compare to such perfection. The other woman was every bit as breathtaking as the goddess rumor proclaimed her to be.

"Thank you, but I'm stronger than you'd think," Airie said.

Nevertheless, as she lifted the hot kettle from the stove, she did so with both hands and great care. She poured the steaming water over fragrant wildflower leaves in a pretty ceramic pot sitting in the center of the table. She returned the kettle to the stove, then eased herself into a chair, her round belly pressing tight against the table's edge.

With a sharp pang, Nieve remembered her own pregnancy. Her final stages had been marked by eager anticipation, but also punctuated with bouts of abject terror.

"Are you afraid?" she asked Airie, looking at her large stomach, then realized the question was far too intimate, and very inappropriate. "Forgive me," she said. "That's none of my business."

The thick black lashes around Airie's eyes fluttered in understanding. She placed a hand on her belly. "I understand. And really, I'm not. Hunter's the one who's afraid. He's seen children born in demon form before and I haven't, but as long as it's healthy, I'm not worried about me. Hunter understands that no matter what happens to me the baby is blameless for it, although there was a time when he wouldn't have." She reached for the teapot and the cups. Her eyes softened and became distant, and her hand stopped in midair as if she'd been caught by an almost forgotten but wondrous memory. "No matter what, this baby has a lot of family watching out for her."

It was odd, to be sitting here drinking tea with a woman who was not mortal. Airie had all of the compulsive allure of a demon—except with Airie, it was her kind and gentle nature that drew others to her. Men and women alike. Nieve could uncover no repressed horror or fear while in her presence. It took her a moment to understand why she did not.

It was because Airie possessed the same type of allure that had drawn Nieve to Creed. The immortal blood in them brought out and enhanced all that was good about their mortal natures, not their demon.

It was far more than demon allure that drew Nieve to Creed. This aching desire she had for him did not disappear when he was no longer near her, as it had with Asher's demon father, because it was with her still.

She would never forgive herself for the expression of hurt on his face when she told him to stay away from her son.

Regret filled her. She wished she had told him before finding Asher that she loved him. Now that she had her son back, alive and well, Creed had no reason to believe he could ever be more than second best in her heart, and that was not true. He had his own place, one that was every bit as precious to her.

She felt as if another piece of her had ridden off with Creed, and she was afraid it might not return to her. Unlike with Asher, if it did not, she would have no hope at all of retrieving it.

Finding Asher sparked other, more troubling, memories. The demon had always called to her in these hours after sunset, becoming more insistent as the night wore on if she resisted. Foreboding settled around her in a way that did not happen when Creed was near. She had taken his protection, and his love, for granted. Now they were gone and she feared she would not get them back.

The silence between the two women stretched to the point of awkwardness. Airie worried for Hunter, and even though Nieve knew that Creed could take care of himself, she feared for him, too.

Abruptly, Airie's eyes turned to twin pools of shimmering tears.

"I won't keep him from you," she said. Nieve's thoughts

had been so caught up in Creed that it took her a second to understand Airie meant Asher. "He came to me at a time when I needed him." Airie dabbed at her eyes with the back of her hand. "I'd just lost the only mother I'd ever known, and was left with no one in the whole world who loved me. I truly believed Scratch was a gift to me from the goddesses. Giving him up won't be easy. Please understand how much I love him."

Nieve's resentment of Airie fled. She had not expected a woman who could literally take anything she wanted in this world to acquiesce to the wishes of another so easily.

"Why do you call him Scratch?"

Warmth glittered behind the tears in Airie's eyes. "He was very dirty when we found him. He couldn't tell us his real name so Hunter started calling him that, and it stuck. I'd planned to give him another one, a better one, but any time I thought of it, I forgot it again." The smile in her eyes fluttered at the corners of her lips, although it remained tainted by a wistful sadness. "He has a way of turning people's attention and thoughts from things when it suits him. I suppose he always knew you would come."

Nieve hoped that was true.

Outside the open window, a murder of crows erupted noisily into the early evening air. Beyond them, spirals of smoke curled from the town in the distance, but the flames appeared to have dissipated. The telltale orange glow was gone, leaving nothing but the encroaching night.

"Not knowing what happened to Ash was the worst thing imaginable for me," Nieve said. "Finding out that he's been cared for and loved makes all of the worry and fear unimportant. Thank you."

As many more questions as she would love to ask about her son, the conversation had now become a difficult one for Airie so Nieve tried to steer it in a different direction. She started to ask Airie a question about the town, and how she enjoyed living so far from where she was born, when the ruckus the crows continued to raise caused her to pause and think.

She looked out of the window again, more closely, and the blood drained from her body. Standing in the yard, all alone, and with tiny, twin globes of fire clenched in her fists, was a woman.

Nieve's throat closed over as if it had been hammered shut.

"What's wrong?" Airie asked. She was much taller than Nieve and had no trouble seeing through the window into the dusty yard, and the paddock beyond it, from her sitting position. Her eyes, rich and brown and flecked with gold, still sparkling with tears, widened. "Is that Willow?"

Nieve nodded, unable to form coherent words. She had no idea what they should do. Airie could not face the half demon. Not in her current condition. Nieve would never forgive herself if something happened to the baby she carried.

She could see the speculation on Airie's face as she considered what to do. Fear crawled into Nieve's chest, burrowing deep. If Airie was anything at all like Creed she would not run and hide, as she should.

And without Creed, Nieve, who was hardly brave, had no demon talents with which to help.

• • •

From their hiding place in the loft of the barn, Ash and Imp watched as Willow walked into the yard.

She looked a lot like Airie, Ash thought, but not in a nice way. The mean woman had none of the *feel* to her that made Airie so special. Her eyes were hard and cold, not soft and warm with tiny sparks of fire. She did not look as if she knew how to laugh.

Imp reached for his hand, her palm rough and warm. "Willow won't hurt us," she said to him, but he heard a tiny flicker of doubt in her voice. Imp was scared of her.

While Airie knew better than to show any fear in front of Willow, Ash wasn't as sure of his mother. He loved her a lot, but she was gentle and timid. He'd hoped the big man, Creed, would help make her stronger, but instead, he'd taken too great a care with her.

Ash was okay with Creed looking after his mother because she deserved to be treated with kindness, and he planned to take good care of her, too, but right now, intentions weren't going to do her any good.

As much as he didn't want to go into the demon boundary when he knew the one who searched for his mother was nearby, he could move faster when he was in it and he had to find Creed right away. His mother would look after Airie, but right after that, she was going to need him.

Ash squeezed Imp's fingers, letting her know what he intended to do so she could get ready to hide once they got there, because no one entered the demon boundary unprepared.

"Remember," he said to her. "If I ever get summoned to the boundary, you can summon me back. Give me some time. I'll be okay for a bit. I can hide, too."

Then, holding tight to Imp's hand, he let his demon cross over, dragging her with them.

• • •

The fire on the walls had been extinguished by the time they reached town.

Creed wondered about that.

As they moved through the near-empty streets, Creed sensed that Hunter was becoming more and more angry. That was because he grew quiet and watchful. He would have made a good assassin, Creed thought. He did not react without thinking—although he did like to provoke. Creed could hardly hold that idiosyncrasy against him.

And Hunter did not exhibit fear. Instead, he beat it into submission.

They found the sheriff across the street from the temple, crouched behind a watering trough, with his gun in his hand and several other weapons, including two rifles, nearby, as if he planned a long siege. He was an older man whose black hair was frosted with gray, and while tall, had a wiry build slowly going to fat around the middle.

The temple in Cottonwood Fall was a simple building, constructed along the lines of the Old World churches Creed had seen in the ancient photos stored in the library of the Temple of Immortal Right. This one was single story, with a plain steeple and bell, and a pitched roof constructed of clay tile. Cottonwood Fall was as far from the goddesses' and Godseeker mountains, and demon territory, as it was possible to be. The goddess boundary, which began in the mountains, extended behind the Borderlands. Creed had asked and been told that a man could walk for days and find himself right back where he started. No one had ever reached it. Therefore, this was not an especially devout region.

The temple itself was in chaos, its heavy wooden double doors thrown wide. From inside came the sounds of glass breaking and wood being smashed.

"I can't say I'm especially fond of the goddesses, except for maybe one," Hunter amended, in reference to Airie, "but I see no reason to destroy a perfectly good building. How many of them are there inside?" he asked the sheriff.

"Ten."

"Are they armed?"

The sheriff spat in the dirt. "I haven't seen or heard any signs that they are."

Creed wondered if Stone had survived the grenade explosion and fall into the sinkhole. It was safest to assume that he had. The boy was well protected by his abilities. He was also going to be more cautious now when using them.

"They won't be armed," Creed said. "They have no need for mortal weapons. The woman and the oldest boy are the ones we want to be rid of. Target them first. The rest are children."

"They're spawn. Whether they're children doesn't matter," the sheriff said.

Creed knew the man's attitude was shared by the majority of people, and that most of them were afraid, and rightly so. There was no point in debating it with him, although he would not stand by and permit the innocent to be harmed. "That would be for the Godseekers to decide."

"The Godseekers don't determine the law here."

"I don't know about you," Hunter said to the sheriff, his mild tone laced with warning, "but I wouldn't want to be offending one of their assassins. It's hard to argue the finer points of the law if you're dead."

The sheriff took a closer look at Creed and went a shade paler. Until that moment, he had taken his affability at face value and barely noticed him.

Hunter turned back to Creed. "Why don't you challenge them and see if you can draw them out?"

Creed had no desire to shift form in front of the people of Cottonwood Fall unless forced to do so, and he would not be able to hide the action. Not even he could accomplish such an enormous act of compulsion on so many onlookers. It was only thanks to Nieve's intervention that he had not revealed his ability in Cottonwood Fall already. Now everyone thought she was half demon. That was going to make it difficult for her to make a new start here.

And the Demon Slayer was a champion to mortal men. If Hunter fought against half demons and won, hope for the world's future could continue to grow. Stone, and others like him, would learn to think twice before terrorizing those they perceived as weaker.

"This is your home," Creed said. "You're the Demon Slayer. How much trouble can a few children be?"

Hunter's expression flattened in a way that did not express gratitude for Creed's show of confidence in him, making Creed grin in response.

Creed examined the temple. "Is there a back door?"

"Yes," the sheriff answered.

"Then why don't you approach from the front, and I'll take the back and make sure no one escapes?" he suggested to Hunter. That might give him some protection from discovery if he should be forced to shift. He spoke to the sheriff again. "Watch out for the oldest boy. He shifts body parts in response to danger, so no matter what, don't shoot at him. A bullet will hit demon's bone plating and deflect off him, and might strike an innocent."

The sheriff's gray-stubbled face darkened. "He can shift?"

"From what I've seen, half demon talents aren't necessarily the same as those of their fathers. They're hybrid. They can be a combination of two or more, or they may be born with none at all and it can skip a generation or two."

"We can't fight that," the sheriff said. His shoulders slumped. "We can't even identify them, as we once thought we could. People are right, then. We're best off to kill any we suspect could be spawn at birth, not just the ones who look demon."

Hunter's neck had gone a dull red. "We may as well begin killing babies that are likely to grow up to be criminals, too. And any that appear imperfect, or deformed."

"Right now, the only ones we have to worry about are in that temple," Creed interrupted. He hoped the sheriff had simply forgotten that Hunter had a child possessing an unusual heritage of its own on the way, and was not sending a subtle message, because if that was his intention, he should be wary of its reception. "And we aren't interested in the children just yet, only the woman and the oldest boy." He thought a moment. "I need some boards and a hammer and nails."

Chapter Nineteen

The sheriff loped down the street to the general store, hugging the shadows, to get the objects Creed requested.

Creed watched him reverse the butt of his pistol and rap it against the store's front window. Shattered glass tinkled to the floor and the boardwalk.

The sheriff stepped over the window's ledge to be swallowed by the gloomy interior. He emerged a few moments later and returned to where Creed and Hunter waited, and passed over several thick wooden four by fours, a clawed hammer and a small tin bucket of nails.

Creed balanced the boards under one arm, and carrying the hammer and nails in his hands, walked around to the rear of the temple. He did not try to hide what he was doing, but strode boldly to the back door.

As he began to hammer the boards in place, the demolition inside ceased with an ominous abruptness.

Seconds later, a heavy foot struck the inside of the door

with such force that Creed's fingers stung from the vibration. He shook his hand, cursing under his breath. If Stone wished, he could put a foot right through it. Creed was counting on him wanting to make the biggest spectacle possible, because that was the obvious intention behind what he was doing.

He wondered as to the reason. Or why Willow had not simply set the building on fire, which was her usual method of destruction.

The kicking on the door stopped. Creed dropped the hammer and the remaining nails and ran around to the front of the temple.

Stone stood on the main steps, the bleached wood risers cracked and sagging beneath his weight. He faced Hunter and the sheriff, but turned as Creed approached. Behind Stone, partially hidden in the shadows, was the young girl with long, honey-brown hair who had lured Nieve into danger. Bright-eyed with interest, the complete lack of concern on her face warned Creed that all was not right with her, and made him cautious.

There was no sign of Willow anywhere.

Creed joined Hunter and the sheriff, who waited across the street from the temple.

"Are you ready for a second round?" Stone called to him.

The boy was cocky in his confidence. So certain of a win. But the first time he had fought Creed, Creed had not wanted to hurt him. Back then, he'd wanted to give him a chance.

Now Creed knew that the boy would never be trustworthy. He enjoyed inflicting pain and suffering. Creed wondered if Stone had ever been salvageable, or if he'd been mostly demon in temperament from birth. They would never know for certain, and that was a pity.

But Stone was only one of the children present, and Creed did not know what the others were capable of, either through their talents or their natures. He wished to observe them before taking action.

"The second round belongs to the Demon Slayer," Creed replied.

Hunter had refused any weapons.

"Those are of little use when fighting a demon, and unnecessary if fighting a child," he said to the sheriff when the man tried to press a pistol into his hand. He tapped the amulet at his throat. "Let's see how much demon the boy has in him."

He entered the deserted street like a gunslinger, his hands low and relaxed, his lean frame moving with the ease of a man untroubled by fear despite the fact he was unarmed.

Creed watched as Stone sized him up, then dismissed him as a mere mortal, and knew that the boy did not know how to read an opponent. While at first glance Hunter might not seem like much of a threat to someone like Stone, who gloried in his demon abilities, there were telltale signs about Hunter that spoke of experience and should make Stone wary of him.

Neither had Stone understood the mercy Creed had extended during their altercation by not killing him. Because Stone possessed no compassion he did not expect any. He saw it as a sign of weakness in an opponent, nothing more.

Creed knew Stone would not receive any mercy from the Demon Slayer. And while he accepted that not all half demons could be spared, or taught something they did not possess because it was never a part of their nature, it saddened him nevertheless. He did not want to accept that people this young could never be redeemed. They were mortal, at least in part, and that was what needed to be nurtured.

Behind Stone, seven more young people lurked in the temple. Several were girls, one of whom was pregnant. Creed accepted the inevitable. In spite of the fact they were little more than children, he could not prevent bloodshed. Soon, shots would be fired by any one of the men he sensed lurking behind the shuttered windows of surrounding homes and businesses. All that stayed them right now was the sheriff's inaction. One signal from him, however, and pandemonium would result. Lives, mortal and half demon alike, would be lost.

These people knew nothing of what they faced. Even the Slayer did not. What worried Creed far more than that was the fact that Willow had not yet made an appearance. Where was she?

Stone swaggered down the low steps, the thud of his boots loud in the heavy silence.

And then Creed heard the single report of a rifle. The shot came from tall, partially opened shutters in the second floor of the general store. The opening was, in actual fact, a doorway through which heavy and awkward goods were lifted by elevator into the building's storage area.

As Creed had warned the sheriff, Stone's rib area shifted and hardened in direct response to a threat. The bullet struck bone plating and deflected, also as predicted, to pierce the shingled siding of the temple.

What Creed had not anticipated was the second shot that rang out. It had not been aimed at the children standing in front of the temple. He heard a woman's screams, and turned to look in time to see a man's limp body tumble from the second floor of the general store to the street below. With sudden dread, he figured out what had happened. The honey-haired girl, with the sweet, innocent face that had charmed Nieve, had caused the man who'd fired that first shot to turn the rifle on himself.

And from a significant distance. Already she used more compulsion than Creed could, and she was not yet fully mature.

"Watch out for the little girl," he called to Hunter.

Surprise crossed Hunter's face first, followed by understanding, then cold calculation when he pieced together what had just happened.

Beside Creed, a thin patina of sweat had broken out on the sheriff's forehead. Twin beads rolled down either temple. "Maybe you're right and the Godseekers are the ones who should deal with these...*things*," he said to Creed. "They look like children. How's a man supposed to tell them apart from normal ones?"

Creed, too intent on making certain Hunter would not be caught in some trap by one of Stone's young companions, and in watching for Willow, made no reply.

She still had not made an appearance. Uneasiness mingled with a growing certainty and shifted to outright worry. She was not here. And if she was not, then where might she be?

He tried to shake it off. Nieve was with Airie, and despite her pregnancy, Hunter believed Airie possessed enough protection for them both.

Hunter had not allowed the shooting to distract him,

nor waited for Stone to make the first move. He didn't aim for the boy's face or stomach, the logical choices, but struck out at what would be a vulnerability on a true demon—the free moving joint in the soft spot beneath one arm. Creed could tell that Hunter had not put a lot of strength behind the blow, no doubt not wanting to break any bones in his hand if Stone shifted.

Stone grunted and took a step back, signaling that Hunter's strategy had been effective.

Creed kept an eye on the girl in the doorway. She watched the confrontation between Hunter and Stone as if not at all worried about any possible threats to her or her other companions. She was undoubtedly correct, and safe enough. None of the spectators would dare fire their weapons again, at least for a few more moments, until after they processed what had happened.

Creed did not want her testing her talents on Hunter.

"Pass me a rifle," he said to the sheriff who, after only a slight hesitation, handed one over from the neat stockpile of arms.

Keeping his movements slow and as unobtrusive as possible, not wanting to draw her attention his way, Creed took the weapon and aimed it at the girl framed in the doorway.

"What are you doing?" the sheriff asked. His hands were shaking. He was unaware of the compulsion that this one had settled over the onlookers, and even though he had seen the evidence to the contrary, to him she seemed no more than a little girl with an innocent demeanor.

Because of the risk that the sheriff might try to interfere, Creed did not hesitate any longer than the time it took him to make certain of his aim. He sighted down the barrel and tightened his finger on the trigger in a fast and practiced motion.

The rifle barked.

With her shoulder sliding the length of the wooden door frame, the girl slumped to a sitting position on the floor. She had a neat hole in her forehead and a look of amazement on her sweet, doll-like face, and Creed squeezed his eyes shut tight for a second to dispel the image. Then, without a word, he passed the rifle back to its speechless owner.

Things happened fast after that.

The Demon Slayer was not having the luck Creed had hoped he might. He'd been truthful when he said that he did not react to a spawn in the same way he did a full demon, and while he was the better and more experienced fighter, Stone's continuous shifting frustrated his offensive efforts. Hunter's face was already bloodied, and his slowed movements became increasingly defensive as Stone landed more blows than he missed.

Creed hesitated. He weighed his options. Stone could not be freed back into the world. Whatever mortality he once might have possessed had been overtaken by demon instincts that he chose to embrace, not suppress.

But in order to defeat Stone, Creed would need to shift to full demon form, something he had not yet done in front of credible witnesses. If he did this, he would be forced to head back to the Godseeker Mountains and the Temple of Immortal Right as quickly as he could in order to reach the Godseekers before word of his demon talents did, so he could attempt to explain the true threat and plead his case for continuing to represent them.

A weight settled into his stomach. He did not want to leave Nieve so soon. He was not yet ready, even though he knew he would have to leave her behind eventually.

Hunter went down, rolling out of harm's way a mere hair's breadth before Stone smashed an enormous clawed, demon fist into the dirt where his face had been.

An immediate decision was required.

Creed shucked off his shirt and stuffed the last grenade into a pocket so he would not lose it. He meant for Nieve to have the proceeds from its sale.

In seconds, his demon was free.

The sheriff, standing beside him, stumbled back with a few choice words on his lips. His gun came up, and Creed grabbed it from him with a swipe of an enormous clawed hand. Even in demon form he had areas vulnerable to gunfire, especially at close range.

"I'm on your side," he reminded the trembling man. The words ground from deep in his chest, unfamiliar and harsh. He tossed the gun back. "Point your weapon somewhere else."

Hunter was back on his feet. Around his neck, the amulet he wore on a plain gold chain had begun to glow. He did not retreat from the fight and allow Creed to take over, as Creed had anticipated, but took a hard swing at Stone's head. When his fist connected, Stone's temple shifted to bone.

Rather than break Hunter's hand, the outcome Creed expected, Stone went down on one knee, shaking his head as if Hunter had managed to hurt him.

Hunter grinned over his shoulder at Creed. He spit a mouthful of blood onto the ground. "I may be slower against spawn, but I seem to respond to the demon in you exactly as I should."

Stone was angry now, and no longer looked as certain of a victory. He shouted to his companions in the temple for help.

"Don't stand there!" he snarled at them. "I'll take the demon. You finish the mortal."

Creed hoped, for Hunter's sake, that the children's combined talents did not add up to more than Creed's demon ones, or he and the Demon Slayer would both be in trouble. As it was, he had little experience with using his assassin training in this form. His demon liked to brawl, to tear its opponents apart, not to strategize.

He had no more time to worry or plan. Stone came at him. He was smaller than Creed, and therefore more agile, and he too knew where to find a demon's most vulnerable points. He'd learned from the last time they'd fought.

Creed, however, was trained to react without too much thought. It did not take him long to find how to balance the extra body weight he carried, and to use it to his advantage. He thrust an elbow into Stone's face and heard the crunch of bone even as it shifted to plating. Stone shook his head, flinging blood from his streaming nose as it reverted to normal. While he tried to recover his senses Creed charged in low, tackling him around the knees with both arms. As he lifted, he threw him, hard, onto his back, and followed through by dropping a knee to the boy's exposed throat. Stone curled to his side and retched into the dirt.

A quick glance in Hunter's direction showed Creed he had not tried to approach the temple, but waited to see what the young half demons inside might do. They were not so quick to follow Stone's command, which told Creed there might still be hope for at least a few of them.

Creed caught a movement at the temple door where a small child had peered outside, no doubt to better see the action unfolding. It was misshapen and demonic in appearance, and the memory of a feral child, possibly this one, tearing a man to bits, made Creed hesitate too long in deciding whether or not the child needed his protection.

Before he could reach any decision, the townspeople sequestered behind closed doors overcame their initial uncertainty and selected their own course of action.

He heard the loud crack of a rifle's report. The child bent at the waist and clutched his chest, then did a slow spin as his legs refused to continue supporting him.

Someone screamed. The pregnant girl dashed forward from inside the temple, dropped to her knees, and scooped the dead child into her arms. Tears streamed down her face. The entire episode had distracted Creed from his downed opponent for a few crucial seconds.

Stone caught Creed by the back of one knee with the toe of his boot and dragged him off balance. Creed recovered, but not before Stone had managed to slide his fingers beneath the bone plating covering Creed's chest. He jerked it, and with a searing agony, Creed felt the muscles and tendons holding it in place begin to tear. He brought a hammer fist down on Stone's arm and the tearing ceased.

Creed punched him in the chest, putting his full weight behind it in a solid and well-aimed blow that should have stopped Stone's heart, but did no real harm other than to knock him down. Creed planted one large demon foot on him so that he could not rise, then pummeled his throat with a bone-enforced fist until the boy choked. When he lifted his arms in an instinctive reaction, Creed extended the claws of his right hand and drove them deep into the exposed flesh beneath Stone's left arm. He dug his claws in as deep as he could force them until he reached the boy's racing heart. With his other fist, he hammered the claws home.

Stone let out a shriek of agony. Creed straightened, retracting his demon's claws, and watched as the boy drew up his knees and writhed in the dirt. Red pooled around him, pulsing from his body with the final beats of his faltering heart.

• • •

Nieve tried to stop Airie from going farther than the front steps, even though she knew the house would not be enough to keep them safe. Willow would simply burn it down around them.

Her concern, when she expressed it, made Airie smile.

"Do you think I'm afraid of demon fire?" she asked.

"I think you're too pregnant to move very fast if you need to take cover," Nieve replied. "What if she isn't alone?"

They stayed on the verandah, forcing Willow to come closer.

She cocked her head to one side and studied Airie. Dust kicked up in the yard behind her, spun by the wind. Fire skipped across her fingertips.

It was obvious to Nieve that the two women shared a common demon ancestor. Willow, too, was a very lovely woman, with the same dark hair and brown, fiery eyes. But she did not possess the ethereal beauty and gentle manner that marked Airie as truly unique. Willow was like a stone image of her—one crafted by a sculptor of no more than average talent. She had nothing inside her that set her apart.

"I would know you anywhere," she said to Airie. "We look alike." Her glance slid over Airie, coming to rest on her round stomach, then jerked up to her face. "I had no idea you were pregnant. That changes things. It means I'll give you a chance. Join me, and save yourself and the child."

"Join you in what?" Airie asked. Sparks glittered a warning in her lovely eyes, changing the deep brown to molten lava.

"There are children who need us to teach them how to survive. Children like yours, who have been abandoned by mortals because they are so much superior to them."

"I don't believe they're superior," Airie said.

The fire trembled on Willow's fingers. "Why do you waste your immortal heritage this way? Don't you hear how mortals speak of us?" She glanced at Nieve, who shrank closer to Airie, and her eyes filled with contempt. "Do you see how they fear us?"

"I don't blame people for being afraid," Airie said. When she spoke, it was with the patience of a mother for its wayward child, even though Willow had to be at least ten years her senior. "I take a certain amount of responsibility for it. If I hadn't banished demons, our kind wouldn't now be terrorizing the world the way you are. Because of me, the mortal world will never again be the same. I'd rather work for a peaceful existence between us all than bring more war and destruction."

The folds of Willow's skirt snapped in the rising wind. "Our kind will make the world far better than it was before."

"No," Airie said. "Not better. Different. We should be

teaching mortals and half demons how to coexist, not force them to persecute and kill each other."

"The time for teaching is done." Willow's face hardened and became ugly with purpose. "If you aren't with me, you're against me. Is that how you wish things to be?" She glanced at Airie's pregnant stomach in a way that made Nieve shiver. "Is that what you want for one of our own?"

All remaining gentleness went out of Airie the instant Willow spoke of the baby with such possessiveness. "You have no claim on this baby and no say in how it's raised. It has two parents to guide it."

"Two parents won't always agree on what's best for the child," Willow said, "especially if their differences are as great as the ones between you and the Demon Slayer." She looked to Nieve. "How do you think your son's demon father would guide him if he were here? Which one of you does your son truly favor? Shall we find out?"

Nieve tried to breathe. Willow planned to summon Ash's father. Wherever her son was right now, Nieve prayed he remained hidden. She had no idea what the demon might do to him.

A circle of fire erupted around Airie and Nieve. And still Airie did not appear at all concerned, although Nieve could not say the same. The catch of her breath preceded a rising panic.

She did not want to face the demon, not because she feared he would harm her, but because she was afraid she could not resist him. And if she did not, while Creed would most likely forgive her for it, he would never look at her in quite the same way again. She loved the way he looked at her, as if she were beautiful and special, and valuable to him.

She did not want to lose that.

She did not want to lose Asher again either, although at least now, she knew he was safe.

"You forget," Airie said to Willow, her voice soft but certain, "that while you may claim the Demon Lord is your father, he's acknowledged me as his daughter. My mother is also a goddess. They're both in perfect agreement as to what's best for me. I can also say, with all certainty, that while I no doubt favor them both, I'm my own person as well. I can take care of myself, and those entrusted to me."

As the flames licked higher, a light mist fell. The mist turned to rain. It did not touch Airie or Nieve, although the fire Willow raised sizzled and died away.

Too late.

He appeared in mortal form, broad-shouldered and terrifyingly handsome, his skin smooth, liquid gold. His thick braid of brown hair swung like a flicked whip as he whirled around, looking for somewhere to focus his resentment at being summoned. Glorious blue eyes, soulless and empty, raked over the three women.

They came to rest on Nieve.

The caress of demon compulsion—sensual, filled with temptation and a promise of pleasure—that had once lured her to disaster called to her again.

Yet this time, as its thoughts slid over her, all she could think of was Creed.

Chapter Twenty

Willow watched the fire disappear. At first she could not credit that Airie had managed to extinguish it, or why she would do so when it left a demon uncontained.

The rain continued to fall all around them, forming a new circle with the three women and the demon at its core. As drops pattered against the ground where demon fire had burned only seconds before, a fine gray mist of steam curled upward, creating a barrier that cut them off from the world.

Airie had spoken the truth when she said her mother was a goddess. She had summoned goddess rain, which when it touched demon fire, turned to steam that held the demon more effectively in place than Willow could ever have managed. It seeped into the tiniest of cracks and between layers of clothing. This was what had banished demons from the world. The damp, pervasive mist was something they could not escape.

The steam gradually drifted, inch by slow inch, toward the

dry center of the circle. Willow touched it with outstretched fingers. While it did her no harm, it would no doubt send the demon back to the boundary in a few short moments if she did not take action.

"I have no desire to hurt you," Airie said to the demon. "Goddess rain banished you once before. Go back where you came from."

"Not until I claim what's mine." He watched Airie the same way a snake contemplated prey. "No one can keep from me the one I have chosen. Not even the Demon Lord's spawn."

"The choice is hers. She says she doesn't want you," Airie said.

The tendrils of steam wrapped tighter around him, and Willow saw her careful plans begin to unravel. She had to do something.

She made a move toward Airie, intending to stop the assault. The mortal woman, however, stepped into Willow's path in an attempt to keep her from reaching Airie. Willow, impatient, thrust her aside with a hard shove that sent her sprawling to the ground.

The demon concentrated those emotionless eyes on Willow in a way that made her more cautious of him, and forced her to consider her next move with greater care, but she would not allow him to believe that she feared him.

The demon took a step toward the quivering mortal woman. She offered too great a distraction for him. Willow needed to shift his attention back to Airie, and find some way to stop the rain that held him in check. He had a promise to fulfill. If Airie would not join her, then she and her spawn could both die.

Willow stretched out her palms. Balls of fire again appeared in her hands, although smaller this time, and not so bright, but they would be enough. They arced into the air, exploding into a sheet of flame that split as it fell so that the demon, the mortal, and Willow were penned into a snug circular dome together, with very little room to maneuver. It was enough to keep Airie outside of it, and the rain at bay, but only for a few precious moments.

The circle tightened, contracted beneath the onslaught of rain. The heat of the demon fire increased, and while it would take far longer to affect Willow and the demon, the mortal woman was not so fortunate. The thought of her screams filled Willow with cold anticipation.

The screams did not come. Instead, the demon positioned his body protectively around her.

The rain began to pour, heavier and harder, and although Willow had been prepared for it, she couldn't continue to hold the fire against it. Airie was stronger than she'd thought.

The demon's head lifted, and he looked at Willow with such hostility that she did not feel as certain of herself as she had only moments before.

"There's no demon in you," he said. "That's why you can't answer my summons. It's why you can't cross to the boundary." His lips curled in contempt. "You're nothing. A mortal no demon would claim."

Anger reddened Willow's vision. She willed the flames to burn brighter and higher despite the effort it cost her. "I am a true daughter of the Demon Lord. I possess demon fire. You'll do what I say, as you promised me."

"I make no promises to mortals."

The demon reached for her throat, too fast for her to

avoid contact. His fingers tightened as he lifted her off her feet. She choked and gasped, and clawed at his hand with her nails. The fire she wielded could no longer be released. It scorched through her veins, bubbling her blood into a boil. Pressure built inside her skull, stretching its ability to contain the contents.

She fought for calm. The demon required proof that she was not mortal. If she did not show fear, he would see the truth of it and he would release her.

She thought she heard a woman's screams. Then her ears popped, and all went silent.

The world shifted and the bottom fell out of the earth.

. . .

In all, when the gunfire ended, five children lay dead. So did several of the townsmen.

While the demon part of Creed normally would have reveled in the smell of blood, and the fear that seeped from mortal and half demon alike, Creed found he could muster no more than a dull and impotent anger at the senselessness of what had transpired. No one with even a trace of mortal compassion could find anything to celebrate in this tragedy. Not even his demon could glory in it.

And as Creed stood over Stone's body, broken and somehow forlorn in death as it lay in the dust and dirt, a great sadness settled in his heart. It had not needed to be this way. While half demons could be fearless, that did not make them unfeeling. He truly believed many could be taught right from wrong, and rules within which they should live, the same as most mortal beings. There would always be an imbalance in the universe. The strong and the weak, the rich and the poor. But there was value in all life.

With a start, Creed realized he retained his demon form. He released it, and in seconds was standing half-naked and exposed to the men silently watching him, fear and uncertainty etched on their faces.

He could not blame them. They had watched him kill Stone, as well as a seemingly innocent young girl—and while Creed did not regret the girl's death either, the need for it sickened him. She'd had all the outward appearance of a mortal, but inside had possessed the very worst instincts of her combined heritage. Her cruelty could not be blamed entirely on her demon heritage. He'd seen no hesitation or conflict in her. Her mortality had not warred with her demon, but rather, encouraged it. Creed had no doubt that there were others like her, or that more would be born in future generations, but hoped they'd be few and far between.

He picked up the shirt he had set aside and put it on, and as he fumbled with the buttons, looked around to see where he could be of most help.

The sheriff had not moved. Hunter was beside him, battered and bloody, but showing no signs of serious injury. Creed limped toward them, rubbing his chest where Stone had torn at his demon's bone plating. The shift back to mortal form had repaired much of the damage, but the fierce pain had not yet dissipated.

The sheriff could not take his eyes off the deformed child, still cradled in the pregnant girl's arms as she wept over his body in the door of the temple. No one seemed to know what to do.

"What is that thing?" the sheriff asked, unable to hide

his horror and revulsion.

"That is a *child*," Creed interrupted, cutting Hunter off before he made some comment he might later regret. Creed knew what the other man had to be thinking, given his wife's current condition. He met Hunter's eyes. "He deserved as much of a chance as any other living being. He never had one. Whose fault might that have been?"

Emotions warred across Hunter's face. Seconds passed. Then, slowly, he nodded. Turning his back to the weeping girl and the dead boy on the steps, he took control of the situation.

"Take the remaining children to the jail and lock them up as best you're able until we can decide what to do with them," he said to the sheriff and a few of the deputies who were not incapacitated by either shock or injury. "It may be time for us to consult with the Godseekers and find a way forward in dealing with half demons. They've already had to do so in the north."

Creed took advantage of the general distraction and uncertainty to walk away so that he could be alone in order to shield himself from those curious and fearful eyes.

He passed the empty mercantile. Beyond it the private residences began, and since he had no wish to be shot at by frightened homeowners, he stopped. He had a burning desire to find Nieve, and to hold her in his arms. To feel that there was at least a part of him that was mortal, and not a monster.

A small hand caught and tugged at the shredded remains of his trouser leg, and he looked down to find Nieve's son, with his solemn face and sober eyes, at his side.

He crouched so that he was at eye level with the boy.

He knew Asher—or Scratch, as Hunter called him—could travel over significant distances, although he was as confused as Hunter with regard to how he accomplished it.

He hoped the child had not seen the fighting. While Asher's unknown past was disquieting enough, it was how Nieve would react to his being here that concerned Creed most. She would want to protect him from this horror—but for very different reasons than Creed did.

Creed knew from personal experience the dangers of exposing half demon children to violence. They thrived on it. It strengthened them. And it brought out the demons they carried inside them.

"You shouldn't be here," Creed said to him. "Your mother and Airie will be worried."

The boy grasped his hand. His fingers were small and barely covered a quarter of Creed's, but in that gentle touch, Creed understood the full force of Asher's demon strength. All of its fearlessness, and the force of its allure, had combined with Nieve's quiet, sweet-tempered determination. Asher had no more desire to harm others than did his mother.

But he wanted something from Creed, and he intended to have it.

"Well, well," Creed said, rocking back on his bare heels in surprise. He did not pull away from that quiet insistence, but neither did he give in to it. He had strengths of his own. "Don't try to persuade me to do something against my will. We both know that's wrong." He studied the boy carefully. Nieve had forgotten this child's existence for more than a year. She had not done so on her own. She would never have put him so far from her thoughts if she'd had any real choice. "You *do* know that it's wrong, don't you?"

The little boy nodded. The compulsion, however, did not abate. He tugged on Creed's hand.

Creed frowned. "Whatever you want from me, you're going to have to ask for it."

A girl responded. "Willow is talking to the Demon Slayer's wife and his mother."

Creed looked up. The girl who spoke was small and thin, and nervous in manner. Her thick hair was a tangled nest of dark ringlets that put him in mind of his sister when she was a little girl. Bare, skinny legs poked like sticks from beneath the hem of a skirt she'd outgrown. She had scabs and ground-in dirt on both knees, and long, shallow scratches on one shin, as if she'd been crawling through bramble bushes. This was another one of Willow's children, and it disturbed him to find Nieve's young and trusting son in her company.

"What are they talking about?" Creed asked. Already he was on his feet and heading back to find Hunter, swinging Asher into his arms as he did. He could hardly leave the children alone. He motioned for the girl to follow them.

She scurried to keep up. "I don't know. But Willow is mad at them."

He had almost forgotten about Willow amid all of the tragedy that had unfolded here in town. Creed slowed. Asher had an arm draped around his neck, and his small fingers played with the tattoo on Creed's shoulder.

"How long ago did you see Willow? How did you know she was mad?" he asked the girl.

"It was just a few minutes." The little girl frowned. "I could tell because her hands were on fire."

Creed's thoughts raced. The girl said she had seen them a few minutes ago, but the trip from Hunter's property to town had taken at least thirty on the back of a hross. Creed looked at the girl more closely. She was several years older than Asher, but still very young. "How did the two of you get here?"

"We came through the demon boundary. We can move faster there," the girl added. She curled up her nose. "But I don't like it."

It was disquieting to discover that demons continued to touch this world, even if from the outside. Airie might know more of it.

And while the thought of two young children traveling in such a place made him uneasy, right now, his biggest concern was for the women he and Hunter had left unprotected.

He was so stupid in thinking, even for a moment, that he could put his duty to the Godseekers ahead of Nieve. That he could ever set his feelings for her aside.

He had not yet been able to walk away from her for long. To do so forever would be impossible. His days with the Godseekers were done.

Creed hiked Asher higher in his arms and took the little girl's hand. He forced himself to be calm. He did not want a re-emergence of his demon. As anxious as he was to get to Nieve, she was stronger than he had thought when he'd first met her. She would not hesitate to do what she had to in order to survive, especially now that she'd found her son.

Creed wanted her to trust him. That meant he had to trust her too.

• • •

Nieve had no idea where the demon had brought her, or

what this place might be, other than that it could not be mortal.

It was filled with sand and rocky cliffs, oppressive and frightening, their juxtaposition impossible to the world she knew. The sky crackled with streaks of red lightning, and the ground trembled beneath the pounding force of the thunder.

The demon woman was with them, although as the demon's strong fingers tightened around her throat, Nieve knew she would not be for long.

A small touch of pity mingled with her horror. Willow should have known better than to deal with demons. This one had what he wanted and no longer needed her. Even if he should release her, there was nowhere in this wasteland for her to run from him.

There was nowhere for Nieve to run either, which was just as well. She knew better than to show fear to a demon, something she had not been able to overcome in the past. It strengthened him and gave him control over her.

She could not believe that she had ever compared Creed to this cold monster. Creed was as beautiful on the inside as he was in appearance, and that inner beauty did not disappear simply because he changed from one physical form to another. It hurt her, deep in her heart, that she had not told him she loved him.

Bright red blood trickled from Willow's ears. Nieve had no love for her. The woman was cruel, and had no use for mortals or those she perceived as weak.

But Willow was far from alone in her cruelty and prejudice. Nieve had experienced more pain at the hands of mortals than she had from half demons, or a demon, and she would forever regret her own inaction in trying to prevent this. She could not stand here and watch the life being choked from Willow.

She scooped up a rock from the ground and threw it as hard as she could. It struck the demon in the shoulder. He did not turn around, or exhibit any surprise, other than a slight flinch.

The fire Willow held flickered beneath her skin, as if the demon had managed to turn it back on her and keep her from releasing it, and Nieve saw that it burned her from the inside. Nieve watched in helpless horror as he squeezed the last bits of life from her. Her legs kicked in the air, her fingers scrabbling at his claws until her lovely features distorted, turned purple, then black. Her eyes burst from her head, and blood gushed from her ears.

The demon tossed her body aside where it lay in a crumpled, broken heap at the foot of one of the jagged cliff faces. Nieve closed her eyes tight, wondering if this was to be her fate, too, and if she would ever see her son or Creed again.

At least she knew Ash would be safe and well-loved. Creed was the one she ached for. She had known, if she should allow herself to love him, how difficult it would be for her if she lost him. Until now she had not considered the consequences her loss might have on him.

She saw no remorse in the demon for what he had done. No regret. It was as if he had completely forgotten the woman he had killed the instant he was through with her.

It was amazing that something so beautiful could harbor such ugliness.

Nieve's back was pressed against a crumbling wall of red sandstone and broken chunks of smoky quartz. She could not move as he reached out a hand and brushed her hair from her cheek with a possessive finger. He traced the line of her jaw, then tilted her chin upward.

"You're mine," he said. "Never forget that. I'll find you wherever you are, no matter how long it takes. We're connected."

She could not tear her eyes from the demon who had fathered her son. Nor did she forget the desire she had once felt for him, even though she had not wanted it. She had been afraid that if she were ever to face him again, as she did now, she would not be able to resist him—and Creed would never again look at her in the same way.

But while Nieve bore the full brunt of the compulsion the demon directed at her, she discovered with a knee-weakening relief that she was no longer bound by his will.

Her heart had chosen Creed. Right now it cried out for him. And he was not here to save her.

But he would come for her. She knew it. He always had, despite his claims that he would not do so again. All she had to do was gain enough time for him to find her.

She pressed the palms of her hands to the stinking wall of sandstone behind her. "I'm not yours. I never was, and I never will be. There's no connection between us."

"No?" He lifted a brow as if her denial amused him. Then he uttered a single word.

"Asher."

Chapter Twenty-one

The girl's name was Imp, Creed had discovered. It suited her, but in a mischievous, harmless way.

He and the children found Hunter near the front steps of the ruined temple, overseeing the care and removal of the bodies. They had been bundled together in two distinct piles—mortal and half demon—and covered with large tarpaulins.

When Hunter saw Creed and his two young companions, he intercepted them and hurried them around the far corner of the temple so they would not have to see what was beneath those tarpaulins. There, he listened to the girl's story without interrupting her, or showing any outward signs of alarm.

That did not mean he was calm, Creed understood, only that he was able to set his emotions aside long enough to deal with practicalities first.

Creed, on the other hand, could not get Nieve from his mind. How many times had he told her that he would not come for her? That his duty came first?

How wrong he had been. He was hers. Nieve would always come first.

He still had her small son in his arms. He held him a bit closer and tried not to worry, not wanting the boy to pick up on his concern.

"Airie has greater protection from demons than you might think," Hunter said to Creed. "I'd worry more if there were other half demons with Willow, but Imp says she's alone. Airie will look after Nieve until we get there." He spoke to the girl. "If you and Scratch are both able to travel in this demon boundary, can you take us through it, too?"

She scuffed one toe in the dirt as if reluctant to come right out and say no because she didn't wish to disappoint him. Creed's heart went out to her. Wherever she came from, he did not doubt that she had been with Willow only because she'd had no other choice.

Cottonwood Fall and all of the Borderlands—indeed, the whole known world—would have to come to terms with a new and widely spreading reality. A sweet-natured child such as this, so eager to please others, should never need to fear abandonment.

Imp looked between Hunter and Creed with doubt written on her face. "Willow wanted me to take her to it, too, but she couldn't cross. And when you're there, you have to be quiet or the demons will find you."

"Can you explain to me how to do it so I can go there by myself?" Creed asked her. "Is there some special trick I should know?"

She lifted her thin shoulders. "I just think about it and it happens."

Hunter raked fingers through his sweat-darkened blond hair. "It's obvious not everyone can do it. Or at least it's not instinctive," he said to Creed. "Would you need to have some sort of connection to this boundary, perhaps? Could it be through your demon fathers?"

It was one possibility. Creed knew Asher's father still lived, so that could be his connection. If it was, it would mean Imp's father likely lived, too. But Creed's demon father had been killed by his sister's husband, Blade. Therefore, Creed had no such link to test.

And demons hated all spawn. Especially their own. Imp said they had to be quiet or demons would find them, so if there was a link, it was a precarious one.

There had to be more possibilities. Their fathers might be the connection that allowed half demons to enter this boundary, but it need not be the only one. Creed shifted Asher so that he settled more comfortably on his arm. The boy had one elbow crooked around his neck. Creed deliberated as to what would make a half demon child seek out such a place, even if involuntarily. It might be out of a necessity to hide from something that was happening to them in the mortal world. To run away from some perceived threat or trauma. Asher had been taken by slavers. He suspected Imp had been turned out of her home.

Creed had never needed to run or hide as a child. His mother might not have loved him, but he hadn't felt threatened, or a desire to escape from the mortal world. He'd had his innate talent for deflecting unwanted attention to protect him from trouble. And he was no longer a child. Perhaps he had outgrown any latent ability he might once have had.

"I have no idea," Creed said.

He watched Hunter assess the chaos in the street beyond the temple, where the sheriff had rounded up the remaining children. They'd either exhausted their abilities in the fight or did not possess any significant amount of demon strength to begin with. Either way, there was no opposition left in them. They simply seemed defeated.

Lost.

"We're wasting time," Hunter said. "If we can't take a shortcut, we need to get moving. The sheriff and his men will have to deal with this for now."

The disquiet that had been nudging at Creed could no longer be set aside. While he would have known if Nieve were in immediate physical danger, his demon insisted she needed him. And that she needed him now.

Creed reached for Imp's hand, wanting to keep her near him to protect her as they went for their hross. He had no intention of leaving her with the others, and the sheriff.

But before he could catch hold of her, Asher's other arm came around his neck. He clung to Creed with his little face pressed against his cheek as if his life depended on it.

Creed heard a single word roll through the child's thoughts.

Asher.

And then the darkened street disappeared—there one second, gone the next. Creed staggered, automatically clutching Asher more tightly to his chest so as to not drop him.

Inside, his demon roared to life, its chaotic thoughts rippling through him with an overwhelming and euphoric speed.

One thought outdistanced all others.

Home.

Creed's demon was home. This, then, was the boundary.

He did not share the same sense of euphoria.

Once he had his feet beneath him again, he looked around. Surrounding them on three sides were cliffs and rock. Beyond the cliffs stretched an enormous desert that stank of death and decay. Waves of heat rippled off red sand. Asher clung to Creed's neck like a burr.

The boy's spoken name, which Creed had heard very distinctly, created at least one connection to the demon boundary. Asher had been summoned here. Creed could think of only one demon with an interest in the child.

His lips thinned. It would not be expecting his presence as well. Let it discover what it was like to deal with him and not a defenseless woman or child.

His demon no longer sang its euphoria into his thoughts. It had fallen quiet, yet remained very restless.

It worried for Nieve.

Creed readjusted Asher's weight so the boy sat on his hip, keeping one arm hooked protectively around him. Nieve was safe with Airie, who could protect her from Willow. Creed would see that no harm came to her son.

He'd find a way to get Asher back to her.

He examined the sheer rock faces, running the tips of his fingers over their rough skin. A small cleft split the rock into two halves, forming a narrow sluice with open sky at the top and a faint crack of light at the far end.

Nieve is in there. His demon seemed so certain.

Creed paused, his fingers glued to the rock. The tattoo on his back itched.

He set Asher on his feet. Other than the forbidding desert

at their backs, there was nowhere else for them to go but forward, between the cliffs.

"Stay behind me," Creed said.

They squeezed through the jagged crack in the cliffs.

On the other side, in a narrow canyon, he found Nieve, just as his demon had known he would.

Her back was to the canyon wall. A man had her pinned against it, his head bent close to hers. One of her hands rested against the rocks behind her, palm down and with her fingers spread. The other hand was pressed to the man's chest. She did not appear to be struggling against him.

This was not a man she was with, but a demon.

Anger clenched Creed's heart in a tight fist. She would not have come here willingly. Inside, where it did the most damage to her, she would be fighting his touch.

Then, unexpectedly, Nieve's free hand came away from the crumbling rock wall to fling a fistful of dirt and broken stone into the demon's face before she ducked under his arm in an attempt to escape. The demon jerked back, caught off guard by this unexpected display of resistance, but still did not shift as he turned to pursue her.

She wasn't running away. Instead, she stooped and grabbed up a larger rock. As she did, she finally saw Creed. Hope and relief filled her eyes, and he read the trust for him that blossomed across her face.

She had not noticed her son's presence though, meaning the boy was hiding from her. While Creed had lectured him for his use of compulsion earlier, now, he was grateful.

He set Asher on the ground, placing him carefully behind him so that he would be protected. The little boy showed no signs of alarm. Creed wondered what all he had seen, and been exposed to, in the time he had been away from his mother, to leave him so calm in the face of danger.

Creed caught the faint sound of a tiny voice whispering, *Asher*. He spun around, only to see the boy vanish.

The demon, too, had spotted Creed now. Blood filled its eyes. It shifted, becoming ugly and horned, and so large that it dwarfed Nieve, tiny beside it. Thick red bone plating creaked as it straightened on squat, solid legs. Creed drew a harsh breath, afraid it might crush her.

And there was nothing he could do about it. His demon refused to emerge.

Nieve's pale blond head drooped. The rock fell from her hand. Then she brought her chin up. Green eyes pierced Creed's.

"What kind of assassin are you if you won't use your best weapon?" she demanded.

You didn't use your best weapon.

She had chastised him for it once before, angry with him for the beating he'd endured. His demon needed no further encouragement from her than that.

Creed set it free. His bones stretched, their joints popping. His shirt ripped to shreds as his body expanded. His hands turned to claws as he assumed his full demon form.

But this time Creed acknowledged a distinct difference as he shifted, because understanding came with it. He was made up of two parts, not one. It had never been his demon that refused to shift in Nieve's presence. It wanted nothing more than to kill any male who dared touch her.

Creed alone had held it back.

He swung his heavy demon head toward Nieve.

"Hide!" he roared at her.

Without waiting to see whether or not she obeyed, he confronted his opponent.

They were evenly matched in size and strength. Creed's demon's protectiveness regarding Nieve surged unrestrained to the surface, and he no longer tried to contain it. While Creed could rationalize that she was unharmed, his demon could not. Another male had dared touch her, and that was not to be tolerated. Creed did not intend to tolerate it either.

He threw one massive fist that connected with the other demon's ear.

It bellowed, fell back, and shook its head. Blood-red rage burned in its glaring eyes. As it regained its footing it exploded toward Creed. One of the sharp horns protruding from its skull gouged at the soft, unprotected underside of Creed's chin where the bone plating parted to form a joint. Creed swung his head to the side and the horn scraped across his cheek. The force of the blow cracked the bone armor and tore the flesh it exposed. A trickle of warm blood dripped from Creed's jowl.

The demon threw a blow at Creed's face, intending to strike the bone he'd already smashed. Rather than try to avoid it, as the demon anticipated, Creed stepped forward and to one side, grabbed the demon's extended arm as it shot out, and yanked. The demon fell against Creed's chest. Creed thrust out his leg, rolled the demon over his hip, and smashed him to the ground. He dropped a knee to his throat, knocking his chin up and out of the way so that the demon's bone plating parted. Creed rammed the claws of one hand between the bone plating, slicing the demon's flesh. Blood squirted in hot, thick gushes.

Creed seized his opponent's head in both hands and

jerked it to the side to break the neck, as he'd been trained. He then followed up with a powerful blow to the chest that was guaranteed to stop the demon's heart in case it still beat.

A blur came at him from one side. His demon stayed his fist when he would have struck out to defend himself.

It was Nieve. Something dull and metallic filled her small hand. A grenade. She must have found it in the scattered remnants of his torn shirt, or perhaps it had fallen from a pocket.

She hooked a finger in the round pin at the top, as she'd seen him do, and dropped the pin on the ground. She went to her knees, shoving the grenade under the demon's inert form between its arm and chest.

Creed scooped her up in one massive arm. He lumbered in a half crouch, with his body bent protectively over hers, as fast as he could toward the break in the cliffs.

His demon was too large to fit, and he could not regain control well enough to shift. Adrenaline surged through him, making it too difficult.

He thrust Nieve inside, blocking the space with his body as the grenade exploded behind him. The ground shuddered. Chunks of rock bounced off his back. Then, the world fell eerily silent.

Creed's demon, however, did not. It still hungered for blood. Changing form would not make him less dangerous, only less obviously so. Instead, Creed fought to retain demon form so that Nieve would at least be warned that all was not right with him.

But Nieve did not seem at all afraid. She threw herself at him, unmindful of the form he wore, and wrapped her arms as far around his bloodied demon body as she could reach.

"I knew you would come for me," she said, resting her cheek against him.

With her touch, and her words, Creed's demon lost all interest in fighting. He shifted to mortal form and gathered her against him. For long moments, Creed could not speak. She, who had so much more reason than he not to trust, had not doubted him.

His entire body ached. His face throbbed, and he knew his cheekbone had cracked beneath the demon's first blow, and that the cut still bled, although not badly.

He would always come for her, but now, somehow, he had to get her home and back to her son.

When he was in demon form he was as close to full-blooded as it was possible to be, with many of its talents, although he had never fully explored them.

Yet he remained mortal, and tied to that world.

He was two parts of a whole. He belonged to two worlds. In this one he had to trust in his demon. In its form, he could carry Nieve across the boundary—back to the world he and his demon had been born to.

"I have to change again," he said.

Nieve didn't turn away so that she did not have to watch, but simply nodded her understanding and waited.

Creed shifted. He pulled Nieve against him, and he thought of Asher, and the mortal world, and what might be happening at Hunter's ranch.

And they were there.

The yard was in chaos. Hunter stood by the stairs to the house, speaking to Airie, holding Imp by one hand and Ash by the other as if he were afraid they might both disappear. Tears streaked his wife's cheeks.

Creed landed in full demon form, his broad feet thudding hard in the dirt, Nieve pressed against him. Everything stopped.

He shifted to mortal form.

Then Asher shook free of Hunter's hand, and came running across the yard toward them, his little legs pumping. He flung himself at Creed, who caught him under the arms and lifted him high.

Chapter Twenty-two

"You shouldn't go back," Hunter had said to Creed when the dust settled and calm returned. "Not yet. Not for a few years. Let Blade deal with the Godseekers and assassins, and show them the value of working with half demons, not against them. He was once one of them. He knows them as well as anyone."

Creed was not yet certain what he planned to do. Blade and Raven had their life together in the Godseeker Mountains. Hunter and Airie were happy in the Borderlands, and had a baby on the way. Cottonwood Fall had seen the benefit of having the Demon Slayer nearby. These were good and decent people, and Hunter was one of them. He'd been born here, and gone to their aid when they'd needed him, and they were not likely to forget it anytime soon.

By nature, Creed was a content and social man. He liked people and companionship. If not for the demon in him, he would never have come to the attention of Godseeker assassin recruiters. He had accepted that life because he'd seen no other options.

And yet he continued to believe in the Godseekers' primary purpose, which was to bring justice to the world. But Creed wanted justice for all. If he went back, he might or might not be welcome now that his demon side had been so publicly exposed. Even if he were welcome to return as a Godseeker assassin, sooner or later he would be forced to choose sides between half demons and mortals.

He would not do it. He could not. He would rather see the world embrace their similarities, not fight over differences.

A lot also depended on Nieve's wishes.

Ash was already asleep in the bedroom that she shared with him. Airie had suggested it, and Nieve had accepted with an alacrity that had hardly come as a surprise to anyone, let alone Creed.

But he had spent weeks alone with her and missed her quiet companionship. The few hours after Ash's bedtime were the only opportunity he had to speak with her in private, and more often than not, he found her too distracted for conversation and unwilling to share her thoughts.

The first time she'd accused him of being a demon, he should have seen how afraid she was of being drawn in and manipulated against her wishes. He should have understood why. Even after she'd gone to live with Bear the only freedom left to her had come from her thoughts, and those, she protected as fiercely as she did her young son.

Getting her to share them with him, even now that Ash's father could no longer reach her, wouldn't be easy. She'd have to trust him. Have complete faith in him.

She would have to love him.

He did not know what he meant to her now that she had her son. The connection between them remained. It had not broken, but neither had it strengthened. An image came to him of the gray-faced sheriff in Desert's End, Fledge, who had clung to life despite death's inevitable approach. If it came to a choice between a fast and painful severing or a slow and corrosive withering of their connection, then Creed would take fast severance.

So, this evening, he had asked Nieve to go for a short walk with him. Even now, as they skirted the edge of the main paddock and followed a worn path to a nearby creek, she would turn every so often as if to guarantee that the house had not disappeared behind them.

In the distance, beyond the shrub-stippled banks of the creek, the lights of Cottonwood Fall twinkled one by one as dusk slowly settled. The town had not been seriously damaged, but only because Willow had concentrated her efforts elsewhere. The inhabitants did not know how lucky they were. In the past, others had not been so fortunate. It was likely that some would not be in the future either, as more half demons emerged from hiding.

The path wound upward for a short while, then dipped downward toward murmuring waters that swirled in fast-flowing eddies before settling into slower, deeper pools.

He had more decisions to make, and Nieve's wishes would figure prominently in them.

Nieve reached for his hand to steady herself as she picked her way over loose rocks scattered along the creek's edge. Hers was warm and small, lost within the enormousness of his, but with much greater durability than it would at first seem. He lifted it to examine it with close curiosity, running his thumb across her rough palm.

She tried to retract it, as if embarrassed by either its condition or his examination.

He pressed a kiss to her palm. "Your hands are very representative of you," he said. "They sum you up well. They're slender, well-formed, and beautiful on one side, but underneath, where it counts the most, they're tough and capable."

Pleasure at his words flooded her green eyes, along with a pretty blush that heightened the loveliness of her face. He had to concentrate on regaining his ability to breathe so he could finish what he had brought her out here to say.

"Ash has done well with Airie and Hunter. He can continue to learn a lot from them," Creed said. Immediately, the pleasure in her eyes died away to be replaced with caution. He tightened his clasp on her fingers. "It's good for him to see what the relationship between an immortal and a mortal should be. That it's not built on domination by one over the other, but a connection between two people who each have something to offer." Nieve did not reply, but she was listening. He took that as a good sign. "Hunter says he and Airie are planning to keep Imp and her companions. Airie wants to set up a community for half demons similar to the one that Raven and Blade have begun. You and Ash should think about staying. You have nowhere else to go."

"I'm not certain Airie and Hunter will find any support from the townspeople for this plan of theirs," she said.

"They'll have mine. I don't want to return to the Godseeker Mountains. Neither do I want to give up on my original purpose, which is to find and save as many half demons as I can. I could let it be known that the Borderlands, and Cottonwood Fall, both have a place for unwanted children. Families who can't cope on their own could bring them here."

Nieve looked at the ground. "Caring for others is what you do best. But I need to find work to support Ash and me so I can take care of us, and I don't think I'll find that in Cottonwood Fall anytime soon."

Creed tipped her chin with a finger so he could read her face. "Do you still want a dozen more children and a place for them to be safe?"

"Yes." She bit her lip, and seemed to choose her words carefully. "But I also want more than that. For weeks I've thought only of finding Ash and never stopped to consider what else might matter to me. I was afraid that if I stopped thinking of him I'd forget him again. Any happiness or pleasure I experienced made me feel guilty, and unfit as a mother. Now that I have him back, I regret not acknowledging other things."

He could see her heart in her eyes.

She meant him.

A heavy load shifted from his heart so that it began to beat again. She had to know that his feelings for her had not changed. Nor would they ever. He had fought a demon for her. He'd helped save her son.

She had claimed him.

But she guarded her emotions too closely for him to be certain what he saw in her was truth. She had to say the words he wanted to hear.

"Putting a child first is as it should be," Creed said. "But there's nothing wrong with also wanting something more for yourself."

"To answer your question, yes. I could love a dozen children or more." She looked into his eyes. Dimples flashed at the corners of her lips, then as quickly disappeared. "But I could only ever love one man."

"Even a man that you fear?" He could not live with that. He wanted her trust as well as her love, because the coming years would not be easy ones. With half demons, discipline would need to be harsh. He'd try to protect her from that, but she needed to know. "I'll use every demon talent I possess if I have to. The world is changing. I can't ignore what I am."

"You are so much more than a demon. I'm not afraid of you. I haven't been since the first day we met. I've been afraid to love you. Because of Ash."

"And now?" She would have to say the words. He did not dare to hope.

"My life will never be complete without you. Not even having Asher back could make up for your loss. Someday he'll grow up and leave me again. That, too, is as it should be. But I've already claimed the man I want to keep me company for the rest of my life. I'll never choose another." She slid her arms around his waist and tipped her head back so that she could see him. Her green eyes softened. "But any claim I have on you is through your demon, and I want more than that. I want your love again. You have no idea how much I've regretted not telling you I love you before we found Asher. I'd planned to tell you that day. And after, the timing seemed wrong."

"Say it again," Creed commanded.

"I love you." Nieve smiled at him. It was filled with a broad and consuming joy that spilled across her upturned face and brightened the evening around them. His heart expanded with the awareness that he had played a part in putting that smile there. Everything she felt—the love, the hope, and the joy—embraced him.

"Could you raise Ash here?" Creed asked. "And a dozen more like him? With me?"

She rested her chin on his chest and appeared to be thinking it over. "He does seem to be taken with you. I suppose the others would be fond of you, too."

"Everyone likes me."

"It's because you're so modest," Nieve said.

Creed took her face in his hands and kissed her lips. A fish jumped in the creek, the splash as it landed loud in the quiet air. Somewhere in the night the wolvens howled, calling to each other as they gathered to hunt.

This land was not so very different from what they had left behind. His goals had not changed. He wanted to make a difference. He did not think he could do that without Nieve. She was his reason for carrying on. His proof that mortals could stand against demons and half demons, and come out the better for it.

"I'll build you a house. I'll spend the rest of my life making you happy," he said. "I want you to have everything you deserve."

"I have everything I could ever want right now. I can't imagine what more you think would make me happy, or that anyone could deserve." A frown crossed her face. "I have no idea what made you help me in the first place. I tried to kill you."

Creed laughed at the memory. "That's right. You shot me."

"That's funny to you?"

She looked so indignant it made him laugh harder. "It's what made me love you." He held her close as he sobered. "You seemed so tiny. So helpless and defeated. And then you proved that you were anything but. You look forward, Nieve. You never look back. That's what makes you a survivor. I can't imagine anyone more perfect for me. I hope I'm worthy of you."

She smoothed a hand over the tattoo on his back, beneath his shirt. It tingled and warmed, sending a thrill of anticipation through him, but it did not catch fire. Inside, his demon purred its contentment.

"You're going to change the world," Nieve said. "I have no idea what the future will bring, but I do know that I want to be standing beside you when it arrives."

Acknowledgments

I'd like to thank Julie Taylor, owner of Skin Decision Piercing & Tattoo Studio, for designing Creed's fabulous tattoo, and also for reading my books.

As always, Kerri-Leigh Grady is an editor extraordinaire. I'm a bit sad the Demon Outlaws are finished. They wouldn't be what they are without her.

My husband and sons, my mother, my sisters, and my brother are all hugely supportive. I couldn't ask for more from my family than what they already give me.

And last but not least, I have some amazing writer friends at Entangled. Thanks to Robin Bielman and Roxanne Snopek for smiling and nodding a lot when I talk all kinds of crazy, and offering to ride shotgun on late-night excursions. Samanthe Beck, Hayson Manning, and EJ Russell are usually good for suggestions on where to hide bodies. I'm so glad that what happened in Vegas didn't stay entirely in Vegas. You guys are great.

About the Author

Paula Altenburg lives in rural Nova Scotia, Canada, with her husband and two sons. Once a manager in the aerospace industry, she now enjoys the luxury of working from home and writing full-time. Paula also co-authors paranormal romance under the pseudonym Taylor Keating. Visit her at www.paulaaltenburg.com.

Did you love this Entangled Select novel? Check out more of our titles!

And for exclusive sneak peeks at our upcoming books, excerpts, contests, chats with authors and editors, and more...

Be sure to like us on Facebook

Follow us on Twitter

Other books by Paula Altenburg...

IN THE *DEMON OUTLAWS* SERIES:

THE DEMON LORD

The Demon Lord has conquered the mortal world and sampled its pleasures. Now all he needs is to conquer the goddess who is meant to complete him. The goddess Allia, however, has other plans. She is sent by her immortal sisters to win the heart of the Demon Lord and make him her slave but soon discovers that the Demon Lord's heart is not easily given, and that in order to win it, she must sacrifice her own.

BLACK WIDOW DEMON

THE DEMON'S DAUGHTER

For the softer side of Paula Altenburg, try her Bliss title...

DESIRE BY DESIGN

Famous architect Matt Brison is unsatisfied with his mundane life in Toronto. So when the mayor of Halifax asks him to spearhead his City Hall project, Matt jumps at the opportunity. There's just one problem: the feisty and beautiful project lead, Eve, isn't exactly thrilled about her new "coworker" hijacking her design. But when the sparks begin to fly, they both find themselves falling for the colleague they shouldn't want. And before they know it, their already shaky foundation might come crumbling down...

If you loved The Demon Creed, try these other books from Entangled...

ANGEL KIN
by Tricia Skinner

When a beautiful woman comes to the Order, half-angel assassin Cain is immediately drawn to her. But when Katie fingers him as the killer, he can come to only one conclusion. His twin, who he thought was dead, is very much alive...and sending him a message. Unfortunately, that message is: "You're next." Now, with Katie's life in his hands, Cain must fight to keep them both alive. But Abel has just one goal: destroy his brother, starting with the woman he's falling in love with.

BY JOVE
by Marissa Doyle

Going back to graduate school to study ancient languages and mythology is a dream come true for Theodora Fairchild. Falling in love with Grant Proctor is an added bonus. But then Theo discovers that being chosen for the prestigious program has more to do with who she is than what she knows. When evil forces threaten Grant's life in an effort to tear the two apart, Theo must rely on her wits and wisdom to save her true love and survive the semester.

CALL OF THE SIREN
by Rosalie Lario

Siren-demon hybrid bounty hunter Dagan Meyers swore he'd never settle down. Tying himself to one woman is so not his bag. Until he meets the gorgeous angel Lina, and can't think of being with anybody BUT her. The last thing Lina wants is to develop feelings for the smooth-talking man she knows will eventually leave her. But as they battle a growing darkness—a powerful dark fae who's harnessed untold power—Dagan and Lina find that love may be their greatest weapon against the evil that threatens to destroy them all.

Night Child
by Lisa Kessler

Issa is one of the original Night Walkers, a proud protector of the mortal world. Now, when the key to the survival of the entire Night Walker race rests on protecting an unborn child, Issa is the only immortal strong enough to defend Muriah and the prophecy. But Muriah's headstrong spirit and soulful eyes awaken feelings in him that are best left buried. When the Egyptian God of Chaos sstrikes, Muriah and Issa must find the lost scrolls to trap him. But as the battle between love and chaos ensues, sacrifices must be made…

Love Single Title Romance? Try these new releases from Entangled Select…

Queen's Wings
by Jamie K. Schmidt

FBI dragon Reed's disdain for humans can't mask the magnetic attraction he has for Carolyn, but when she tells him she's going to shift into a dragon he thinks she's crazy. A female hasn't been hatched, or shape shifted, in over a thousand years. He's proven wrong after Carolyn shifts and is named the new Queen on the block. When the Cult of Humanity kidnaps Carolyn to sacrifice her, Reed must face his fears—and feelings, racing to save the woman he realizes he can't live without.

CRIMSON HEART
by Heather McCollum

Highland warrior Searc Munro's dark, killing magic must never be known. But when his father's life is threatened, Searc's secret is revealed. When Elena Seymour's lineage as the illegitimate daughter of King Henry VIII is discovered, she runs for her life. Teaming up as exiles, Elena and Searc seek refuge in Edinburg. With a series of ritual killings haunting the city and a traitor attempting to assassinate Scotland's regent, suspicion turns to Searc. Now the two must find a way to trust each other, despite their secrets, before it's too late.

Short on time? Read these novellas from Entangled Select...

HEALING HER HEART
by Audra North

Dr. Greg Stanton is looking for ways to de-stress in the aftermath of losing a patient, and getting hot and heavy with Emily Jankowski sounds like just what he needs to forget his high-stress life for a while. He doesn't have time for anything long-term—his only focus is and has always been the well-being of the patients whose lives are in his hands. But when Emily accepts his straightforward terms of a no-strings relationship, they realize too late that they won't be satisfied with sex alone...

OPENING ACT
by Suleikha Snyder

Reporter Saroj Shah has been in love with bass player and bartender Adam Harper since her first day of college—seven years ago. Forever thinking of her as part-friend and part-little sister, he's just been too blind, and too clueless, to see it. Until one pivotal moment pulls her into the spotlight. The moment Saroj steps on stage, Adam can't take his mind off of her. But after seven years, Saroj is ready to move on. Adam will have to hit the right note if he wants to prove to Saroj he was worth the wait.

Three in one! Grab these Select anthologies...

SPELLBOUND IN SLEEPY HOLLOW
by Patricia Eimer, Rosalie Lario, and Boone Brux

The Von Tassel sisters are in deep. With a new inn opening up to non-magic guests, these three witches have enough to worry about, but after a deal with the Headless Horseman, all three Von Tassel sisters must find their true loves by All Hallow's Eve. Will Stephanie be able to forgive her playboy ex? Will Bri be able to win back her childhood crush-turned-ghost hunter? Will Lexi be able to sway her supernatural employee? Or will each be forever trapped as ghosts in Sleepy Hollow like their ill-fated aunties.

CURSE OF THE PHOENIX
by Rachel Firasek

Book One: The Last Rising

Saving souls without any hope for her own redemption isn't how Phoenix Ice imagined spending eternity. Fed up, she decides her next death will be her last. But when she sacrifices her own life for a sexy Texan in a catastrophic plane crash, she has no idea the consequences will be so great. When the mysterious Ice comes into Turner Alcott's life, he knows she's the one. If he wants to win her heart, Turner must teach Ice how to forgive herself, and prove that love is the ultimate sacrifice.

Book Two: The Last Awakening

Ex-soldier Greyson Meadows desperately wants to be freed from the nightmares and guilt that haunt him. Arabella's been gifted her mortality and long-gone voodoo magic. She must save her next soul within a week without using magic, or she'll lose her power forever. When Greyson is confronted by a waif of a woman who forces him to face the truth about his past, he runs fast and hard. Now one will have to give up everything so the other can have peace, but will love's magic withstand the loss?

Book Three: The Last Beginning

Though she's always hated being a phoenix, Sadie has to admit immortality has its advantages. She's seen and done more in the last 150 years than she'd ever dreamed of, but she can't get past the fact that Osiris has done nothing but manipulate her and her fellow phoenixes. Sun god Osiris is ashamed of his role as ruler of the Underworld, but unless he can figure out how to save Sadie, that's exactly where she's going to end up. Permanently. He'll help her the only way he can—even if it means she'll hate him forever.

CPSIA information can be obtained at www.ICGtesting.com
Printed in the USA
LVOW07s1526180615

442985LV00005B/571/P